TO STAND IN A FALL

How far can we Fall?

BY

H. L. FOREST

Published by Hemingway Publishers
Cover design by Hemingway Publishers
ISBN: Printed in the United States

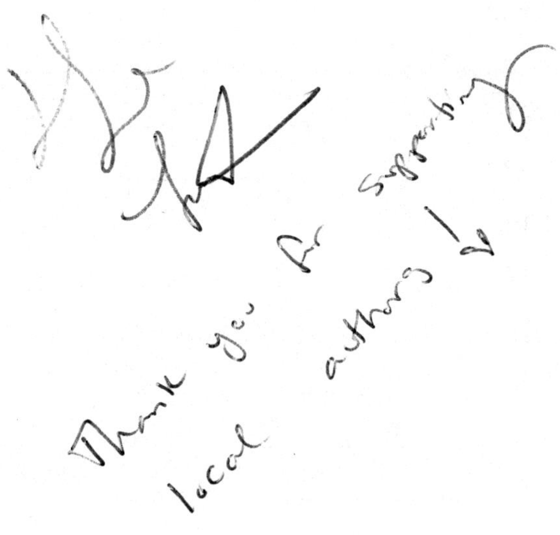
Thank you for supporting
local authors!

Table of Contents

DEDICATION

For Hubbs, Bestie, and Both of my Mommas.

PROLOGUE

The day began like any other: cold, dull, lonely. I couldn't feel my pillow beneath my head. I must have lost it in the night again. I wanted so badly to just roll over and go back to sleep in my warm bed, ignoring the icy world outside and all the terrors it held. If I could just close my eyes for a minute more…

But no. I needed to get moving on the day. The cold, gray daylight would only last so long, and there was always much to be done.

I slipped out of bed, pulled on my jeans, wool socks, and hoodie, then quietly exited my small bedroom in the tiny cabin. It wasn't much, but it was more than most people were able to get to after the Fall. Slipping into my boots and heavy coat, I peered out the door's tiny window. The area around my cabin appeared clear all the way up to the tree line, about 50 yards away. That's always a good start to the day. I pulled on my rabbit-skin hat and mittens, then opened the door to the bitter wind that tried its hardest to steal my breath as I plunged out into the morning light.

I suppose I should start at the beginning. As the song says, "A very good place to start." I'm Noah. Yes, I am a woman, and yes, I know that is a man's name. I'm also aware that I can change it legally. I have been given all the advice I could possibly choke on in my 30 years. I'm not conventionally pretty, but I am sturdy, a little weird, and always up for an adventure, as long as it's in a paperback and I don't need to talk to people. Listen to me, saying that like the world didn't go to hell two years ago, and I haven't been forced into a tiny cabin in Minnesota's northern forest. Let me take you back to two and a half years ago when I was a simple girl living in a much less lonely world…

CHAPTER 1

"Noah, you got that round for table 7 yet?" Nancy, the manager, yelled across the bar, her voice barely audible over Hank Williams singing about something I didn't care about.

"Yep, on it." I handed her a tray with 12 amber bottles and silver labels that I cared for even less. Friday nights in a small town is just not a time or place I like to tend bar. It is not the worst job out there, but the same old faces ordering the same old drinks to the same songs, getting hit on by every single guy who walks in, and then the guys whose dates are in the bathroom always left me feeling like there was more to life. This rat race felt more like a rat ball, speeding along with no rhyme or reason and no discernable destination. My apathy was rivaled only by my dislike of drunk people. If I don't like drunk people, why did I work in a bar, you ask? You have never lived in a small town, huh? There aren't exactly many options.

It wasn't all bad. I had a few regulars who, while I didn't know them personally, were always friendly and stood up for us bartenders when things got out of hand. Nancy's husband was the local sheriff, and his boys would hang out sometimes, which helped keep the riff-raff under control. The owner, Buck, was a bit of a slime ball, but with so many cops frequenting his establishment, he kept his hands to himself for the most part. We also served some of the best fish and chips I have had on this side of the pond. The head cook, Dane, was a marvel with a fryer. I even had a few girlfriends that I would have brunch with once in a while after church on Sundays. They didn't go to church with me, but we met up afterward for eggs and mimosas. I also had a few guy friends who would take me out to the movies sometimes, and I even dated one guy for four months. I had a pretty nice life going on, even if, on this night, I felt annoyed by everything.

A new face took a seat at the bar across from me and flashed his most winning smile. It was not very winning, but I smiled back like a good little barmaid. "What'll you have?" I asked him loudly.

"Hey there, little girly. What's a pretty thing like you doing on that side of the oak?" slurred Random Drunk Guy.

"Living the dream, Buddy. What can I get you?"

"You know, you look like that one actress. You know, the one in that movie about a building and that guy-"

"I don't really watch TV. What would you like me to get for you," I asked, growing a little short with Random Drunk Guy.

He didn't really seem to notice. "How about a tall glass of," He glanced at my name tag, "Noah? You take the wrong tag, baby? Or is Noah your man? I bet that's it, huh? Noah is your man?" His smile turned into a sickening grin. I took a deep breath, ready to have the conversation I had a thousand times before about my given name.

"That's her name, you jerk," Drunk Regular, three stools down remarked, not looking up from his phone. "It's a pretty name for a pretty girl. She is single, but she won't go home with you. Try Molly by the Juke over there. She likes her martinis dirty."

Random Drunk Guy blinked a couple of times as this information sank in, then turned to Drunk Regular. "This nice little thing and I are having a little A-B conversation, so why don't you see your way out of it?"

Drunk Regular snorted a little laugh, still scrolling his phone. "Are you in 5th grade, Bro? Trust me when I say that you are out of your league here, both with Noah and with me, so why don't you just do yourself a favor, order your drinks, and let the lady work."

Drunk Random looked from me to Drunk Regular a few times, then ordered two dirty martinis. Glad to turn around to grab a bottle, I rolled my eyes so hard; I'm pretty sure I knocked down all the pins in my head. After mixing up the drinks, he grabbed them and headed towards Molly, the owner's daughter. She giggled as he walked up, tossing her hair over her shoulder as she accepted the drink. Too bad I already knocked all those pins down. Molly had gone home with half the guys who frequented this bar. It was sick to think of Buck hiring her as entertainment for his guests, considering she was barely over 21. I shuddered and turned away. Like I said, Buck was a slimeball. I pushed the thoughts away and turned to Drunk Regular.

"Thanks. I appreciate the preemptive stupid question answers."

"Mmm hmm," he mumbled, his eyes still on the phone. I grabbed him a fresh beer, which he barely acknowledged as he scrolled through his phone. I smiled to myself. There were a few regulars that I liked to see here, and this guy was one of them. He never hit on me, never tried his luck with Molly; he just sat at the bar reading books on his phone while enjoying a couple of cold beers. In my opinion, he was the best kind of regular.

The football game on the big screen roared. Hank had finished his song, and Johnny Cash stepped up to the Juke. Molly's obnoxious laugh rolled over the bar. Small-town folks talked about small-town politics. The night rolled along. The boring, the mundane. The beautiful in retrospect.

Closing time crept up, and I rang the bell to warn all the stragglers of last call. Random Drunk Guy seemed to have struck out with Molly as she hid in the back, crying while he roamed the bar, an angry look on his face. I had a few dishes to wash up, so I invited her to chat while I worked. "Date go bad?" I asked her.

"Always," she said, her mascara running down her cheeks. "I hate this place. I hate these men. I hate what I have to do here."

I looked at her with a bit of confusion. I had always thought that she was a barfly because she liked it. "You don't… like what you do here?"

She cawed out a laugh. "No. My daddy threatened to kick me out if I didn't agree to it. I have nowhere to go, no one but him in this rotten world. Sometimes, I wish I could just run away and start over. I mean, I'm still young. I could still go to college. I always wanted to be a vet when I was a kid, but every time I brought it up to my daddy, he… Well, you know how he gets when he is mad."

I sat there stunned, hands in burning hot water. How had I never known this? How had I never cared enough to ask her about her life? "Why don't you just save up and get out?" I asked her.

"I don't get paid. Sometimes, the johns in the bar will give me a 'tip,' but it is never much. They pay my daddy directly."

"So, he has been… prostituting you out?! In his bar?! Right under the police's noses?" I was shocked at this revelation. That man was sicker and more twisted than I had ever known.

"Some of those boys in blue are his favorite customers," she said sadly.

I wanted to vomit. I pulled Molly in for a hug, wet hands and all. She cried into my shoulder. I suddenly felt terrible for being annoyed by her all the time. She didn't want this for her life.

"Hey," I said. "Let me talk to Nancy. She can talk to her husband, and he can sort this out."

"No!" she practically yelled. "I mean, no, she can't do that. I mean, it's a job, right? We all have bad days and good days. Some of the guys are really nice. Maybe I will meet one who will want to marry me and bring me away from this town."

"Molly, you can't live like this."

"Oh, I'm just being dramatic. I really do love this place. I just needed to cry a little, I guess." She took a deep breath and used the paper towel dispenser as a mirror to fix her makeup. “You have a good night, Noah. Thanks for listening.” And then she was off. I heard her high-pitched laugh and an “Oh, THERE you are! I’ve been looking everywhere for you!” from the door. I shook my head. That poor girl was a mess and in a bad situation. I needed to do something. I would call Nancy the next day and talk to her about it.

Once the dishes were all washed, tables wiped, and the register closed out, I was finally able to leave the stale beer smell of Buck’s and escape into the warm August night, filled with buzzing bugs, a soft breeze, and a billion stars. The walk home was always a little nerve-wracking until I got out of the bar zone downtown, but I had my pepper spray in hand and my 9mm in the small of my back, so I let myself enjoy the night.

A truck horn honked behind me, making me whip around and squint into the headlights of the offending vehicle. I was vaguely aware of my gun’s grip in my hand under my shirt as the truck rolled up on me, the window rolling down. Drunk Regular leaned out. So much for the best kind of regular.

“Hey, Noah. Want a ride?”

“Hey…. Guy. Nah, I’m good. The walk is a nice way to wind down,” I replied to him.

“It’s Duke, actually. And I’m fine. I only had three beers, and that was over a few hours. If that is what you’re worried about. If you think I might be a serial killer luring young ladies to my dungeon, then I can assure you, I am probably not.”

I couldn't stop the laugh that bubbled out. "Duke? Like Prince? Earl? Baron?"

"Those are my brothers, actually. And the whole serial killer bit doesn't spook you?"

"I mean, really, what are the chances of us both being serial killers?"

He grinned at me. It was… a really nice smile. I had never really looked at Duke as more than a generic face in front of a bar I hated being behind, but now that I really looked at him, he was pretty easy on the eyes. Dark hair long enough to tell me he didn't spend a ton on cuts, framed sharp cheekbones, a square jaw, and cool, smoky eyes.

But I was not born yesterday, and a handsome face does not a gentleman make.

"Thanks for the offer, and it was nice to actually meet you, Duke. I really am fine and enjoy the walk. Get yourself home safe. G'night."

"You got it. I don't suppose I could talk you into texting me when you get home so I know you made it safe?" he winked.

"Not a chance," I smiled sweetly back.

Grinning, he nodded once. "You got it, killer." And then he was off.

I watched his taillights for a while down the tree-lined street, my mind humming with the strange exchange between us. "Well, that was the best turndown I have ever given." I had to admit to myself it was refreshing. And it almost made me want to actually text him. Too bad I didn't get his number.

Ten minutes later, I was unlocking my bright blue front door. Bob, my giant golden retriever, bounded up to me with his leash in his mouth, his tail threatening to lift him off the ground with how fast it was going.

"Seriously, Bob, it's two in the morning. You should be sleeping."

His big brown eyes sparkled as he beamed a dopey grin at me. "You get a 10-minute walk! That is it!" I told him. He barked, spun in a circle, and sat most of the way down as I hooked him up. "You are pathetic," I said, smiling at him and giving him a kiss on the head. Bark. "Yeah, I love you, too."

By the time we got home from our 30-minute walk, I was exhausted. It had been a long day, and I was ready for it to be over. I made a salad, filled Bob's water dish with fresh cold water, and plopped onto the couch, flipping on the TV for some late-night garbage. The local sports team won. Go sports team. A politician did something bad and made up for it by doing something menial. A famous person ate something ordinary people eat every day and made the news for it. Seriously, this is why I never turn on the TV.

I was about to flip it off when something scrolling along the bottom caught my eye. "13 dead in metro area after bus station collapses." Why was that not a story they were covering? That was odd, even for this station. I pulled my phone out and searched for more details, salad turning soggy on the couch next to me. It didn't take me long to find the story. A sinkhole had opened up beneath a bus station in the city, causing the building to collapse onto 11 people waiting for their bus, plus a janitor and a homeless woman.

But why hadn't the news covered it? Maybe they had, and I just missed it. After all, it was approaching three am, and the news had been recorded hours before. I just caught the fluff stories. That had to be it. I was about to close it down and shut off my phone for the night when another story caught my eye. "Sinkhole in Ashlan causes interstate closure." Another sinkhole? In Ashlan? My mother lived in Ashlan. I would have to call her in the morning to see if she knew anything about it. Opening up a new search window, I type in "Sinkhole Minnesota."

Three thousand articles popped up. I clicked on the first one, which brought me to the article about the bus station. The next article was about a city farther north that had four sinkholes opened up in the city within an hour of each other. Eyewitnesses claimed they saw monsters in the dark of the holes— some dismissed them as crazy rednecks. The subsequent article was about aliens zapping large chunks of earth away. I snorted as I turned to Bob.

"What do you think of that, Bob?" I asked the dog, who was so kind as to clean up my dinner dish for me. He smiled and laid his head on my lap. "Good call. Let's head to bed."

Weird things happen all the time—no need to lose sleep over it. Still, 13 people lost their lives. Sinkholes were opening up all over the place, and no one seemed to notice. That should have been more significant news.

CHAPTER 2

I got up bright and early the next afternoon. Bob was already in the kitchen, sitting by the fridge, awaiting his morning feast. Seriously, this dog eats better than I do. I filled his bowl with a pound of fresh beef, some shredded carrots, steamed broccoli, three raw eggs, and a dollop of Greek yogurt. He cocked his head at me as I set it on the floor in front of him.

"Go ahead," I told him. He cocked his head and whined. "Seriously, you are ridiculous." I pulled the blueberries out of the fridge and tossed a handful on his food. He smiled at me and began greedily eating it up.

I began to undress for a quick shower when my phone rang.

"Hello, mother," I answered, bracing for the spillage of gossip, concern for my social life, and questions about grandbabies. Her weekly calls were both a comfort and a cause for irritation. However, I had a few things to ask her about, too, so I was glad for her call.

"Noah, how much money do you have?" Her voice was full of desperation and fear.

"What? Mom, what is wrong? You sound sca-"

"Noah! How much money do you have? In cash, not in the bank?"

"Why does that matter? What is wrong? What's going on?"

Her voice suddenly came out full of fear and warning. "Sweetheart, something is happening, and you need to get out of town. Take all the cash you have, fill every gas can you have, grab all the nonperishables you have and get out of town."

Confusion and fear filled me. My mother was flighty, loved gossip, and had a light-hearted nature. I had never heard this desperation in her voice before. It chilled me to the bone.

"Mother, what are you talking about? I need more than a scared warning. What is going on? Where do you want me to go? Do you need me to come see you?"

"Noah Elaine, listen to me. Turn on the news. Something bad is happening, and you need to get safe. Get out of town."

I walked back to the living room and grabbed the remote. "Mom, if you are being a drama queen, I am going.... To..." My voice trailed off as the television screen filled with scenes of skyscrapers disappearing into the earth, mobs of bleeding, dirt-covered people running and screaming, water pouring down wide streets, washing away cars and people alike. I stared in shocked silence for a moment before my mother's voice brought me back.

"Noah, sweetheart, get in your car. Drive. Get as far from the city as you can."

I was already on my way to the bedroom to grab my emergency fund. I was so glad that I decided to keep it in cash. Who knew if plastic would be any good any time soon? My mind raced. What was going on? Where should I go? Is anywhere safe?

My heart sank as I had a horrible realization.

"Mom, where are you?"

She sighed, and I could hear the smile she was forcing into her voice. "Noah, get yourself safe. I will be alright."

"Mother, that is not what I asked. Where the hell are you?"

"Watch your mouth. Cursing is not ladylike."

"Mother."

She sighed again. "My building is flooding. Thankfully, I am on the 3rd floor, but…. Well, it won't be long now. Everyone left is heading to the roof and hoping for a rescue crew, but… well, this is a large city."

"Um, no, that… no. They will get you. Get to the roof. I will call the police. There is… They…" I was at a total loss for words. I just couldn't believe what I was hearing.

"Noah, my beautiful, perfect baby girl. Get yourself safe. I wil—"

And the line went dead.

I stared numbly into space. I might have sat there forever numbly processing what was happening, but Bob seemed to notice something was awry and head-butted me back to reality.

I snapped back to the present moment. Okay, what do I do now? Call Nancy? The bar manager was probably the one who would have more information. Her husband was probably at the station now, so maybe she would know more. I dialed her number, but my phone would not work at all. Towers must be down. How bad was it here? We were miles away from the metro area, but the havoc seemed pretty widespread. I looked out the window to see my quiet neighborhood, with its tree-lined streets and tidy homes. No signs of mass hysteria, disappearing buildings, or flooding streets. What was going on?

My thoughts were interrupted by a pounding on my front door. "Noah! Noah, you home?!" I ran to the door and opened it. Duke practically fell into my house.

"Um, how do you know where I live?" I asked incredulously.

"We need to get out of here. Now," he replied.

"Not until you answer my question." I insisted.

"Seriously, Noah, it is on your mailbox. You have a huge dog that everyone knows. You live a straight mile from the bar you work at. And I happen to be a police deputy. Nancy's husband is my boss. He called me on my radio to check on you. Any other stupid questions, or can we get moving?"

I blinked at him a few times, not sure what to make of this. As of 12 hours ago, he was just a faceless regular at the bar. Now he is in my house trying to convince me to go with him?

Then, my brain snapped back from the shock of everything.

"What is going on? I just saw on the news I lost contact with my mother, who lives in Ashland.

That's just outside of-"

"I know where Ashlan is. We don't have time. Can we talk while you grab some essentials?" Duke pushed me toward my bedroom, which Bob took as aggressive and lunged at Duke, sinking his teeth into his forearm, causing Duke to scream a most undignified yelp.

"Bob!" I screamed, grabbing the golden fur and pulling back. "No, Bob, let him go! No!"

Bob glared at Duke, letting out a low growl, releasing the arm, which he thankfully decided he didn't need to bite hard to get his point across.

"Control your animal." Duke snapped at me, pulling up his sleeve to see the damage.

"Excuse me, you pounded down my door and shoved me in my own home! You control YOUR animal!" I snapped back.

Duke looked at me for a second, then sighed. "I'm sorry. Hard to turn it off. Good boy, Bob.

Seriously, who names their dog Bob?"

"Can we please focus here? This whole thing is like a vaudeville skit. Packing, walking, talking, m'kay?" I led him to my room, where I had thankfully put my dirty clothes in the hamper and not left them on the floor like I normally do. Small mercies, I guess?

I grabbed a bag out of my closet and began filling it with clothes. "Duke, talk. What is happening?"

He began grabbing blankets and random things from my closet, setting them on the bed for me to choose from. "About three months ago, sinkholes began forming all over the US. They were small to start with, but they have been getting larger and larger, causing more damage. Yesterday, 13 people were killed by one when a bus station collapsed on top of them."

"Yeah, I saw that on the news," I said, collecting paperbacks off my shelf and stuffing them in the bag. "What is going on? Where did the sinkholes come from? I mean, I'm no geologist, but they don't usually come in spurts, right?"

"We don't know. The official word is that swamp gas pockets are bursting, but there has been chatter about terrorist groups claiming that they have been pumping methane into underground caverns, causing the surface to flex."

"Okay, less official. What. Is. Going. On?"

"The surface is falling apart. There is nowhere officially safe because there is no rhyme or reason to what is happening, but it seems the trend is cities are where the majority are. We just don't know for sure. The best thing to do is just get out of town and… Pray, I guess."

I snatched a second bag and ran into my bathroom, tossing in toiletries, towels, and makeup.

Back in the bedroom, I filled the rest of the space with a few more books.

"So, foodstuff next, right?" I asked.

"Probably, if you want to eat," he replied.

We stared at each other for a moment, then both cracked a grin. "Duke, why are you here?"

"To warn you? I told you, my boss is Nancy's-"

"Duke, why are you here instead of getting your friends and family ready?"

He looked at me a little blankly for a moment. "I don't… have… anyone."

"Oh," I said, not really knowing what to make of anything that had taken place today, let alone this strange conversation. I started gathering canned foods out of the pantry and putting them in a third bag. "So where are you going? Any suggestions on which way I should go? I just…. I've never been in an apocalypse before and have no idea what to do."

"We could go together? I mean, if you want to. I'm not trying to…. I just meant…" He looked away quickly, color touching his cheeks.

"Duke? If you are worried that I think you are trying to flirt or get lucky while the world is literally falling apart around us, you are insane. I have my car, but it does make sense to just go in one if you don't mind. It's only for a few days, right? The government will figure out safe zones and get everyone back home. Right? That's the plan?"

"Officially, yes."

"I really don't like that word as much as I thought I did."

"I really don't know, Noah. It could be days; it could be weeks. I just know that it seems that the best, safest thing to do is get away from towns. Believe it or not, this is my first apocalypse, too."

I looked around the pantry—too much to process. I needed to get to my mother. I needed to get out of town. I needed to get my head on straight.

Taking a deep breath, I scooped all the dried beans and rice I had and tossed in a few boxes of mac and cheese for good measure. I turned a half circle, then swiped back to grab the bags of coffee.

Who knew how long, right? "Did you grab food, too, Duke?"

"Yeah, I did. I was planning to stop at the grocery on the way out of town and see if they had anything left. Most people cleared out this morning." He took the bag from my hand. "Let's get moving."

We loaded everything up in the bed of his pickup. I ran in one last time to see if I had forgotten anything. My head was spinning with the reality of what was happening; I grabbed my Bible off the coffee table, my first aid kit from the cupboard, my 9mm, and all the ammo I had in the safe. As I turned all the lights out, I had the weirdest feeling that I would never see this little house again. I shook the thought away. Seriously? No need to be dramatic about it, Noah.

I hopped in the front seat and called for Bob, who took a firm position between me and Duke, giving a side eye and a deep growl for good measure.

"Noted. Bob does not like me," Duke said, putting the truck in drive.

"Don't take it personally. He is a momma's boy."

"I learned that the hard way."

"He didn't break skin, did he? On your arm?" I had forgotten about the initial meeting between you two.

"Nah, it was just a love nibble. Isn't that right, Bobby Boy?" he reached over to rub Bob's ear, only to receive another deep growl. "He will warm up to me, right?"

"Oh, no. His mind is made up. You are doomed to be his chew toy for life. So sad."

"Really?"

"No. Not really. He's a Golden. They love everyone." As if to prove my point, he laid down and put his head on my lap, looking up at me with his huge brown eyes. "Yes. A puddle of butter."

"Weird dog."

CHAPTER 3

e sat in silence until we reached the Quick Mart on the town's edge. The doors were broken. Looters had already come through.

"Well, might as well see if there is anything useful left," Duke said as he opened the door. "You want to wait here with Bob or come see what we can find?"

"I'll help," I said, sliding out of the truck. "Wait here, Bob. I'll be right back." He gave me a sad look and laid his head back down. I smiled, following Duke to the shattered remains of a door.

"Stay behind me until I make sure the coast is clear."

"Seriously? What are you expecting? Pirates?" I rolled my eyes as he held up a hand.

"Noah, desperate people do desperate things. Behind me, please?"

"Okay, Duke. I will follow you. That way, you can get shot, and I can be the hero that pulls you to saf-"

PAH! PAH! PAH!

Three shots tore through the air. I screamed, grabbing my gun and diving behind the door frame. Duke was lying three feet away in a pool of blood that grew by the second. Panic tore through my chest as I sat there, holding my gun against the wall beside me. I had never fired it outside of the range before. My hands were shaking too badly for it to be of any use. Duke groaned and moved.

"Cease fire!" I shouted. I had no idea if that was the right thing to say, but it sounded official, maybe. "Cease fire!" I added it for good measure. Hushed voices argued, glass broke, and then silence ensued. I sat for a long minute, trying to breathe and listen, but all I could hear were my own terrified heartbeat and Bob barking like crazy from the truck. I waved at him, then realizing that was dumb, quickly put my hand back. I was so unprepared for this apocalypse thing.

Taking a deep breath, I flipped around the corner of the doorway, firing blindly into the store. A chip bag exploded as I leaped for Duke, shielding his body with mine. "I got you, Duke! I'm here! I gave us some cover," I yelled as I started pulling on his body. He let out a loud groan and then began laughing.

"Noah, you shot a bag of chips. The bad guys ran out the back. And one shot is not how you cover somebody."

"No, I did it! I shot, and now they… And you…. Shoot. Where are you hit?"

"Left arm. Through and through."

You got hit twice?!"

"What? No, that's what you call it when… Oh, never mind. Just help me up."

I had thought my adrenaline would make me lift him so fast that he'd fly into the ceiling. That was not the case at all. In fact, Duke was a heavy man. He groaned again as I helped him upright. "Let's just go," I said, my voice trembling with urgency.

"No, I didn't get shot for nothing. You grab, and I will keep watch. Keep your gun easily accessible, though I hope not to see you shoot it ever again. That was ugly."

"Hey, I was scared, ok? I have never been shot at before, never had someone shot in front of me; this is a day of firsts for me!"

He gave me a thin grin. "I'm just teasing. You were very brave. Now, help me tie this thing off. I don't need to lose any more blood." I removed the bandana from my hair and tied it as tight as I could around his bloody arm. He grunted but didn't complain, pulling out his gun and asking me to cock it for him. "I will cover you from here." He positioned himself against the doorframe with his gun pointed at the floor in front of him.

I started searching the aisles for any remaining items, which wasn't much. Thankfully, there were some medical supplies left, so I seized as much as I could carry and hurried back to the store's front to stash it on the counter. "Paper, please," I asked, smiling sweetly at my bleeding comrade. He rolled his eyes at me and shuffled to the counter, constantly watching behind me and glancing out the door every few seconds to check on the truck.

I ran down the canned food aisle, looking for something useful. I like canned cherry pie filling as much as the next guy, but is it really emergency food? Yeah, it is. So, I grabbed a few.

I heard sounds coming from the back. "Noah, hurry up. We have to get out of here."

I began grabbing everything in sight, then ran to the front. "Ok, that should do it, I think. Can you carry some of this? I'll pay."

"Are you serious right now, Noah?!"

"I am no thief!" I shot back defensively.

POW POW!

Shots rang out from behind us.

"Never mind!" We grabbed our booty and sprinted to the truck, hastily throwing everything except the medical supplies into the back before jumping in the truck.

"I'll drive, you patch," Duke instructed, grunting as he slammed the door shut.

"Is that a good idea? You lost quite a bit of blood." I asked, hopping in the passenger seat as Bob licked my face.

"No kidding? Did you remember the French-fried onions for our baked potatoes later?!"

"I said we should have just left after you got shot!" I snapped back.

POW POW! Shots rang out at us as he slammed the truck into the gear, skidding out of the lot.

"Defensive pirates! I was even going to pay you!" I shouted through the closed window.

"Noah! Can you please help patch up this gun wound instead of yelling at the nice pirate man?!"

"He is not nice!"

"I changed my mind. Can I apocalypse with someone less crazy?"

"Oh, you big baby. Give me your arm."

I pushed Bob into the back and moved closer to Duke. He carried the scent of cologne and something peppermint. I swallowed, forcing myself to ignore how nice he smelled. "I can't reach your left arm very well, Duke. Could you have been shot somewhere else?" I grumbled, turning around in the seat, my back against the dash so I could reach across his chest.

"Next time, I will ask the nice pirate to shoot me in the other arm, okay?" I rolled my eyes but couldn't help the smile that pulled at my cheeks. Duke slowed to get around a broken-down car partially obstructing the road, and I swallowed my feelings of intrigue.

Suddenly, the truck lurched, throwing me head-first into the seat.

"Hang on!" Duke yelled, steering the truck wildly.

"Hang on to what?!" I yelled back, hitting my back against the dash. Out the back window, I saw dust filling the air and a large hole in the road where the abandoned car had just been. I took a deep breath and pushed down my fear.

"Let's just get a little way out of town and pull over. I don't think I can take any more of your driving backwards."

Duke kept his eyes on the road, looking calm, considering what we narrowly avoided. I was glad for his calm as my heart was racing.

"We can do that. There is a pull-off a few miles down."

"Good," I said. "It would probably be best for me to get you out of your shirt anyways." The words were hardly out of my mouth when I realized what I had just said. Duke continued to watch the road but let a slight smirk cross his lips. "You know what I mean!" I snapped. I pulled Bob back up front just for good measure. I couldn't help but steal a glance at Duke as he drove. His smoky eyes flicked over to me, capturing my gaze for a beat, then back to the road.

He was good enough not to mention the blush.

We pulled over at a small scenic lookout offering a great view of a very run-down old farm. I hopped out, let Bob jump down, grabbed the medical supplies from the store as well as my first aid kit and went to the driver's side. "Okay, you big baby, let's see this wound of yours," I teased as I opened his door. Duke grimaced and exhaled heavily as I loosened the bandana and pulled off his shirt. I gasped. The wound was an ugly, bloody mess. His bicep muscle twitched, causing blood to seep out of the hole that yawned at me. Tears came unbidden to my eyes.

"Duke, this is…" My voice trailed off as guilt tore through my heart.

"It's really not that bad. I've had worse. Just do what I tell you," he said gently, handing me a bottle of water. "We have to clean it first, get all the extra blood off."

I looked up at him, my eyes brimming with tears. "Duke, I am so sorry. This is my fault. I should have just listened to you and let you focus. I… got you shot. I'm-"

"Noah, it is not your fault. I'm a cop. I have been shot twice before, and both were worse than this. If anything, you saved me by being there and helping me get out before they came back." I dropped my eyes, and his hand lifted my chin, directing my gaze back to his. "Noah, this is not your fault."

I gave a quick nod and wiped away the tears threatening to spill down my cheeks.

"Now, let's get this cleaned." I opened the bottle and started to work, following his directions. I retched a few times but managed to get the wound cleaned, slathered with antiseptic, and tied up to the point that it could close. Once he was patched, I asked if he wanted me to take over driving for a while.

"Probably a good idea. I need to take some painkillers and rest. I lost a lot of blood," he said

“Where do you want me to head?”

“North. I have a friend who owns a remote cabin a couple hours from here. We should be able to make it before dinner time.”

At the mention of food, my stomach growled loudly. I realized I hadn’t eaten since my lunch break last night. “Let’s grab something now. I’m starving.” We loaded back into the truck with some nuts, water bottles, and a couple of apples from my pantry at home. Within a few minutes, we hit the road again.

We rode in silence for a while. Every so often, Bob would sigh and move his head around. He really didn’t love car rides like most big dogs, but he took it in stride. After about an hour, we passed by an abandoned car on the side of the road. I got sudden goosebumps. “Hey, Duke?”

“Mmm?” he mumbled from the passenger side.

“Are you awake?”

“Nope. This is the Pope using Duke’s mouth. What a handsome little puppet.”

“I’m serious. When was the last time you saw a car? I mean, a moving car?”

Duke sat up and looked out the windshield.

“You know, I don’t think we have seen a car since we got out of town. That is odd.”

“Where do you think everyone is?”

"Hopefully, somewhere safe. We can't really worry about that now. Let's just get to our destination."

Bob suddenly sat up straight and let out a booming bark. "Woah, buddy, it's ok! We will get out soon. You're okay," I said soothingly, but he remained unsettled. His hackles raised. "Hey, Buddy. It's okay."

A sudden movement on the road in front of me snapped my attention back to the road. I gasped and slammed on the brakes, sending the truck into a skid. Duke grabbed the Jesus Bar and screamed, "Look out!"

As quickly as it was there, it was gone. We sat in shocked silence, the air filled with the smell of burning brake pads, breathing heavily. My mind could not accept what it had just witnessed.

CHAPTER 4

"What… What was…. Did you see…" I tried to form a cohesive sentence. It was not going well.

"Noah, please tell me with as much detail as you can what you just saw."

My mind sputtered, and my mouth tried to make sense of what my eyes had told it. "It… Was tall. I think it was a giant toad. On two legs. With a mouth on its chest."

"Good. Good," Duke said. "I am certain that we are both hallucinating the same thing."

That was really the only reasonable explanation. What I had seen was certainly not human, but it was definitely not a native species to this part of the universe.

"What should we do? Keep moving?" I asked.

"I think so. I am not sure what just happened, but I do know that it can't be good."

A low rattling sound, barely audible above the truck's engine, sent goosebumps over every inch of my skin. I peeked in the rear-view mirror and peed a little.

“Duke, don’t look now, but our hallucination is watching us,” I murmured. His eyes quickly shifted from one mirror to another until he spotted it. His breathing stopped as he slowly reached for his gun.

“Noah, I need you to cock this for me slowly and hand it back. Then put the truck in gear and slam the gas like it owes you money,” he breathed back, then, very carefully, his hand with the gun rose. My eyes fixated on the creature, in total shock of what I was seeing.

It stood at least 9 feet tall. Its legs, with an excessive number of knee joints and folded in an accordion-like manner. Its arms reached the ground at its sides and ended in what must have been hands but looked more like a magnet in a knife drawer, wicked claws hooking out in all directions. That would have been bad enough, but its face really was the source of nightmares for life. Its four eye sockets were sunken into a tiny head, and colorless, glassy eyes stared at us, unblinking. It had a shiny bald head and a mouth that was a slash, full of red-tinted teeth.

And then there was the second mouth on the chest, about 18 inches across, with what was clearly a human foot sticking out. The large mouth moved up and down slowly, almost thoughtfully, as it watched us.

Duke poked me with his finger, reminding me that we should probably not sit here and invite this guy to lunch. I grabbed the gun, cocked it, and handed it back, slamming the truck in gear and peeling out, screaming as I did. Both hands on the wheel, I looked in the mirror only to see the creature running after us.

And catching up.

"What is that thing?!" I shouted.

"Just drive! Drive! Keep moving forward!"

We sped up, approaching 80 miles per hour. There is no way the thing could be that fast. And yet…

Duke rolled down his window and spun around, holding his weapon out the window awkwardly with his right hand. He fired off three shots. I glanced in the mirror and watched the thing go down. I let out what was something between a "caw" like a crow, a snort like a pig, and a bark like a seal. It was anything but ladylike; my mother would be proud. Duke grimaced as he turned back around and rolled up his window. "Well, that was… something," he said.

"Duke, in case we die by getting eaten by a weird black frog monster, I just wanted you to know something," I replied. "I just have to get this off my chest."

He glanced at me and raised his eyebrows. "Yeah?"

"Your name is Deputy Duke. Seriously, who is named Deputy Duke?"

He took a deep breath and let it out slowly. "Yes, that is correct."

"I just wanted to make sure that you were made fun of for it. You know, before we die later today," I said, keeping my eyes locked on the road.

"Thank you, Noah. I can die humiliated now. You are the yin to my ego's yang."

"I do what I can."

I burst into tears. I'm not one to cry. I don't usually get emotional over movies, and I didn't even cry when my last boyfriend dumped me at work. I keep it together. But that day, that moment was different. I flat-out blubbered, full-on snot-sobs.

Duke reached over, taking my hand in his. "Noah, pull over. I can drive for a while. We will be getting off the main road soon anyways."

I didn't argue. I pulled over, unbuckled, and hopped out, blowing my nose on my shirt sleeve as I walked around. Duke stopped me before I got in and pulled me into a much-needed hug. He held me until my breathing evened out, watching the tree line the entire time. I let go first, pushing back to dry my eyes. "I'm sorry. I don't know where that came from," I said, avoiding his eyes.

"Hey," he said, gently holding my chin in his hands. I looked up into his eyes, feeling so vulnerable, so scared, so lost. I don't know what came over me. I grabbed him by the neck and kissed him. I kissed him hard. My hands eagerly sought out as much comfort and physical contact as they could get as the seconds ticked by. Duke seemed just as shocked as I was by my actions, freezing for a moment before kissing me back.

When I came up for air, he looked into my eyes. "Noah, we are not going to die today," he firmly assured me.

"How can you know that?" I sniffled.

He took my hands in his, even though it must have been extremely painful to move his wounded arm. "I will not let you die today. I don't know what is going on, where the sinkholes are from, what that monster was, or what to do other than drive far away, but I do know this: When a beautiful woman kisses you out of terror… you count your lucky stars because she is never going to do it again."

I laughed and leaned in for a hug. We stood there holding each other for a minute.

"I still don't really like you, just so you know," I said into his shoulder.

"I would expect nothing less. Now," Duke said, stepping back. "We need to keep moving. It's about another 100 miles to my friend's cabin, so we should make it before dark. Hop in, take a deep breath, and keep watch in case there are more of those things around. Can you do that?"

"Yes," I said with more confidence than I felt.

"Good. Let's get moving, Killer." I smiled at him and gave his hands a gentle squeeze.

"Thank you, Duke. For everything. I don't know what today would have looked like if it weren't for you."

He leaned in and kissed the top of my head gently. "What can I say? I love a damsel in distress." "You are a chauvinist," I grumbled, pouting a little.

"I like to think of myself as a knight, actually. You know, brave, handsome, heroic, saves the girl and slays the dragon."

"As I recall, I was the one who saved you in the shootout," I said indignantly as I walked back to the passenger side and climbed in.

"I know, I saw you," he said in a mocking voice. "Those chips didn't know what hit them."

We both laughed as we continued down the road. Bob gave a little bark to remind us that he was there. "You are a good boy, Bob. You told us when the monster was coming. You get extra belly rubs before bed tonight!" He tilted his head back and smiled his big doggy smile at me.

We were coming upon another car on the side of the road. A chill ran down my spine. Was the driver of this car the foot we saw being chewed on by the monster? A wave of nausea swept over me as I thought about it. As we passed by it, I saw massive damage to the front door and a bloody trail where something heavy was dragged across the road. "Oh," I moaned.

"Keep watching. There might be more of them around here," Duke said, eyes sharp, scanning the tree line as he sped up.

"Duke," I said, my own eyes scanning around me.

"Yeah?"

"I am scared."

"Me, too, Noah. But we have a pretty good team here. We are going to be ok." He took my hand and gave it a gentle squeeze before grabbing the wheel with both hands again.

I took a deep breath and blew it out slowly, watching the tree line. What was happening? I was so confused, so angry, so many emotions that I could not keep a thought straight in my head.

"So, what is your favorite type of book to read?" Duke's voice shook me out of my thoughts.

"Really? You want to talk about books? Right now? As we avoid man-eating-monster-toads?"

"Well, we could talk about the toads, or we could pass the time a little more cheerfully. Up to you."

I thought about it for a moment, then decided I would be crazy to want to even think about those things. "I really love a good murder mystery. Suspense, danger, who-done-it, spy versus spy, gripping, thrilling roller coaster of a read. How about you?"

"Well, if I could read every romance novel out there, I would be a happy man," Duke said while watching the road.

I stared at him for a moment. "Well, that's… cool," I managed, shifting a little closer to the door.

"I kind of figured you for a sci-fi guy."

"Oh, man, I read this amazing book once about this woman who falls in love with an alien, and the alien takes her back to his home planet to meet his people, and she meets his old alien girlfriend, and the woman thinks that he is still in love with the other woman, but he kissed her and…"

Duke looked over at my horrified face and burst out laughing. "I'm sorry, I can't keep that up. No, I don't read romance novels. I am more of a historical fiction and suspense guy. Wow, the look on your face was priceless."

I laughed along with him as we eased into comfortable conversations about favorite books, authors, book stores, and on and on. It provided a peaceful way to pass the hours of driving despite the spooky eyes glinting from the forest edge.

CHAPTER 5

We got into the denser evergreen portion of the drive and passed a few more abandoned cars, some of which crashed into the tree line. Whenever I saw blood trails, my stomach turned over. We passed a sign that said "Carlston, 3 miles" and a few amenities the town offered.

There was movement to my right, and I got a glimpse of something large and dark in the trees. "I think I just saw another one," I told him quietly.

"You did. We have passed three in the past few miles. We should be able to stop safely for gas if there is a station in the open at the edge of town. Then it's a road change and cabin, but on smaller side roads, so we will have to be extra cautious, keeping both guns out and at the ready." "What if we can't find gas? Will we still get there?"

Duke's lack of response was answer enough.

The turn-off for Carlston—population 32,857, home of the World's Largest Dreamcatcher, came upon us sooner than I would have liked, not knowing what we were about to face. As it turned out, I didn't need to worry about it. Carlston was gone. I sat in shocked silence as we came to a stop on the shoulder of the off-ramp. It looked as though a giant had taken an ice cream scoop and scooped out the whole town. Mile after mile of deep, black holes with sometimes rubble visible and a few places flooded from broken water mains was all that remained of the town. It was my first glimpse of the sinkhole devastation, and it was, well, simply devastating. We stared at it in shocked silence. Bob let out a whine; the nothingness of it all was haunting. All those people, all those lives. Did they hold each other as their world collapsed? Had they started their day normally, with a cup of coffee and pancakes shared with their children? Were moms and dads on their way to work, babies in daycare, buses filled with children, grandmothers playing cards, uncles planning surprise camping trips, young women applying makeup and styling their hair?

So many lives, so many timelines—just gone.

I couldn't breathe. I couldn't cry. I couldn't tear my eyes away from the nothingness. Choking out a ragged breath, I noticed movement in the rubble far away. I wish I hadn't noticed, for now, it was all I could see. There were the monsters —some larger, some smaller, all with those long arms and accordion-like legs, climbing nimbly over the smashed-up buildings, leaping yards at a time over openings. A small group sprang out of a hole, dragging something bulky behind them. Once they were on the solid surface of a hole's rim, they began tearing into it.

I couldn't hold my nausea upon realizing what it was. I managed to open the truck door in time to vomit violently. They had a human. They were eating a human. The beasts were scavenging the ruins of this city and eating the inhabitants. I was dimly aware of Duke's hand on my back. I spat out the bile and grabbed my water to rinse my mouth. "We need to keep moving, Noah."

With a burning throat, I turned to face him. "Duke, we need to stop this. They are eating…"

"I know. But there is nothing we can do right now. Let's get safe and make a plan. We are low on gas and vastly outnumbered. Even if we weren't, we can't spend our ammo this way."

I knew he was right, but the idea of leaving these monsters to continue this vile debauch was unbearable. Turning away, I closed my door on the gruesome sight.

"Let's get gas and get to the cabin," I agreed. "Can you figure out an alternate route, as we can't get through Carlston?"

"Sure thing. We will get back on the main road and—" his sentence was cut off by Bob barking loudly, snarling, and jumping toward the window. We had been noticed.

Three dark shapes grew larger as they sped toward us at a frightening speed. Duke slammed the truck into gear and sped off, hoping to gain some distance before the beasts could reach and rip us apart and then eat us alive. "Grab your gun!" he shouted, glancing in the mirror and pushing the truck into overdrive.

I drew my weapon, checked the mag, chambered a round, and swung around in my seat to roll down the window. "This would be way easier if you had a sunroof in this thing," I groaned as we rocketed on, leaning out slightly to see how close our company was.

“Yeah, I should have thought about that when I was looking for a reliable vehicle. How will this sucker do in a road way shoot out? Is it going to work well in all end-of-the-world scenarios? What is the monster-proofing on the body like?”

“I know, right? Who taught you to shop for cars?”

The three monsters behind us lagged; we had at least a half-mile head start, and there were easier meals to be had. Facing forward, I rolled up the window and tried my best not to think of what those meals were.

Leaving Carlston in the rearview mirror, we sped down the quiet road. Duke knew the roads well and circumnavigated the town in less than half an hour. Fortunately, we didn’t encounter more creatures.

Our luck continued as we arrived at Papa Ray’s Gas and Shop. A few frightened people were filling up their cars, gas cans, and every container they had. An old guy by the front door sat with a shotgun on his lap, smiling with his weathered face. We pulled into the line and waited.

“Do you want to see if they have any more supplies left? Water, bullets, maps, the works,” Duke asked me.

“Sure,” I replied, unbuckling my seatbelt and climbing out of the truck with shaky legs, approaching the old man on the overhung porch. “Hey,” I greeted wearily. “You must be Papa Ray.”

With a smooth motion, he leaped from the rocking chair, lifted his rifle, and aimed at my head. Dumbstruck, I collapsed to the ground as his shot rang out, dead.

Well, not dead, but definitely in shock.

Duke was by my side instantly, his face pale as he screamed my name. "Noah! Noah! Can you hear me?"

Blinking, I looked at him. "I think I just died. Did I get shot in the head by an old guy with a rifle?"

"Who you callin' an old guy, little missy?"

I looked up and I saw the old man cradling his rifle yet again and the same smile playing on his lips.

Sitting up, I was not sure what to say or what had just happened. I didn't need to worry about saying anything, though. Duke took care of that for me.

"What the hell is wrong with you? You almost killed her? That was-"

"Hold up, sonny," the Old Guy said, holding a hand out for peace. "No need to get uptight. There was one of them beasties over yonder in the trees, by that big ol' pine tree. S'prolly still there if you care to take a look. I been keepin' my eyes out for the rascals so folk can load up on what I have left. S'not much, but if it helps keep 'em going 'til they can find safety, then it's worth it. I'm Papa Ray; this here is Bessy." His eyes looked meaningfully at the gun in his arm.

“Now I am terribly sorry to cause such a fright to a pretty little thing like your wife here, but them things is fast. Not much time for small talk when they get close.”

Duke took a deep breath and touched my cheek one more time to assure himself (and me) that I was still alive. Then, he stood and extended a hand to Papa Ray.

“I’m Duke. Nice to meet you, sir. This is Noah. We are in need of gas. And ammo if you carry it?

We have plenty of cash. Not sure what your prices look like right about now.”

“Oh, Duke, I can’t take yer money anymore that I can take yer lady’s life. We are all human beans here and needin’ to work together as much we can. Come on in and have a look around when yer done fillin’ yer tank.”

“We appreciate it, though a word of caution to people before you open fire on them might help with your road-aide manner.”

“My apologies, little missy. I will certainly give a holler before I shoot at you again. Deal?”

I nodded as Duke helped me up, brushed off my clothes a bit and led me back to the truck. Bob jumped out and ran straight to the man who had shot at me a minute before. He leaped on Papa Ray, smothering him with kisses and wagging his tail like a playful pup. Duke’s jaw dropped.

"What… did… Is he… Oh, never mind," Duke muttered. He hopped in beside me and drove up to the pump. I smiled at Bob as I calmed my breathing. Duke began filling the tank and then opened my door again.

"Noah, I need to ask you something."

"No, I will not marry you," I smiled as much as I could muster.

Duke smirked back. "I can work on that later. For now, I need you to think open-mindedly and listen carefully." He took a deep breath. "I want to bring that body with us."

I stared at him for a second.

"I'm sorry, what?"

"Noah, if we can learn about these things, we can see if they have any weaknesses. We can study it up close; we can see how it is put together so we can see how best to take them down." "Duke, are you crazy?! What if they carry diseases? What if it rots and fills everything with a smell that we can never get rid of? What if it comes back to life and eats our faces?!"

"I know that it sounds terrible, but think about it from a greater good standpoint. We have no idea how long these things will be around, where they came from, anything about them really. A chance to get one dead to look at, cut open, learn about- It might just save our lives and many others. That is worth the smell haunting us, right?"

I took a deep breath. "I super hate you right now, Duke. You know that, right?"

"I do, yes." The gas pump clicked, alerting us that the tank was full. He turned around and put the hose back. "Just think about it for a few minutes while I talk to Ray. Are you okay to drive the truck and park it over there so the next cars can get in?"

I sat there for a moment more. "Yes, I can move the truck, and maybe I will think about the corpse absconding. Good enough?"

"Good enough." He leaned in and kissed the top of my head. In a barely audible voice, he said, "I thought I lost you."

Then he turned and walked away. I felt the color rise to my cheeks. I hardly knew Duke, and yet here I was, wanting to call him back to me. Life-and-death situations have a way of lighting sparks you never wanted to be lit, I guess.

After I moved the truck, a minivan pulled into the vacant space. A woman around her mid-thirties stepped out and began pumping gas, looking over her shoulder. She looked so scared; I felt like she needed me to talk to her. I climbed out and walked over to her.

"Hey," I said.

She startled at the sound of my voice. "Oh, hi."

"Are you doing okay? Where are you heading from?" I asked her.

"I don't know, I don't know, I don't know," she moaned. Peeking into her car, I noticed two empty car seats.

"Are you… are you alone?" I asked in a hushed voice.

She fell to the ground beside her van. "They're gone! My babies! They're gone!" she cried out.

I choked on my own tears, watching her anguish. "Hey, it's okay, Sweety. What is your name? Where were you? Do you need help finding your babies? How old are they?" I desperately fought for the right words as I sank next to her and stroked her dark hair. She continued to scream, clutching at her chest.

"My babies! My babies! They were taken from me!" she wailed. Other people from nearby vehicles began to wander over. Her grief-wracked face was stained with tears and dust. I sat helplessly holding her, eyes searching for Duke. He emerged from the store and was looking our way with a pale face.

At least a dozen people had gathered around us. I looked desperately from face to face to see if someone would help share this burden. A movement caught my eye. Bob burst out of the store and began barking furiously. There were three men in the bed of our truck, unloading it into their van as fast as they could.

"Hey! Stop that!" I yelled, struggling to free myself from the grasp of the woman. "Someone, stop them! Duke! Duke!" Snapping out of his moment of shock, Duke saw the pillagers taking all of our much-needed supplies and ran towards them.

The woman clutched my arm tightly and moaned, "Oh, my babies! They're gone! Gone!"

I tried to pull free. The group surrounding us charged at the men in the truck, but they saw their window was up. They quickly jumped into their vehicle and sped off.

Duke drew his gun, firing a few shots. One hit a tire, causing the van to careen off the road and into the ditch. The men jumped out, one limping badly, and tried to run off. Duke was on them in a flash.

"Freeze!"

Two of the men stopped, while the third just bolted for the trees.

"I said FREEZE!" Duke's voice boomed out. His tone was deep and commanding. The runner just kept going and disappeared into the underbrush. I finally freed myself from the woman's grasp and hurried across the dirt parking lot to Duke's side. I pulled my own weapon as my stomach dropped out of me. From the woods, a sickening clicking sound and a rattling growl emanated, followed by gurgling screams, sloppy crunching noises, and, then, silence. Duke sucked in a breath, looked grim, and shook his head. "He didn't have to run. I just wanted our supplies back. It wasn't worth his life."

I placed my hand on his arm, glancing at the bandages from earlier and shook my head. So much pain—what was happening to our world? How could people, even in desperation, become so cruel, heartless, thoughtless, and careless?

The screech of tires snapped us back to reality as the minivan sped toward us. We jumped out of the way as it pulled between us and the looters. The woman slowed down and then hustled away, leaving a cloud of dust where the men had been a moment before.

We both took a deep breath.

"Duke, can we go now? It is the worst pit stop I have ever made in my life, and I have driven across Montana."

He chuckled and pulled me in. "Yeah, let's get out of here," he said. "Papa Ray has some supplies left that we can take a look through if you are up to it?"

"Yeah, I think I can handle that, but we should leave Bob to watch the truck."

"Agreed."

Lowering the tailgate, Bob hopped up into the back. I opened a fresh bottle of water and filled Bob's bowl, which I had brought from home. "You wait here, boy. Let me know if there is any more trouble."

Bob gave me a sloppy kiss and then settled down by his water bowl.

Duke and I entered the old shop and saw Papa Ray gazing out the dusty window. "Well, that sure was quite the performance, huh?" he asked, shaking his head. "Had a few dishonest folk come through today to try that kinda garbage. Makes me feel like there ain't any reason to care 'bout 'em."

"I hear you there, Ray," Duke said, striding over to the old man. "Been a cop for about six years now, and there are more people that need to be saved from themselves than you would believe."

"Oh, I sure do believe it," Papa Ray said, shaking his head sadly.

"Mind if we take a look at what supplies you have left?"

"Yeah, come on, kids." Papa Ray said as he led us around the store, handing us cans, bags, bottles, and batteries as he saw fit. As few other people came in, he directed them to the supplies they needed, ensuring no group received more than another. When someone was looking for an item he was out of, he helped them find a suitable substitute. This man really was here to help every person who came along. If only the world had more people like Papa Ray.

We thanked Ray for his generosity and walked back out to the truck. More cars were pulling in with weary travelers and injured survivors.

Climbing back into the truck with Bob, I watched Duke share some parting words with Papa Ray. He handed something to the old man and then turned to walk away. After climbing in, he pulled up to the now-wrecked van the looters had used. We both jumped out and started reloading the bed of the truck. There were a lot of supplies in the van that didn't belong to us.

"I'll tell Ray to get this stuff in his store for those who need it," Duke said. "You sit tight."

As he walked away, Bob started growling again. I pet his head before burying my face in his silky, golden fur. “Bob, what is happening?” I murmured, allowing a few tears to spill out. Although Ray was a great human, the face of the crying woman haunted me. The woman had used motherhood as a weapon. She used my compassion as a tool against me. It was so hard to believe that people could be that dark during a time when working together was so vital. On the first day of whatever was happening, I wondered how much worse it would get?

I really didn’t want to know.

Duke huffed as he climbed back in the truck. “Ray is going to keep his eyes open for more road pirates, warn people as they stop. I gave him directions to the cabin in case he needed a safe place. He just laughed at me and said his place was here, where he could do the most good. Why can’t the world be full of Papa Ray’s?”

“I was just thinking that,” I said, sinking my fingers into Bob’s comforting coat.

I took a deep breath and said. “I really don’t want to bring the body of that monster with us, but I think it would be best if we did to learn as much about it as we can so that we don’t have to get eaten and can hopefully learn the best way to kill them.”

Duke glanced at me. “Noah, as much as I was hoping you would say that, I think we should just get out of here and get to the cabin. Once we are safe and have a routine, we can come back and look for a fresh one. I do think we need to do this. I don't think we should do it now."

"Oh, I am so glad to hear you say that!" Grasping his hand, I gave it a squeeze.

"Well, Wifey, shall we be off?" I quickly released his hand.

"Okay, you did correct him, right? Papa Ray?"

"Nah, why would I do that?"

I grumbled something to Bob about not even liking Duke as we put the gas station behind us. A close call with a bullet, looters, and monsters is a bit much for one stop. "How far is the cabin?" I asked Duke.

"About 20 minutes from here, so close enough that we could come back for supplies as we need them if Ray can stay alive and keep the looters at bay."

"I hope he does. I like him. Even though he almost shot me."

"Yeah, that was off-putting, but," he slipped into a lazy drawl like Papa Ray's, "he shore do grow on ya, hey missy?"

I laughed, and Bob barked. We smiled despite the weight of the day's heavy events.

CHAPTER 6

The cabin was a little piece of heaven. Down a long dirt road, followed by another dirt road, a trail through the undergrowth brought us into a clearing about a hundred yards across with a tidy little cabin plopped right in the center. It was not much, maybe 25 feet wide by 20 feet deep. The front door was sturdy, and a little chimney told me that there was a cozy fireplace right in the center. We pulled up and hopped out.

"Your friend is really fine with using this place? He doesn't need it for himself?"

"Nah, he doesn't come here much anymore. He lost his family a few years back, and this place is one of the reminders he tries to avoid. He told me to use it as much as I can so it stays in good repair."

"That is terrible! What happened?" I asked him. "Is he okay?"

Duke paused for a beat. His face took on an expression I hadn't seen before. He cleared his throat before answering. "Yeah, he is doing better, but he hasn't been the same since it happened. It's his grief, so I'd rather not get into it right now. We have a few things we need to focus on."

We began to unload the truck, this time into a safe haven. The beauty of the cabin was overwhelming. Pine logs stained a rich, deep brown, curtains a light gold hue, hand sawn furniture adorned with thick pillows and blankets tossed around flooded my tired senses. The fireplace was in the center of the main room and opened from both sides, with cozy chairs positioned perfectly for making s'mores and reading into the night. The kitchen to one side had a sturdy little table with four chairs, a small refrigerator, and a small wood-burning stove with a cooktop. On the opposite side, there was a small bathroom and another door that must have led to the cabin's single bedroom. The man had a few homey pieces that made the cabin so cozy and inviting: a throw pillow with handprints painted on it, the names Tim and Trinity written in it in bubbly letters, a poorly done cross stitching that said "Welcome to the Cabin! Get toasted with the S'mores!" and a few books with labels on the spines declaring "Our Family" and "Best Year Ever." No wonder the guy never wanted to come back. The place screamed of a loving family. I pushed the thought away and helped Duke with the unloading.

We got our supplies in and began to unpack as much as we could, keeping everything as orderly as we could manage. If this friend came here for refuge as well, we didn't want him to think we didn't care for his family's fireside. I got a stack of firewood brought in and placed it in the holder. Meanwhile, Duke climbed up to the roof to do whatever he had to do to turn on the solar panel and give us some lights before he started making something for us for dinner. I was starving, but I made him stop long enough to clean his wound and apply a fresh dressing to it.

Our meal was rice with stir-fried veggies, and a can of tuna plopped on top. It was amazing, even if Bob turned his nose up to our peasant food. He would come around.

After we ate and washed up, I went to the bathroom to shower. The cabin had a well, so water was not an issue, but the water heater hadn't heated much yet. I hate cold showers, but I needed to get the grime of gun battles, monster chases, and marauders off of me, so I sucked it up and felt a thousand times better when I emerged and pulled on clean clothes. The heat of August is short-lived, but I still pulled on my favorite sweatpants and hoodie. Duke was sitting by the fireplace, thumbing through a novel he had pulled from my bag. He looked so peaceful sitting there, the fire's glow reflecting his sharp features, and his breathing was calm. I just stood there for a moment to admire his good looks.

"Do I need to arrest you for stalking?" he asked, not glancing up from the book.

"Find anything you like in *my* bag?" I asked, plopping on the couch next to him.

"How could I not? You brought a small library with you," he replied. "Do you remember when I said that we only had room for essentials?"

I grinned at him. "This is the essentials. Just be glad I left the box sets at home."

He smiled back and turned his attention once again to the book.

"So, Tim," I said, picking up the hand-printed pillow.

Duke froze for half a second, then said, “Are we really doing this now?”

“Well, I think we have the time,” I said, turning the pillow to face him. ‘Tim and Trinity’ would love for us to share their story as we are staying in their cabin. Tell me about Tim. Is he another cop?”

“Yeah, Tim and I worked together for a few years right out of the academy. He was cocky, headstrong, loved the ladies, you know, the kind.”

I rolled my eyes. “Boy, do I ever.” He smiled a sad smile back.

“Tim was on the fast track for promotions, awards, accolades, and then he met Trinity. He fell hard for that girl. I had never seen him so unsure of himself yet so happy. He smiled all the time, texted her while he was on duty, met her for lunch practically every day, and talked about her constantly. I thought she was going to be another notch on his very long belt, but she was different from him. When he introduced me, he couldn’t let go of her hand. He waited on her hand and foot, and she did the same for him. They were made for each other. Then, one day, he told me that they were having a baby and he was getting married. I was so happy for him. Tim was always a devilish rogue, and this girl made him want to be better. They bought this little cabin for their honeymoon. I helped him build the furniture, source the supplies, and his sweet little bride decorated. Poorly, I may add.”

He gave the cross-stitching a meaningful grin. “She was a great woman, the best he had ever met and more than he deserved. Then, one day, we were on shift together, and he got the call. His wife and their unborn baby boy were killed in a hit and run."

My eyes filled with tears as Duke stood up and walked to the kitchen. "The fridge hasn't had time to cool much yet, but would you like a beer anyways?"

"Sure," I mumbled. Suddenly, the pillow in my hand was like lead, poisoning me through its touch. I set it down and took the lukewarm beer. I could hardly taste through the sadness in my throat.

"Is Tim still working with you?"

"Yeah," he said. "We delved into the investigation, off the books, and found the guy who hit and killed Trinity and made him pay."

"You guys arrested him?"

"We killed him."

I stared at him in shocked silence for a minute. "You murdered him?" I whispered.

"No," Duke said, suddenly with flames in his smokey eyes. "He shot first."

I was dumbstruck. Duke was a much more dangerous man than I realized. Was I in danger? Did he have a violent temper? Questions swam through my mind as he watched me over his beer.

"When it was all over, he wanted to quit the force, but a group of us from the department talked him into staying, telling him that he was needed and that staying busy, helping people would be a great therapy all on its own. He is doing better these days, but he is still a mess."

"How long ago was that?" I asked carefully.

"Four years ago. A lifetime it seems, but Tim is still hanging in there, putting one foot in front of the other every day, keeping on. I hope you can meet him someday. He is like a brother to me."

"I would like that," I said, still a little uneasy about what he had just shared with me. I emptied my beer and put the bottle in the recycling bin, though that seemed a little silly with the world falling apart, in more ways than one, really. "I'm going to go out with Bob. Do you need help with the shower?"

Duke laughed. "No, Wifey, I can shower myself, thank you."

I rolled my eyes. "You know what I meant."

"Yeah, I do. Be careful out there. We don't know if there are any of those monsters around here.

Keep Bob close to you, and use the lantern in the kitchen."

"Will do. Now go clean up. You stink," I lied as I grabbed the lantern and took Bob out on the fresh summer night.

It was so peaceful. There were more stars than I had ever seen before in my life. The moon was a day or two from full, and its silver light bathed the cabin's yard in a soft, cool glow. Bob ran a bit, always staying near me but still stretching his legs. The lantern gave a pool of warm glow around us. I was enjoying the peaceful night, pushing away the memories that the day had brought. I couldn't start thinking, or I would fall apart. Was my mother even alive? Was my little town wiped from the map? Tears began to well up in my eyes. There were too many questions without answers, so I contented myself watching the fireflies in the distance. Most of them flickered on and off, choreographing mystical dance routines to entice the others. A few of them just hovered in the same spot for a full minute, then disappeared. I began counting them to see if I could find a pattern in the insect dance—too many dancers to count. I noticed a group of insects frozen in time, just hovering in a tidy little pattern—four of them.

My blood ran cold.

"Bob, come on, boy," I urged softly, keeping an eye on the four still lights glowing in the dark. He gave out a slight growl and trotted over to me. I began walking backward, slowly, not making any sudden movements. From somewhere behind me, I heard a scraping sound, followed by a series of clicks. I spun around, squinting to see the tree line in the dark. More terribly still, fireflies hovered in a formation of four. Bob sensed something was wrong. He let out a booming bark that echoed around the clearing, silencing the wildlife around us. "Bob, come!" I yelled, turning and sprinting back to the cabin. Bob and I dashed inside, slamming the door and bolting the latch inside. I leaned my back to the door and slid down to the floor, breathing deeply as scraping sounds came from the other side. *Scritch scritch scritch.* I squeezed my eyes shut, willing the beast away.

"Noah?" Duke stood outside the bathroom, a towel around his waist. "Everything okay?"

"There are at least two out there," I managed. If I had not been so terrified, I would have noticed how great he looked, half-naked. I was almost too terrified.

"Over here," he beckoned me to the bedroom away from the door. "I don't know how smart these things are, so let's wait it out where it can't see in the window."

I turned away so he could dress, then sat on the edge of the bed. From outside, we could hear at least two sets of clicking and rattling sounds. We sat together in silence for what felt like hours.

When the noises had gone silent, we talked in whispers, too nervous that they would hear us and figure out how to get in.

"We need to fortify the doors and windows. And it would be a good idea to begin gathering more wood." Duke's voice was gentle and comforting in the darkness.

"How long do you think this will be going on?"

"I don't even have a guess. We should figure out how we plan to catch one so we can learn about them. I don't relish the idea, but if it gives us an advantage, we should press it."

"Can we talk about something else?" I asked softly, laying back on the bed, yawning. "I really don't want to think about those things anymore tonight."

"How about we just go to sleep? I know I am exhausted after today. I will take the couch. Do you need anything else?"

I was silent for a moment. "Duke, don't take this the wrong way, but will you sleep in here with me? I don't want to… be alone." I felt like a child asking to sleep in Mommy's bed, but I really needed the comfort.

"Sure thing. I can bring some cushion from the couch-"

"Or you could share the bed with me? That is the 'don't take the wrong way' part I mentioned."

He was silent for a moment. "Noah, I just don't think I should. I will sleep on the floor. If you need me for anything, I will be right there. Alright?"

I couldn't help but feel a little put-out. "Yeah, of course. That's probably best anyways." I did not feel that way, but I also didn't want to push him. I was not looking for sex. That was about the farthest thing from my mind at the moment, but I desperately wanted intimacy, closeness, touch. I pulled the blanket over me in the humid cabin, more for that comfort I was seeking than for warmth. Duke made himself a bed next to mine and lay down.

Before sleep overtook me, I whispered, "Hey, Duke?"

"Yes?"

"Thank you for coming to me. I would be dead if it weren't for you. So, thank you."

"I wouldn't have it any other way, Noah. I'm glad to be stuck here with you."

I smiled for a moment, but it quickly melted away with thoughts of the day's crazy events. My last thoughts before sleep overtook me were of my little house, my quiet neighborhood. My mother.

CHAPTER 7

Morning sunlight streamed through the window. Bob was warm on my legs, and I could smell coffee brewing. Did I actually remember to set the timer on the pot last night? I wondered.

It took me a moment to remember the previous day's events and come back to reality. The bright light seemed to dull as my heart sank. How many lives had been lost yesterday? How many people I knew were gone? How many that I love?

I pushed the thoughts away as I climbed out of bed and went out to the kitchen area. Duke sat at the table with a legal pad and pen in front of him and a gloriously steamy cup of coffee. He looked up as I walked in. "Good morning. Sleep well?"

"Hey. Yeah, I slept amazingly, actually. How about you?"

"Fine. Coffee is ready. No cream and sugar, but it is hot."

"Black is beautiful," I said, grabbing a mug off the rack and pouring the black gold. It was bitter and too hot and perfect. I took a sip and moaned. "Oh, I love you."

Duke looked up from what he was working on and cocked an eyebrow at me. "Beg pardon?"

"Don't flatter yourself. I'm talking to the coffee."

He smiled a small smile and went back to work. "What are you working on there?" I asked, peeking at the yellow paper.

"Planning out short- and long-term goals so we can survive as long as possible and not end up in a hairy situation where January comes and we have no food or ammo," he said, punching some numbers into his phone's calculator.

"Are you thinking we will be here that long?"

"I have no idea how long we will be here, but I would rather be prepared and not need the plans than not plan ahead and, well, die."

"How sensible of you. Want some help?"

"Sure. Can you take a sheet and write up an inventory of all of our food supplies, including net weights?"

"Wow. Sounds fun," I said, making a face at him.

"I can do that while you calculate gas rationing, firewood collection, trap locations for fresh meat, defensive alterations-"

"Yeah, yeah, yeah. Give me that paper."

"You got it," he smiled, handing over a sheet and pen. "And don't forget the weights."

"Yes, Sir, Deputy Duke, Sir," I saluted, clicked my heels, and turned to the bags we had stacked neatly in the living room. I heard Duke chuckle a little under his breath and smiled to myself at the sound.

Our planning process took most of the morning, and by the time I had cataloged all of our dry goods, I was hungry. We prepared another stir fry, using up as much of the fresh stuff as we dared. I scooped some in three bowls and set one on the floor. "Sorry, no blueberries, Buddy," I said when I was given big, sad eyes. Bob cocked his head and begrudgingly ate his portion.

"What kind of food is Bob used to? I can see if we can find some on our next excursion into the wild world," Duke offered.

I gave a little laugh. "If you could source out his food, our troubles would be over." I told Duke about Bob's special diet, and he gave a snort.

"That dog eats better than I do!"

"Yeah, me too," I replied, giving Bob a scratch behind the ears.

While we cleaned up the dishes, we discussed our plans for the near future. We agreed that when either of us goes out, we either go together or take Bob. Lantern usage was to be rationed, and we would use renewable firewood and scavenged things as much as we could. We would plan a trip back to Papa Ray's in a week and see how he is faring, check to see if he had any supplies we were low on, and, if possible, bring back a monster corpse. That last bit made my stomach flip over.

We used the sunny, hot afternoon to gather firewood and forage the tree line. We kept Bob within sight and called out to each other every 30 seconds. It seemed to be a good system, though the calling was redundant as the trees were fairly far apart, and there was so little undergrowth between the tall pines. It was peaceful, like a family outing. I could almost forget scary man-eating beasts were hunting us.

Then Bob began to bark.

I looked up from the mushrooms I was picking to see Duke. He already had his gun drawn and was cautiously walking towards me. He handed it slowly to me, whispering, "Cock this. My arm isn't ready to." I checked the magazine to count rounds. He must have filled it because it was full. I pushed the mag back in and chambered a round, handing it back to him and drawing my weapon, repeating the process. I had not reloaded my own gun, but I still had 11 shots. After chambering a round, I nodded to Duke and faced away from him. I called Bob. There was no reply.

"Bob?" I stage-whispered into the forest. I couldn't see or hear him. "Duke, where was he? Where did he go? Did you see him?" I asked, a panicked hand squeezing my heart.

"Bob!" Duke yelled out loudly. "Bob! Here, boy!" A rustling deeper in the woods caught our ears, followed by a deep growl, a squeal, some loud clicking, and the heart-wrenching sounds of a dog fight. "Noah, stay behind me and watch my back. We will get to Bob."

"10-4," I whispered back, hardly able to breathe. I turned my back to him once again and set my shoulders to fire.

"Ok, with me," he whispered. We went toward the sound, keeping our steps as in sync as we could. I kicked him a few times, but Duke was gracious about it. We got closer, and the sounds grew louder, this time accompanied by a sickening wet rattle. I choked on a sob, slamming my hand to my mouth, eyes roving the forest behind us. Duke froze, and I read the silent cue. "Noah, listen to me. Walk back to the cabin. I am going to cover your back. Straight to the cabin." His voice was barely more than a breath.

"Bob?" I asked, my voice shaking.

"It's too late. Back to the cabin now. We have to get-"

I flipped around and shoved my way through the raspberry bush that we were tucked behind, gun at the ready.

The next bit gets fuzzy. I remember hearing a woman scream, a bunch of gunshots, a lot of blood in both red and startling yellow, and what appeared to be a black basketball rolling into the underbrush. I wish the next part were fuzzy, but it will be burned into my memory for the rest of my life.

Bob lay there, covered in blood, his silky fur full of leaves, his eyes terrified as he looked into mine. A small whimper escaped him as I ran my hand over his face. "Hi, baby," I cooed to him. "Hey, look at mommy. Good boy. Bob is the best boy." His tail trembled as he tried to wag it. The effort caused more blood to erupt out of the gash to his torso. I could see his organs peeking out of the bloody mess.

"Noah, we have to get out of here," Duke urged, grabbing my arm gently.

“Not without Bob,” I said in the same soft sing-song voice. “We have to get him home and patched up.”

“Noah, listen to me; we have to go now.” I could hear rattling and scraping sounds ring around me, but they seemed so insignificant compared to what was happening in front of me.

“Noah!” Duke was yelling now, but it didn’t seem to get through the fog in my mind. All I could focus on were Bob’s eyes, the blood all over the litter of the forest, and the voice of a panicked woman rambling. Rough hands pulled on my underarms, standing me up straight. Gunshots rang out. Someone pulled me around the thorny raspberry bush and urged me to run. I ran until it was dark all around me, and a door slammed somewhere, and then I collapsed.

CHAPTER 8

When I came to, there was a cold cloth on my forehead and a blanket over my body. I sat there for a moment as, for the second time that day, I remembered events that made me want to shoot something. I sat up slowly as a wave of nausea swept over me; I paused and sat in silence at the edge of the bed. When I was able to stand, I left the room and stopped in my tracks.

The kitchen table was covered in blood. The first aid kit, gauze, a few open books, and a pot of hot water sat around Bob's very still form. Duke had a headlamp on and was bloody up to his elbows, his shirt, pants, and face splattered with gore. He was working feverishly on the dog, every now and again slipping a stethoscope in his ears and listening to the dog's chest.

I blubbered out some kind of noise and covered my mouth. At the sound, Bob's tail twitched.

Duke looked at me, his face pale, his eyes desperate.

"I think he might make it," he said, then returned to his task with a needle and thread, stitching the angry gash closed.

"What? How? Why? How is this possible? Where did you get a stethoscope?!" I exclaimed, barely able to form the words.

"Let me finish this up first. Then we can talk. We should probably clean the blood up, too. In this summer heat, it won't take long to begin to rot." He checked Bob's heart again, added a few more stitches, and snipped the thread. I just stared at him, mouth hanging open.

"Noah, I need you here with me. You went into shock, but I need your help now. Are you going to be able to do it?" Duke looked exhausted. I had no idea how late it was, but the sun was down. He had to have been working for hours on Bob.

I jumped into action, boiling more water, wiping things down, helping move Bob gently to a blanket on the floor, and cleaning everything Duke had touched. It took the better part of an hour to clean up the gore, and then Duke went off to shower. We would have to make something to help with the smell the next day, but for tonight, we drank warm beer and sat together, watching Bob breathe.

"Okay, Doctor Duke. Any more surprises I should know about?" I asked, trying to break the silence.

"Noah, you need to know that he might not make it. I have never done anything like that before. Trinity was going to nursing school and had a box of books and her stethoscope in a closet. I was entirely guessing about a lot of the anatomy based on the diagrams of humans. I may have only saved him to have him die of my mistakes later. I did my best, but it might not be enough."

I took his hand in mine. "Duke, you tried. Even if he doesn't make it through the night, I am forever in your debt. I am amazed that he is still alive. I am amazed by you." I leaned closer to kiss him, but he looked away quickly, clearing his throat.

"Well, you would have done the same, I'm sure." He pulled his hand from mine. We sat awkwardly for a minute, with me feeling a little put off by the denial.

"So, what exactly happened out there?" I asked, breaking the silence again.

"Can we talk about it in the morning? I need to process a few things. And I am beat. You want to sit up with Bob for a while, or are you going to turn in, too?"

I stared blankly at him. I had no idea what to make of this evening. Had I done something in the forest while I was in shock? Said something that offended him? Shot him again? I quickly regained composure. "Yeah, I will sit up with him. You can have the bed tonight; I will sleep out here. Good night."

"Night," he said, and then he was off to bed.

I let out a slow breath. Bob opened his eyes and looked at me. "Hey, Bob. You are the best boy ever. You are not nearly as complicated as human boys."

He tried to lift his head but whined and laid back down, panting. I grabbed some water for him and dripped it into his mouth. He swallowed it greedily and closed his eyes again. I picked up a paperback and curled up on the couch. I scanned the same page for an hour, then decided to just sit and watch Bob. He slept peacefully, his chest lifting gently; I smiled as he farted and wagged his tail in his sleep. I was getting groggy and knew I would need to be at peak performance tomorrow, so I pulled up a blanket and let my eyes shut. I didn't know what I would wake up to in the morning, but there was only one way to find out.

CHAPTER 9

I had a very broken sleep; every hour or so, I would wake to Bob whimpering. I found some painkillers in the first aid kit, crushed them up, and mixed them with some peanut butter. Bob ate it slowly, looking up at me with a sorrowful gaze. I haven't felt any heartbreak like this before. I wanted to do more, but I was helpless as my best friend lay there, broken. I couldn't see the wound as it was wrapped in gauze, but I knew from the amount of blood we cleaned up that it was not good.

I lay back on the couch and closed my eyes. Sleep drifted over me again, and I dreamed of Bob standing on his hind legs, playing soccer with the head of a monster, while my mother scolded me about my posture. When I woke up again, it was still dark, and the fire burned down to embers. I added a few small logs to reawaken it and checked on Bob. His tail flopped weakly as I spoke to him, but I gave him a kiss on the head and returned to sleep, this time on the floor right beside him. I fell back to sleep with my hand tangled in his silky fur.

When I woke again, the sunlight was peeking through the windows. I checked on Bob, ran to the bathroom, and started stoking the stove's fire to make some coffee.

"How is our patient doing?"

I turned to see Duke crouched over Bob, petting him gently. Bob managed a low growl, then a woofing sigh. I smiled as Duke rolled his eyes. "Give me a break, man. I performed my first-ever surgery on you, and you are still alive. Cut a guy some slack."

I poured two mugs of coffee and joined them in the living room. Duke was not wearing a shirt, and his muscular chest and arms were somewhat distracting as he stretched, running a hand through his dark hair. I turned my eyes quickly to the floor as I handed him his cup.

"Thank you," he said while sitting next to me. "How did you sleep?"

"Okay, I guess. And Bob is still here with us, so I can't complain."

We sat in silence and enjoyed our coffee. Duke took a deep breath and turned to me.

"Noah, we need to talk about yesterday."

"Yes, for sure. I don't know why that happened. I just had a moment of weakness," I told him, turning my eyes away.

"It's no problem. I'm just glad we got out of it without any more damage done."

"Damage? I wouldn't exactly call it damage," I said, feeling slightly put off. I mean, I'm not that experienced with men, but I couldn't be that bad of a kisser?

"Well, disaster? Close call? Whatever we call it, I know mistakes were made, but we can put that behind us and move forward."

"Yeah, I mean, for sure. I will make sure it doesn't happen again. I was just… feeling a lot of things at the moment."

"Most people experience that when they are in shock."

"Wait, shock? What are you talking about?"

He looked at me, a little confused. "Yesterday? In the woods? The close call with the monsters?

Bob being low-key disemboweled? What were you talking about?"

"Oh, that, yeah, I… um… monsters. Yeah," I gracefully worked my way out of the confusion. I guess we were not going to discuss that avoided kiss.

"I know you couldn't help it when you heard Bob, but next time, please just say, 'Hey, I am going to run blindly into the dark bushes to face the monsters.' That would help a little."

"Yeah, can you fill me in? It is all a blur. I'm not sure what happened after I heard Bob fighting… Was he fighting that beast?" I choked a little.

"I think so. I'm pretty sure he ran to the monster to protect us. He did a lot of damage to it, too. Did you see it at all?"

I thought back. "Not really. All I could see was Bob. Everything else was a jumbled mess in the background."

"Well, I think that the monsters are… well, two monsters each."

"….. What?" I looked incredulously over the top of my coffee mug, making eye contact with Duke for the first time all morning.

"The body of the monster, the part with the giant mouth, I think that is one monster, and the tiny head is a symbiont to the first. When the body fell, the head wiggled free and ran off on spindly little legs. I would like to get out there while the sun is high and check it out. It might help us to understand them. And if that is the case, how to kill them efficiently."

I sat there, staring at him. "The head came off and ran away?"

"Yep."

"Did you go into shock, too?"

He smiled at me. "This was not my first blood bath. I've been through a few ugly situations."

"Did you find the woman? The one that kept screaming?"

"I did. Once I got her to the cabin and wrapped up in a blanket, she calmed down. She makes terrible coffee, by the way." He winked at me.

"I wasn't screaming. Was I?"

"Yep."

"Oh," I felt a blush spread across my cheeks. "Thank you for getting me out of there. And for getting Bob out. I will try to do better the next time we see them."

"That might be sooner than later. I don't know if they cannibalize, but if they do, that carcass may have attracted others. We should grab a bite and head out there."

I took a shaky breath, the thought of those creatures being cannibals making my stomach turn.

"Yes. We should do that."

"If you aren't up for it, Noah, I can go alone."

"No, I will be there with you. You have saved me twice now, and I have only saved you once, so I need to keep close so I don't miss my chance to even the score."

He grinned at me. "Then let's get moving."

An hour later, we were armed with our weapons, safety whistles in case one of us got lost, a legal pad with pens, and the cabin's ax. The body was not far, but we weren't taking any chances. I took the rear, Duke taking point, both guns drawn. Duke had me clean and redressed his gunshot wound before we left, and it looked so painful I had to swallow my breakfast again, but he didn't complain. The man was a stone.

I followed him into the tree line and kept watch while he found our trail out of the woods. The blood trail was attracting swarms of flies and bees. We traced the trail back into the woods to the raspberry hedge. We made eye contact, and Duke made some gestures similar to those they do in cop movies that probably mean 'keep eyes open and follow me,' but could easily mean 'don't poke your eyes out on this stick.'

The buzzing of flies was overpowering as we made our way around the hedge. The body was still there, yellow blood congealed in odd clumps that made me think of a honeycomb. We scanned the area for more monsters. Maybe they didn't eat their own kind because it was clear as far as we could see into the forest.

I kept watch, occasionally glancing over to see what Duke was doing every few minutes. He sketched the body's location, marking out trees, stones, and other landmarks. Then he pulled out a measuring tape and wrote down a few measurements. He took out his phone and captured many pictures of the body from every possible angle. I turned away as he opened its giant mouth and poked around inside. He paid close attention to where the head had dislodged and cut open the vacancy, making notes the whole time. After at least an hour, he stood up, sighed, and turned to me.

"I need a shower."

"I didn't want to mention it, but…"

He grabbed everything he brought with us, and we turned back to the cabin. It was surprising that we didn't see or hear any monsters throughout our time in the woods, but who knows how they travel, hunt, or think? We got back to the safety of the cabin and locked the door. The day's heat made the inside of the cabin feel like a furnace, so we opened the windows. Duke took his shower while I tended to Bob. He was lethargic and barely drank any of the water I gave him. His eyes were glassy, and his breathing labored. By seeing him, tears stung my eyes. Were we being selfish by making him suffer? I pushed the thought away as Duke entered the room, shirtless again.

Was he trying to be a tease, or did he really not know what this was doing to me?

Whatever the answer, I pushed that thought away, too. We sat at the table and ate the rest of the remaining fresh produce we had. I tried to savor every bite, but I kept looking at Bob, and the food turned to sawdust in my mouth. Duke watched me for a moment, then pulled out the notes he took.

"Let's study this. See what we can learn from it," he said gently.

I nodded and mumbled, "Okay."

He smiled at me and handed over a new legal pad and pen. "Write down everything you think of as you read the notes, and look at the pictures and sketches. Whatever thoughts come to mind, get it on paper. The thoughts will branch out and we can compare a little later."

"Got it," I said, taking the paper. I slid the phone toward me and looked at the sickening pictures.

The subject is gross. Black, dry-looking skin with green and brown blotches. Yucky in appearance. I wrote. I hoped this was what Duke wanted from me. I peeked over at his work. His page was nearly half filled with tidy, blocky writing, his eyes roving the sketches, his hand moving feverishly over the page. I sighed, and Duke looked up at me.

"You can't copy my work. The teacher will notice," he said. I rolled my eyes at him.

"I have no idea why we are doing this or if I am going to be of any help at all."

"We are doing this to learn all we can from our resources. Just a steady stream of thought put to paper is all you need to do. Trust me when I say it will start to flow, and you will have an amazing discovery to share."

"Can we make more coffee? Or open the door for some fresh air?"

"Yes, and yes. But I will make the coffee." He wrote a few more words and hopped up to get the stove going. I opened the front door and breathed deeply. It was hot outside but not as bad as inside. Bees droned along, birds sang to each other, and clouds moved briskly across the sky as if heading to their next appointment. I would have definitely preferred to be outside on a day like this.

"Noah, let's get working. We need to do it while it is fresh in our minds. You're doing great," Duke coaxed.

I huffed and returned to the table.

The body is dead. Bite marks on the torso from Bob. Good boy, Bob. Blood is yellow, for some reason. Head is missing, presumed escaped. Whatever that means. I reviewed the pictures of the mouth. *Mouth is large. Four rows of sharp teeth. Black tongue.* Then, I flipped to the pictures of the legs. *Weird multi-jointed legs, good for jumping, as we saw. Wait, no visible sexual organs?*

I looked up at Duke. "Hey, I don't know if this is important, but did you notice any sexual organs?"

He looked up from his page.

"I just mean, on a bi-pedal creature like this, don't you think you would be able to see, you know, the dangly bits?"

"Hmm," he pondered. "That is good. Let me buy you a cup of coffee."

I smiled, proud of my insight, as he brought me a mug and took a sip. Shoot. His coffee *was* better than mine.

"Maybe this one is the female, assuming they reproduce sexually," he mused over his own cup.

"Should we cut that one open and see?" I asked, then made a face at myself. Why would I have thought to do that? Gross.

"I think we should. Maybe the main body is the female, and the smaller one is the male? There are certain types of fish that do that, the male fusing to the female for life."

"But they aren't fused. The other one bailed as soon as its mate died."

"True," he said. "They must not mate for life. They can detach and get a new partner if they choose to?"

"This is a lot of guessing," I sighed.

"It's more of a hypothesis, actually. And science always starts with a hypothesis."

"So now you are Doctor Deputy Professor Duke?"

He grinned at me. "Or just Duke. Some people call me that. You know, the ones that aren't calling me 'Your Highness'." We laughed a little. I smiled at him, then remembered the denied kiss the night before and looked away.

"I better check on Bob," I said, excusing myself from the table. Bob was barely still alive. He drank a little more water and ate a few small pieces of apple I had saved for him. This was tearing my heart out.

After a while, Duke came and sat on the couch behind me. He put a hand on my shoulder.

"Noah, about last night," he started.

"Oh, that. No, don't worry about it," I blew it off. "Nothing, really. I get it; we are here to survive. I just thought… I mean, you asked for my number… I kissed you on the side of the road…"

He gave my shoulder a gentle squeeze. "I just don't want to complicate things. If this were a different situation, a different time…"

"I get it, no worries. You thought I was your type, and you discovered that I'm not. I'm a big girl; I can take the hint. Let's just move on."

He removed his hand from my shoulder. "It's really not that," he began.

"It's not a big deal, okay?" I snapped at him. I can take rejection, but I can't take sympathy.

He stood up without a word and walked to the door. He paused for a second, then disappeared into the bright daylight. We were both feeling stung by the conversation, but we would be fine by dinner. I thought about our rule for not going outside alone and tried to convince myself that it was a stupid rule, but even I, despite my infinite stubbornness, could not believe that. I grabbed my gun and followed Duke out into the sunlight.

He stood close to the tree line, hands on his head. I approached him slowly, my pride still stinging. He was muttering to himself in a low voice, so I cleared my throat as I got closer. As much as I wanted to eavesdrop, we didn't need any more strife this early on.

"We should start getting firewood tomorrow. I don't know if my arm will be any good for swinging an ax, but we can at least get some downed logs brought into the clearing." He didn't turn to look at me.

"That sounds like a good idea," I said softly. "Do we want to dissect that thing in the forest today?"

"Probably for the best. It will be pretty smelly, and tomorrow will just be worse." He spoke with a professional tone. He sounded like a cop. I didn't like it.

"What do we need to get together for that?" I kept my voice even.

"The ax and the hatchet from the woodshed, buckets of water, a few knives, a notepad, and a pen. Probably want to bring the tarp from the shed along, too. We can try to haul the carcass into the clearing to have a more secure location to work from. The clearing is more defensible."

"Shall we get started on that? Or you need some time to cool?"

"Nah. You want to start filling buckets? I will get the stuff from the shed."

"Sure thing." As I turned to go, Duke spun around and caught my wrist.

"Noah, please believe me when I say that it had nothing at all to do with you. I have some things I have been working through, and I am just not ready for intimacy."

I looked into his eyes silently for a few seconds, trying to read his expression, then nodded slowly.

"I respect that. Can we pretend that this never happened?"

He held on for a moment more. "Yes," he answered softly, then released my wrist. "Let's get started."

CHAPTER 10

It took us about half an hour to get our gear ready for yet another trek into the forest. The sun was dipping behind the tops of the trees in the west, so we knew the clock was ticking. Finding the trail was easier this time, as we had already been down it multiple times. The sound of buzzing flies was sickening as we approached the raspberry hedge. I swear I could hear them crunching away at the corpse. The smell of the rotting beast hit me like a heavy-weight boxer with a grudge. Duke kept his composure in total cop mode as we approached. His steps were calculated and precise, and I had no idea how he kept it together so well as we rounded the hedge.

We were greeted by three giant, blackish monsters feasting on the corpse. I was shocked and let out a sharp yelp, then shut my mouth tight, frozen with fear. I had seen how fast these things moved, and there was no way we were making it to the cabin alive. A ragged breath escaped me as Duke made a very low shushing sound. While we were more than eight feet from the creatures, they hadn't attacked. Duke stood rooted in place, staring down the closest one, its four eyes flicking around us like it was watching the flies swarming. After about a minute, the creature moved a small appendage on the side of its tiny head, tapping the large body, which went back to feasting on the dead body. While I was terrified beyond the ability to put two words together, I had to admit it was gruesomely fascinating watching them eat. Well, watching them eat something other than us.

The tiny heads would wiggle the side appendages in different patterns, and the lower body would respond by slicing off a small chunk of the meat with their many claws and gingerly feeding it to the tiny head's mouth, then go back to their gorging. It was definitely looking like these were symbiotic creatures. Duke slowly moved his hand behind him and touched me, waving me back out of the area. I took a slow step back, then another, then another. Duke matched my steps with perfect timing. We cleared the hedge, and Duke leaned close to me to whisper, "Run back to the cabin. Do not look back. Do not wait for me."

"What are you going to do?" I whispered back, hardly more than a breath.

"I will be right behind you running. Go now."

I took a few tentative steps, watching the edge of the hedge as I walked backward. I turned to begin my sprint to the safety of the cabin and nearly ran into a tree with a gaping mouth full of angry teeth. The clicking sound that had begun to make my heart falter when I heard it emanate from the huge gullet that could literally bite in half. I screamed and dropped down as long, flabby arms wriggled around, trying to catch me in the wicked claws at the ends. Three shots rang out, and I lost my breath. The huge beast was on me, teeth pressed against my face; I clenched my eyes shut, feeling the skin on my cheek rip open and smelling the reek of what could only be likened to the gym socks of a zombie football team. This was how I would die: unable to breathe, in pain, and surrounded by stench.

Dying took a lot longer than I thought it would. I heard more gunshots and sucked in a glorious lungful of clean air. I opened my eyes to see Duke's hand extended to me. "Come with me if you want to live."

I looked around a moment, very confused as to why, in heaven, I was covered in sticky, yellow gore. Duke's hands wrapped around my torso and heaved me off the ground. I looked around and saw four dead monsters lying about the area. I looked at Duke wide-eyed. "What the actual hell just happened?"

He smiled as he ejected his magazine, fitting in a replacement. "I guess the brain is in the head." He gestured to the body that had been on top of me. There was a clean hole through the head, just below one of the top eyes. The bottom body was untouched. I lifted a hand to my cheek to feel where its teeth had opened the flesh. It stung like crazy, but it was really just a scrape. Duke had already begun yanking on one of the creatures' heads to try to remove it, and it held fast. Pulling a multitool out of his pocket, he began extracting teeth from both mouths, and I had to look away. Keeping watch was probably the best option right now, right?

"What do you think it means that they didn't attack us?" he asked as he worked.

I was still in a fog from being almost crushed and eaten. "I'm pretty sure that one was attacking me," I said, pointing to my face.

He grunted as he worked the head free, revealing an appendage that looked very much like that organ we were searching for earlier. "Well, here it is," he said. Turning back to me, he held the head up, giving me a good look at the tiny monster's tiny monster.

"Lovely. You were saying?"

"I was just thinking they didn't seem to be able to see us. The one that looked at us couldn't seem to focus its eyes while we stood still. It only looked at us when we made noise. Once we were silent and still, it went back to eating. Maybe the flies were interfering with its vision, or maybe they just don't see well."

I thought about this, trying to ignore the sounds coming from behind me while Duke worked. "You have a point there. I was too terrified to think that far, but I think you are right. The one that almost ate my face could have just been following along for the carcass and came upon us by chance."

"Yeah, and the ones that came after us in Carlston didn't come at us until you opened the door and closed it again."

"That is helpful to know," I said dully.

"Do you want to go back to the cabin to clean up while I work on these things?" Duke asked. "What are you planning on doing?" I asked, keeping my eyes away. My near-death experience had left me in rather wet pants, and a shower sounded like a great idea.

"All I want to do is cut one open and see what I can about their systems. I'm not an expert at all, but I did dissect a frog in 7th grade. Plus the whole surgery thing."

I groaned. “I will help. Can we agree that we are done in one hour?”

“Agreed. Help me roll this thing over.”

We spent the hour cutting, poking, taking notes, puking, taking samples, and discussing our findings. I had to admit, after the first few cuts, it was pretty fascinating, though not any less nasty. We finished our research and headed back to the cabin, exhausted, sore, and pretty much ready to sleep for the night. We added our notes to the growing stack on the table, then took turns showering and checking on Bob. He was hanging on and maybe even improving; he lifted his head to drink and ate the food I gave him with almost gusto. I smiled when he licked my hand.

We had accumulated quite a yucky pile of clothes that needed to be cleaned, so we started boiling water to wash them. Tim and Trinity had obviously spent a lot of time here as there was a retractable clothesline between the cabin and the woodshed, along with an old-timey wash bin. I felt very 1840s chic, scrubbing the sweat from Duke’s trousers, wondering where I had misplaced my bonnet.

We ate a light dinner and lit a fire, chatting idly by the fireplace. We didn’t need the heat, but the coziness was a blessing. It was nice after the day we had. We talked to Bob and stroked his fur. I cleaned Duke’s bullet wound, and he cleaned my monster fang bite; it was very sweet. We agreed that we needed to begin preparing for the cold in case we were stranded out here for longer than a month. The heat and humidity of August would give way to the sleet of October pretty quickly.

"How long will our dry goods last, do you think?" I asked him.

He thought for a moment. "Maybe a month. We will need to figure out alternate food sources. There are some traps in the shed for catching small game. A rabbit every other day would do us all some good."

"I can't eat a bunny!" I said, much more loudly than I meant to. Bob lifted his head and whined. I softened. "I mean, have you ever seen a bunny? All cute and fluffy? Totally innocent with their little boopy snoots?"

"Oh, please don't do this to yourself. Or me, for that matter. Where do you think meat comes from? Are you going to tell me now that you think cows are cute?"

"They are! With the big eyes and sloppy noses, that big old purple tongue that licks your face!"

Duke just rolled his eyes. "Noah, you are insane. You know that, don't you?"

"If I knew it, then I wouldn't be insane."

"Well, whatever you are, we will need to eat, and canned pie filling won't cut it. Thanks for that, by the way. You really know how to get the essentials. Like the half a ton of books."

"You leave my books out of this! They didn't do anything to you." I stuck my tongue out at him, to which he put his thumb to his nose. We laughed and then fell silent.

"Duke," I asked, taking a deep breath. "Do you think that there is anyone left? You know, back home?"

He closed his eyes and leaned his head back. "I don't know. I hope so. I don't even know if our town is still standing."

I felt tears prick my eyes again as I thought of the sight of what used to be Carlston. Were the monsters jumping into the pits that remained from where my house once stood, eating my neighbors? Was the bar gone? What about Nancy and her husband? Molly?

My Mother? Were they all just gone like that? It seemed impossible.

"I think I am going to turn in. You want the bed again tonight, and I can stay with Bob?" I asked.

"No, you take the bed. I'll keep up with Bob. We can talk about all those bunnies we are going to murder together."

I gave him a sassy look. "Fine, you two heathens sit out here and plot. I'm going to get some sleep. There had better be coffee for me when I get up." I didn't actually feel the cheerfulness from our banter, but I needed him to think I was okay. I needed to believe I was okay. And more than anything I really needed to go cry myself to sleep.

I shut the door to the little bedroom and stripped off my outer layer. Climbing into the bed felt good as I wrapped up in the safety of the quilt. No monster could ever penetrate the safety of a quilt fortress; that is just science.

I faced the wall away from the door and closed my eyes. The blankets smelled like Duke. I inhaled slowly, allowing myself to relax, and snuggled in closer. I needed to feel safe tonight, so the smell was a blessing. I lay there in the dark, allowing tears to leak from my eyes. Soon, I was wracked with silent sobs. I released all the fear, all the anger, all the pain. I cried until I hiccuped, and then I needed to blow my nose. I took a deep breath, sneaked out to the bathroom, blew my nose, and splashed water on my face.

Back in the bedroom, I tried to get comfortable, but now I just felt alone. I wanted to be near Bob and maybe near Duke, too. So, I wrapped up in the quilt and crept out to the couch where Duke lay sleeping. He had pulled out one of the photo albums and had fallen asleep while flipping through it. There were pictures of flower girls, old people dressed up in wedding clothes, and a beautiful bride being held up by groomsmen. I spotted Duke right away, his gray eyes laughing at me from the picture. I pulled the book gently out of Duke's hands to put it away. As I closed it, I took a sharp breath that made him jump and look at me. My eyes filled with tears anew as understanding dawned upon me. The front of the wedding album had golden lettering declaring "The Dukes, Timothy, and Trinity." Our eyes met for a moment before he dropped his. I sank to the couch beside his stretched-out legs. I placed the album gently back on his lap. He laid a hand on it and sighed, caressing it gently with his thumb. I sat in silence, letting him make the first move.

"Noah, I haven't been with anyone since Trin. I hadn't even kissed someone until you got me on the way here. It's been four years since they died, and yet I still can't believe that it's true. I always think that she is going to walk through the front door with our little boy on her hip, an arm full of wildflowers that they had collected, singing an old show tune badly. Trinity was my world, carrying my world. And I lost them. I lost them, Noah. That woman at Papa Ray's wailing and weeping over her missing babies, I couldn't even look because I knew her pain. And then to see that it was all a sick ruse to steal from others, I… I wanted to throw her to the monsters." He took a shaky breath.

"How long were you married?" I asked gently.

"Six months, twelve days, twenty hours, and forty-one minutes. She was due to deliver Matthew within a month. I had planned to take a month off to be with them when he was born. Man, I was so excited to be a father. I bought four different cribs before I liked the one we had in his room. I repainted the walls six times before I liked the shade of green. Trin teased me that she was supposed to be the one nesting." He smiled and ran his hand over the book.

"And then I got called into the chief's office. It was a Thursday, rainy cold. Trin was meeting her parents for brunch at her favorite bistro. It was ten in the morning, and the man who hit her was so high he jumped a curb and ran down four people without noticing; he just drove off. Chief said that they got a few details from witnesses but not enough to go off of. It took me months to track the guy down. When I did, he pulled a gun. Killed my partner, Martin, and put two rounds through me. I don't remember the incident, but another officer said she had to pry my bloody gun from my hand. I had beat him to death with it once I ran out of bullets."

I wanted to say something, but there was nothing, no words. I laid a hand on top of his, and after a minute, I asked, "Where did he shoot you?"

He stood up and lifted his shirt; there was a long scar along his rib cage. "Here is one," he said, letting his shirt drop and pulling the waistband of his pants down, revealing a round scar. The bullet must have torn right through his intestines. "I nearly bled out on the way to the hospital, but I never stopped smiling. They say that revenge doesn't make it better, but I felt better that day than I had in a long time. I put that dog down."

Bob lifted his head and whimpered. "Ok, dog is too kind of a term, monster. I put that monster down."

Duke sat back down next to me and placed his hand on mine. "Noah, I really like you. You are funny, quirky, tender, thoughtful. Sexy, if I am being honest about it. But this place…This was ours. I just can't be with you here. I can't make love to you in the bed I shared with my wife."

I laced my fingers in with his.

"Duke, I wish I could take away your pain. I wish I had a magic wand that made it all just go away. Your unbelievable loss, the monsters taking over the world, all of it. But I don't, and I can't. What I can do is be here now. I really like you, too, Duke, but I will not pressure you in any way. This was your home away from home with your wife. That is a beautiful thing, and I won't undermine that. If you are ever ready to get involved, I will be here. If that day never comes, I promise to be your teammate and friend to the end of the road. I am not Trinity, and I could never replace her. But I could be the next chapter if you ever wanted that."

Duke laid his hand on my cheek, and I leaned into it, closing my eyes. When I opened them, Duke was watching me intently, his smokey eyes burrowing into me. "I want to kiss you right now."

I smiled at him. "Not today, Duke. We both need some time. But I will allow you to share this very comfortable couch with me." We grabbed pillows from the bedroom and laid our heads on either side. It was nice having him close, and we both fell into smooth breathing rhythms in a few minutes. I whispered to him, "Duke?"

"Yeah?"

"Is it okay if I still call you Duke? Or do you prefer Tim?"

I could hear the smile in his voice. "Whatever you want to call me, Noah. Good night."

"Dream sweet," I said, drifting into my dreams, feeling so close yet so alone.

CHAPTER 11

The next morning came too soon. The sun took a day off and dark storm clouds made us rethink our previous day's plans for collecting wood. A steady rain began after breakfast. We took the opportunity to plan out more long-term goals. Duke sketched the property, and we plotted out possible garden locations, places to set traps and escape routes in case the cabin was ever compromised. We made to-do lists, wish lists, shopping lists, and a list of things we could use for bartering if we found more survivors. We went over the photos, notes, and sketches again and spent some time discussing the previous day's events. Once our brains were thoroughly exhausted, we found cozy nooks to read from the myriad of books I had brought along.

The day was peaceful. Duke and I ate dinner, then boiled some water to clean each other's injuries and made some tea, which was lovely. The bonding time spent together was invaluable, forming a connection of friendship and camaraderie that would not have occurred on a busy day running for our lives through the woods. I said a little prayer of thanks to God for the rain that day.

Time trudged on. We healed, we worked, we chopped, and I learned to skin a rabbit. As much as I hated the idea of it, rabbit stew turned out to be pretty damn good after weeks of canned food. Bob was up and running like a puppy before I knew it, and I made sure to give him a kiss every chance I had. Duke showed me a stream about a mile north of the cabin, which I marked on his map in case we lost water. The fact that it was teeming with trout was just a bonus. We worked on curing meats and drying herbs and roots that grew naturally around the clearing. The days marched by, and the trees began to blush as the first frost was approaching quickly.

On the day we made the last of our coffee, Duke turned to me and said, "I think it is time we go see if Papa Ray is still operating. We have some rabbit skins and dried fish we could trade for other essentials he may have acquired. If nothing else, it would be good to share the knowledge we have gleaned about the beasts and see if there is any news from the rest of the world."

I chewed my dried fish, thinking. "You might be right. Winter is closing in quickly and I am beginning to think that no one is getting this whole thing solved anytime soon. We don't have any cold-weather gear at all. This place is pretty perfect, but the weather will keep us stuck here once the snow gets deep, and I don't want to run out of supplies and have to eat you."

"Not going to start with Bob?" Duke asked, cocking an eyebrow at me.

"Nah, I already lost him once. I'm not doing that again," I said with a smile. Bob wagged his tail so hard it beat my leg, and he looked up at me with a smile.He still walked with a limp, but that dog being alive was a miracle. I gave him the last of my breakfast, which he gobbled up happily.

"Still a weird dog."

Bob had warmed up to Duke quite a bit since his brush with death. He still insisted on wedging between us when we sat too close together. Having a four-legged chaperone helped keep us both honest with the whole 'just friends' thing.

It was certainly getting harder to stand that, though.

I have never been married, but I imagined that this is what it would be like. We spent every day together, talked about the books we read, and bickered over where we would be planting the carrots. We shot monsters together and stitched up bullet wounds. Normal, everyday married-people stuff. It made me think about all the other married people stuff. Not just the after-bedtime stuff, but the closeness, the intimacy, the kissing and holding hands and snuggling by the fire. I often wondered if Duke felt the same. I would occasionally turn to see him watching me, a soft smile playing at the sides of his mouth. Other times, while we slept, he would turn over on the couch in his sleep and hold me close, but he was always up before I awoke. Once, while we were out foraging and decided to split up, he had said, "Be safe, love you," and turned before I could respond. We both pretended it didn't happen. If he felt the sexual tension, he didn't show it.

We made a new inventory of what we had left, and it was pretty sad. The rabbits around were plentiful, and we had begun to amass quite a collection of hides. We were getting down to only a few cases of bullets left. Canned goods were as good as gone. A trip out into the world would be necessary soon if we were to beat the cold.

Duke searched all the closets to see what we had that we could part with for trade. He tried to convince me that the books could be valuable. I almost let Bob bite him again. We decided that we could part with some extra clothes, a dozen rabbit skins, a few pounds of dried fish, some of the wild flower tea I had made, a length rope from the shed, and a few knives we had made from the claws of the monsters we slew. Turns out those suckers are sharp and remain sharp for a long time. We also made multiple copies of our research and discoveries about the creatures. If the information could help save a life down the road, it was worth the hand cramps from copying all those pages over and over again.

We loaded up in the pickup at sunrise the next morning and took a deep breath. We hadn't left the cabin in over a month. What would be waiting for us down the bumpy dirt road? Duke reached over and grabbed my hand for the first time in weeks. "You ready, killer?"

"I was born ready," I said, with more bravado than I actually felt.

I looked over at Duke and smiled. His hair had grown out a bit, and his lack of a razor meant that he now wore a scruffy beard. It was a great look on him.

"Let's do this." He started up the truck, and we began our journey down the road. The twenty-minute drive to Papa Ray's was made longer due to a tree down across our path. I kept watch while Duke worked the tree off the road. There were scurrying and clicking sounds from the monsters deeper in the woods, and I was sure I saw a few sets of four eyes, but we were back on the road before they got too brave.

Once we reached the small road, Duke stopped the truck. “When we get there, we stick together, alright? No matter the reason, we do not leave each other’s sides. We will leave Bob with the truck to protect the supplies while we talk to Papa Ray about some trading. That is if the place is even still there. We have our needs list and our wants list. Anything off of those lists needs to be agreed on by both of us. For safety, it would be best if we refer to each other as husband and wife. And no mention of the location of the cabin. Are we agreed and is there anything else we need to discuss?”

“Yeah, how is being ‘married’ safer?”

Duke looked at me like I asked why rain falls down and not up. “Do you actually not know, or are you being obtuse?”

“A little of both, I guess.”

“If you are just my friend, you are more expendable. If there are bad guys here who would want a little happy ending to their shopping trip, a single female won’t be as fought for as a wife would. I don’t know what has happened out here in the past month, but on day one, I was shot ten minutes into our escape over some Doritos. Desperation brings out the savage in some.”

I swallowed. Could it really be like that? Could there really be people who would steal a woman just to rape her? I guess that sort of thing happened far too often before the world had begun to crumble physically and not just socially, so it would make sense that the trend would continue. The color must have drained from my face because Duke reached out and stroked my hair.

"Hey, I'm sorry. I still slip into cop mode when things are scary. That was insensitive of me to say it that way. I just mean that if perps think you are married to a cop with a gun, they are less likely to target you."

I grabbed his hand and exhaled slowly. "It's okay. I would rather hear the ugly truth than a sugar-coated version. I mean, it sounds much less scary, but the world is running low on sugar." I managed a smile and let his hand go. He held it to my face a moment longer before he continued driving.

"Noah, you are the bravest woman I have ever met."

My heart skipped a beat at the words, and I felt a blush creeping into my cheeks. Even after the month we had spent in isolation together, there was still a flutter in my belly when we gave my praise or when our eyes met.

We rode in silence the rest of the way. When we arrived at the old service station, Duke slowed to a crawl, and we took stock of the situation. The place was technically still standing, but it looked like it had been through a war. A crude fence topped with barbed wire surrounded the place. There were a few men with long guns of assorted types posted along the perimeter. A tower had been erected in the middle of the parking lot, equipped with what appeared to be a loud speaker attached to it. The station itself was boarded up in many places, and I was pretty sure I could see some blood splatter and bullet holes along the front wall. Duke looked at me. "It is not too late to turn back. We can make do with what we have and what we can forage."

My eyes scanned over the forbidding looking compound and then returned to Duke. "I think we should go for it. At the first sign of trouble, we leave. What do you think, Bob?"

A deep, menacing growl answered me. Bob didn't like the station's facelift any more than I did.

We were low on supplies, though; we needed to at least try.

"Let's go for it," I said, Duke's words of my bravery helping me along.

"Got it. Don't use my name. We will call each other pet names for an extra layer of protection.

Anonymity could be useful right now."

"You got it, Cookie-Butt."

He looked back at me. "Really? Straight to Cookie-Butt? Not going to warm up with a Honey or Sweety?"

"Oh, that is the warm-up."

Duke chuckled as he pulled up to the makeshift gate, rolling down his window to speak with the rather large, stern-looking woman holding what I would guess was an AK47. "Hey there. Is this place open for trades? My wife and I have some goods we can give and a list of things we are looking for."

The woman cocked her head to the side, glancing at me, then at Bob, and back to Duke. "We are open for trading, but you must leave any weapons here at the gate. Too many roving bands of innocent-looking pillagers have stopped by to 'trade' their goods."

"I would feel better if we would be allowed to remain armed. All due respect, ma'am, but I am a police officer and still take my sworn duty seriously. We are just as leery of you as you are of us."

"No exceptions, sir."

"Daisy, would you stop harassin' every single face that drives up on your shift? Fer Pete's sake, search the truck, pat down the people, and tell them the weapons remain visible at all times. We aren't running Camp David here!"

Papa Ray came limping up to the gate. We had been so preoccupied with the guard that we didn't see the old man with his trusty rifle in tow hobbling along. He looked exactly as he had the last time we came through, probably even the same outfit.

"Yes, Sir," Daisy said, throwing a salute.

"And would you knock that off? I told yer a million times ta stop callin' me 'Sir.' I ain't never been a Sir in my life." The wizened old face smiled at us. "Hey, I think I remember you two. Came through the day of The Fall, right?"

"The what?" I asked. Duke kept his mouth shut, looking much less foolish than I did.

"'Member when the holes tore apart this peaceful land and the Rovers started eatin' everybody up?"

"Oh, yeah," I said, looking away in embarrassment. Of course, there would be names for the event and the beasts. Duke came to my rescue.

"We were wondering what to call the things. We have been so busy trying to survive that this is our first trek out of the forest."

"Makes sense. Now, you both agree to a vehicle search and a pat down? And the whole bit about not concealin' weapons inside the gate?"

"You got it, Ray. We can really just unload what we have for trade and work from there. Honey, you want to help me with the supplies?"

"Sure thing, Babe. Pat downs first?" I asked, looking at Ray.

"If you don't mind, Darlin'. I gotta keep my people safe, too."

We hopped out of the truck and laid out guns and knives on the hood of the truck. A man stepped up behind me for the frisk. He asked me to put my hands on the hood away from the weapon and spread my legs, which I did. He spent a little too long searching for me and made sure he got a few cheap gropes in. Suddenly, I could feel his obvious erection rubbing up against me, grinding hard and forcing my hips into the truck's fender. I gasped in fear, looking for help from Duke, who was not facing away and chatting with Ray. The man moaned in pleasure, then hissed in my ear, "You like that you feel? There's more where that came from, Doll." Then he grabbed my backside, squeezing hard, before sliding his hand between my legs for one last cheap grope. "All clear over here, Chief." His voice was back to a normal tone as he stepped back to his position along the fence. I glanced his way, and he made a rather rude and explicit gesture at me. I whipped my head back around. Duke was still talking to Ray, and Daisy was searching the cab of the truck. I glanced back at the man, who winked at me and blew a kiss. I strapped on my gun and knife, refusing to give him the satisfaction of letting him see how rattled I was.

I felt dirty; my stomach was trying to turn itself inside out, and my hands were trembling as I climbed back into the cab. *Don't look at him again. Don't look,* I told myself. Duke joined me and pulled into the lot. He took my hand. "We're okay, don't worry. Ray is an honest man." I'm glad he assumed that was why I was shaking. I didn't think I could put into words what had just happened.

Duke backed up to the open bay door that served as Ray's trading house. The inside of the store must have been changed into something else because everything had been moved into the two bays. "Let's go shopping, sweetheart," he said, smiling at me. I returned what I hoped was a convincing smile. He gave my hand a squeeze and then turned to Bob. "You stay here, Buddy. Keep the truck safe."

Bob gave a small woof and licked Duke's shoulder. The moment grounded me back to the mission. I needed to be strong for my little band of misfits.

We unloaded the goods we'd brought and carried them into the shop. A few tables had been set up for sorting and bartering, and we began to lay out what we had. Duke chatted with Papa Ray while he took stock of all the goods we brought. For a guy who seemed ready to give away anything and everything just over a month ago, he sure seemed diligent as a trader. It occurred to me that for an old-school shopkeeper, this was probably a more natural way to run his business.

Once he had cataloged everything we brought for trade, he gave us a total that we had for credit. As money was no longer valued as currency, he had created a credit system for anyone who came through with needs. He seemed to have a little of everything, which surprised us greatly. "Have you had many people come through with trades? This seems like a pretty well-balanced inventory," Duke asked. Ray smiled, cradling his rifle. "It's the Hunters that gave me all this stuff."

"Hunters?" I asked.

"There're a few groups of folks who have the skills and know how to get into the remains of the collapsed cities. They form their team and make expeditions into the holes. They dig into the rubble of buildings and bring up what they can find. There was a shoppin' mall almost at the edge of Carlston where they have had a bit of luck. Food, clothes, batteries, medicine. It is not all salvageable, and it is pretty dangerous, but they seem to have a system. They stop by every week or so with new supplies for me."

Duke had switched back to cop mode, and I could see a plan forming in his head. “When are they due to come back with another load for you?”

“I don’t rightfully know. There is no schedule to it, they just come when they have something to work with. Is there something that you need them to look for?”

“We might have some information about the Rovers that could help them. I have a copy for you, too, in fact. We took a couple apart to learn about them and their weaknesses. I don’t know if anyone else has been doing research on them, but if they have, I would love to compare notes.”

“Well, I would be mighty pleased to see what you have. We ain’t been doing nuttin’ but blastin’ the buggers when we see them. Had a few get in the station before we put up the fence. They jump pretty high, but we can pop ‘em while they’re in the air. They take a few shots each to get ‘em to go down.”

“They are actually two creatures in one. The larger one with the chest mouth can’t survive without the smaller head attached, but the head can detach and search for a new host. A single shot to the tiny head had worked for us,” Duke explained. “My wife here is quite the tiny head killer,” he said as he reached around my hip and pulled me in. The unexpected contact made me flinch. Duke gave me an appraising look, to which I gave my most convincing smile.

“Yeah, I have taken a few of the males out.”

"The males?" Ray asked, appearing not to notice anything out of the ordinary.

"Yeah," I continued. "We think that the larger body is the female and the smaller head is the male."

"We are also fairly certain that they detect motion rather than traditional sight," Duke continued. "If you hold still, they get confused and can't find you. Think of the T-rex in Jurassic Park. Not sure about smell or sound. We have thankfully not had too many run-ins."

"Well, they don't really like anything 'round 25 hertz. We keep it pumpin' though this speaker round the clock, helps keep 'em away."

Duke cocked his head at the surprising comment from the old man. "Good to know."

"Daisy over there has a dog whistle. She was callin' her mutt when one of them buggers got in, and it just about tore through the fence tryin' to get away. Been a good tool for keepin' the station safe for tradin'."

"You happen to have any of those on hand?" I asked hopefully.

"Shore do," Ray replied.

"That should be added to the needs lists," I said, looking to Duke for confirmation.

He nodded, then reached his free hand into his pocket and pulled out the needs and wants lists. Showing them both to Ray, we began to work our way through the crowded shelves, Duke and Ray chatting all the while. I just kept quiet, occasionally peeking out to the truck to check on Bob and make sure that creep wasn't close by.

We managed to get 10 pounds of canned goods, boots in both our sizes, duct tape, coffee, bleach, a larger trap for a bigger game, and a pair of shiny new whistles. As we loaded up our treasures, we said our goodbyes to Ray.

"If you need a hand around here, you know where to find me," Duke told the old man. "And thank you for everything. We will hopefully be back with more to trade. One last thing. Are there any of the Hunters that you know and trust?"

"My nephew is one of them. Good boy. Brave to the point o' stupid sometimes, but a good head on his shoulders. Why, you thinkin' about joinin' up?"

"Well, my wife and I need to discuss it, but I think that may be something I would like to try. I have some skills that could come in handy. If there is a group going out soon, can you tell your nephew where we are and have him come talk to us?"

"Shore thing, Sonny. You three take care now."

"Hopefully see you again soon," Duke said, shaking the old man's hand.

We climbed into the truck and pulled away. I glanced at the guard as we drove out the gate and quickly turned away when he licked his lips and grabbed his crotch. I shuttered a little and instinctively reached back for Bob to sink my fingers into his comforting warmth.

"Well, that went better than I could have even hoped! Not a hitch to speak of!" Duke exclaimed as we followed the road that would bring us to the safety of our little cabin.

I wanted to tell Duke about the guard with the wandering hands and threatening whisper, but then I remembered what he had told me before. You don't defend a friend as you would a wife. We weren't together, and we were basically roommates. It was not his job to protect me. I turned to him, the words burning in my throat. He looked so pleased, so proud of our day and what we had accomplished. How could I selfishly tarnish that for him? If I cared about him at all, I could not. I pushed down the anger, fear, disgust, and shame down and smiled at Duke. "That was great! We should be set for a while, at least until this coffee runs out."

On the dirt road to the cabin, we came back to the place where the tree had been on the road. Someone had moved it back.

CHAPTER 12

We sat in silence, looking at the log that blocked our path. The warm fall day seemed to drop twenty degrees. Duke met my eyes, the joy and pride now gone. "What do you want to do?"

I bit my lip as chills crept through me. "Well, we have to get it out of the way again. I watch, and you move, like last time?" He nodded. Bob growled from the back of the truck. There were Rovers nearby. We checked our magazines, chambered a round each, and cautiously opened the doors. The woods were dead silent; not a bird or bug made a sound. Duke held his gun out in front of him, arms straight, eyes alert. I mimicked his actions, scanning the area, and took a position with my back to him. A loud clicking sound came from somewhere in the foliage, followed by a wet, rumbling rattle from elsewhere. I could hear movement in the forest, seemingly all around us. I didn't know where to point my weapon or what to do next.

"Duke, better get that thing moved fast. We have company, and I think a lot of it."

He grunted as he moved the log a little at a time. I backed closer to him as I saw eyes appear in the gloom between the trees. Had the Rovers moved the log? Had they set a trap for us?

A drop of rain brushed my cheek. I scanned the left side of the road, then the right, watching for movement, which there was now a plethora of. Dark eyes appeared all around us as another raindrop landed on my shoulder. I glanced up and screamed.

A woman was staring at me from the trees; at least, her head was. The rest of her body dangled from the branches higher up the trees. Duke turned to me and dropped the log. He followed my gaze and gasped.

In an instant, the road was flooded with Rovers. They came at us from every angle. Shots rang out as we fired on the beasts, but it was not enough. They just kept coming at us, keeping us surrounded. Duke shouted, "Get to the truck! Noah, get to the truck!" We were only a few yards away, but we would not get there in time. There was no way. I shot a rover that leaped at us over the tops of its buddies. I turned to sprint to the truck, but my way was blocked by a Rover. I pulled the trigger to no response.

"Duke, I'm out!" He spun around me and shot the Rover in the face. If fell with a heavy thump, blocking the door shut. Bob was inside the truck, barking and snarling like mad. The chaos of the moment swarmed me. I let out a scream of rage, fear, and frustration. The rovers were closing in, close enough for me to smell their horrid breath, and they weren't stopping. "The whistle!" I shouted. "Where is the whistle?"

"In the truck!" Duke yelled back over the cacophony of rattling and clicking voices. "Dash board!"

“Cover me! I’m going for it!” I lunged for the driver’s side door, and instantly, razor claws were ripping through my side. I yanked the door open, jumped in, and slammed it shut as Duke shot two more that charged at him. Tears were blurring my vision as Bob jumped on me. I shoved him off and grabbed the shiny little tube.

“God, please let this work,” I prayed and blew the whistle as hard as I could. Bob let out a horrible shriek and jumped to the back of the truck. I threw the door open and blasted it again. It felt silly since it made no noise that I could hear, but the Rovers certainly heard something. They dropped to the ground, their long arms pulling them away from me as quickly as possible. I blew the whistle until I was light headed, and then I blew again. The Rovers emitted all sorts of squeals and gurgles as they fled from the sound. Within a minute, it was silent again.

Duke was lying on the ground holding his face, with blood blooming from between his fingers and his arms covered in clean slices. “Duke!” I said, kneeling next to him. I lifted his head and laid it on my lap. He gasped and grabbed my arm with his free hand. “Let me see, Duke. I need to see how bad it is.”

“Noah, get in the truck. They’re coming back,” he stammered. His eyes were wide, and his face pale beneath the blood. A deep gash had sliced through the right side of his face, from his jaw to his eyebrow, less than a centimeter from his eye. He jumped as a squirrel rustled and leaped from one tree to another.

“Duke, I’m going to get you out of here. Can you stand?”

His wild eyes roamed around. "Noah, I can't lose you! Get to the truck! They're here! Lookout!"

I glanced around and saw nothing but Rover carcasses and still forest. Worry creased my forehead as I ran my hand over the uninjured side of his face. "Duke, let me get you home. We need to get off the road. Can you stand?"

"Noah, I can't lose you! Get to the truck! They're here!"

He was in shock; I took a deep breath. "Stand up, Duke. That's an order," I commanded. I pulled on his arms as I stood up, bringing him with me. I got under his arm and helped him towards the truck. My side screamed out in agony as we hobbled forward, trying to ignore the decapitated body leering at us from the trees above. The passenger side was still blocked by the dead monster, so I helped him to the driver's side and pushed him over to the passenger seat. I felt hot blood running down my side. I looked around for something to help slow the bleeding. With nothing available, I pulled off my shirt and tore it at the sections where the claws had sliced through. I made a few long strips and tied them around myself as tightly as I could handle. I took another strip and reached over to Duke. His face was still pale, and he was staring blankly ahead.

"Hold this to your face," I instructed, placing it tightly on the wound. *From now on, we don't leave without a first aid kit,* I said to myself. I looked at the tree that had stopped our progress; it was still impassable. I took a deep breath and climbed out. I blew the whistle hard as I struggled to move the obstruction. Duke had struggled with it, and I felt pretty hopeless. I managed to move it a few feet by pivoting the end, all the while blowing the whistle. The tree bark scraped my bare torso as I worked to move the tree away enough to get around. Exhausted and hurting, with sweat stinging all the open wounds on my skin, I climbed back in the truck. Bob was lying on Duke, leaning his head against the shirt on Duke's face. I smiled and started the drive home.

When we arrived, I looked at Duke. He was holding the shirt to his face, watching me, his head leaning back against the seat.

"Hey. How are you doing?" I asked softly, giving him a brave smile, feeling quite self-conscious sitting there in my bra.

"You saved my life," he said while taking a deep breath and looking away.

"Duke, we saved each other," I said, reaching over to touch his leg.

He grabbed my hand and squeezed. "I thought we were done for back there. I forgot about the whistle, and if it weren't for you, we would be dead right now. And we got home somehow. Noah, I owe you my life."

"No, you don't. We are a team. We save each other all the time. It's our thing." I smiled at him. He lifted my hand and tenderly kissed my fingers.

"This is one of those times that I really want to kiss you."

I smiled, pushing away the thought that I wanted that more than anything. "You always say that after almost dying. Let's get in and clean up. I, for one, think that I will splurge for a bath."

He held my hand for a moment longer. "I always want to kiss you, Noah," he whispered.

He released my hand and climbed out of the truck. I took a deep breath and climbed out after him. Bob followed me into the house, and I began boiling water to clean out our myriad of new wounds. I laid out the first aid supplies and told Duke to sit for clean-up. I started with his face, which would need stitches.

"So, you want me to do the stitching?" I asked.

"It will go better than if I do it," he replied. "There could be something in the nursing textbook about stitching. Want me to grab it?"

"Yes, please," I said, relieved to put it off for a while. He fetched the book and began searching for the section on suturing faces back together while I worked on his arms. There were many cuts from the claws of the Rovers, but they were shallow and just needed to be cleaned, medicated, and wrapped up. He found the chapter on sutures, and thankfully, there were illustrations.

I cleaned the wound again and moved the lantern as close to us as possible. It felt awkward because he was so much taller than me. I had him lay his head on my lap and took a deep breath. "You are going to do fine, Noah. Just follow the patterns in the pictures, and you will be great." I knew his words were meant to be comforting, but they made me more nervous.

I held the sides of the skin together and brought the needle down. The first push-through made my stomach turn over. My hands started to shake.

"Duke, I don't think I can do this. You don't mind being hideously scarred for life, right?"

He looked at me, thinking for a moment.

"If you do it, we can have coffee with dinner."

It took me about fifteen minutes to finish up the gash. I messed up a few of the stitches and had to pull them out and redo them. Duke was a great patient, sitting there as if it was nothing. Maybe he was still feeling the effects of being in shock.

After he was all fixed up and had taken some pain medication, it was my turn. I lay on my side on the couch so Duke could get a good look at the gash. He boiled more water and started sanitizing the suture kit. I glanced at my side and looked away quickly. It was longer than the one Duke had on his face. It was deep, too. I squirmed a lot while he sewed me up. I was secretly relieved that he had practiced on Bob once before.

After getting put back together and washing up (no bath for me on new stitches), we made dinner and started a fire. The events of the day crashed around me like a hailstorm. I set my bowl of chili aside and grabbed my coffee. The aroma filled me with a sense of security and normalcy. I closed my eyes and breathed in deeply. When I opened them, Duke was staring at me.

"Noah, is something on your mind? You have been a little off since Ray's."

I looked away quickly, the thoughts of the man touching me tearing back into the forefront of my memory. A shudder tore through me before I could stop it.

Duke set his bowl down and got off the couch to kneel in front of me. "Noah, what happened? What is going on?"

I looked into his eyes and thought about lying to him. Then I saw the angry gash on his face. He deserved the truth from me when he asked for it.

"At the compound, when we were being searched.... The man that searched me... He touched me. He grabbed me and whispered in my ear some creepy things."

After saying it aloud, I was stung by shame. Here I was, making a big deal out of something as seemingly simple as a grope and a dry hump. I mean, it's not like he raped me. How could I be so selfish as to let it bother me?

Duke sat in silence for a few moments, looking into my eyes. He took a deep breath. I was mentally preparing for him to give me a tongue-lashing for my foolishness.

"Noah, why didn't you say something?" His voice was soft, almost a whisper. He shook his head, turning away, his lips pulled tight.

"I'm sorry, I shouldn't have mentioned it. You have so much to worry about, and I am not your responsibility, and-"

"What?" He looked back at me, his eyes sharp.

"I'm not your wife. I'm not even your girlfriend. It's not your job to protect me, and I need to be able to handle things on my own. I mean, I had things like that happen all the time tending bar."

He pulled my face towards him and kissed me. He ran his hands through my hair, caressed my neck, and gently traced his rough fingers along my jawline. I melted into him, running my hands along his arms. The tension of the day was erased by his soft touch and tender caresses.

He pulled back from me and tears were glistening in his eyes. "Noah, you are everything to me. When I said that men don't protect a friend like they do a wife, I certainly did not mean that I would not protect you. You are the reason I keep going every day. When you brush against me as we work side by side, it is like moonlight dancing on my skin. My heart was my wife's, but she is gone. I will always love her, but if you can accept that and love me anyway, I would swear my heart to you right now.

"Noah, I love you. And I swear that I will protect you from anything that comes to harm you."

My breath caught in my throat. "I… I can't make you do that, Duke."

"No one ever makes me do anything that I do not do." He took my hands and stood me up.

"Come with me."

He led me to the door and peered out the small window. It must have been clear because he opened the door and led me out into the warm fall evening. A few fireflies still danced around as he led me to the center of the clearing. The stars were just beginning to appear as twilight swept over us.

Duke stopped me and took both my hands in his.

"Noah Elaine, here in the presence of God and each other, I take you to be my wife. I promise to protect you, love you, and be the best teammate for you as long as we both shall live. I vow to be yours and yours only, forsaking all others and leaving behind the heartaches of the past. I will be yours for better or worse, in sickness and in health, as long as I breathe. Will you take me?"

I smiled at him, taking half a step closer. "Timothy Duke, here in the presence of God and each other, I take you to be my husband. I promise to love and protect you, be the best teammate I can, and follow your leadership as long as we both shall live. I vow to be yours and only yours, forsaking all others and moving forward with you. I will be yours in safety and injury, in times of plenty and times of need, as long as I breathe."

An owl screeched in the night air as our lips met again, this time as husband and wife. Duke lifted me gently and carried me to the cabin. He carried me straight to the small bedroom and softly laid me down on the quilt. He laid down next to me and pulled me close.

"Mrs. Duke, I want to make love to you."

"Then what are you waiting for?" I asked, caressing his muscular arm.

"Well, we both had massive injuries today, so there is that."

I laughed and pulled him in to kiss him. We snuggled together in the bed that we had avoided for more than a month. Now, it was our bed, and we fell asleep in each other's arms.

CHAPTER 13

A beautiful fall morning glistened through the small window of our bedroom. I took a deep breath and smiled. Duke was up making coffee, and I smelled something I hadn't smelled in a long time: eggs.

I hopped out of bed, straightened the bedding, then walked out to greet my new husband. The thought made me smile.

Duke didn't turn from the little stove when I walked in. "Good morning, lovely," he said. I walked over to him and wrapped my arms around his waist, and he chuckled. "I take it you are looking for coffee?"

"You got it," I said into his shoulder blade.

He turned around and smiled down at me. "You have to earn it."

I smiled and lifted up on my toes to kiss him. "Now, feed me?"

He grinned and turned back to the stove. I pulled out some plates and mugs while he brought the food over to the table. "Now, where did you get eggs?" I asked.

"A gift from Papa Ray. He has a few chickens behind the station. He gave me a dozen." He groaned a little as he sat down.

The wound on his face looked angry, and his left eye was black and nearly swollen shut. He must have been in so much pain.

"How are you feeling today?" I asked, probing just a little.

"Well, I am married to a beautiful woman. I am eating the best eggs I may have ever made, and the sun is shining. I think that I am feeling pretty amazing," he said

I smiled at him. "That bad, huh?"

"Worse. I feel like my head went through a buzz saw, and I have a couple bruised ribs. How about you? How is that side feeling?"

"I might be sharing your buzz saw. Is a buzz saw a thing?"

"I think so. I'm not a carpenter."

We smiled at each other and enjoyed our meal. It was wonderful. After eating, we cleaned and redressed each other's wounds. There was really no covering the angry gash along Duke's face, so I just cleaned it as best I could and slathered it with antibacterial goo. Then, we went out to the truck and began unpacking our hard-earned treasures. We updated our inventory lists, planned out how we would use the canned goods sparingly, set the new game trap, and searched the forest edge for sticks and kindling to use. It was a warm, clear fall day, and the woods were clear of Rovers as far as we could see. We took a break to eat lunch and reclean our wounds. I couldn't decide which hurt worse: the gash or the ragged scrapes.

After lunch, we continued our winter preparations by searching through the clothes we had traded for and those already in the cabin. Trinity had been a little smaller than me, and it felt odd wearing Duke's first wife's clothes, but staying warm was more important than not feeling awkward. We went through the cabin inch by inch to see if there were any repairs that needed to be done before the snow flew. We found a few small areas that would need patching, but nothing major. Duke went to the woodshed to grab a few tools while I took the ax to some nice dry wood to make thin slats for the patching. While working, we chatted, planned, and stole kisses. The events of the day before seemed miles away.

I climbed onto the roof to check for any places that required our attention while Duke boiled some water and started on the laundry. I found four places that needed some waterproofing and new shingles. "Hey, Duke? Can you toss me the hammer and a few of those slats? Also, do we have any tar or weatherproofing stuff? I found a few small places that could use some attention."

"Yeah, here you go," Duke mumbled as he walked around the side of the cabin and looked up at me. I burst out laughing at the sight. He had donned a slightly frilly apron over his bare chest, with three clothes pins lined up in the side of his mouth. He rolled his eyes at me and tossed the hammer my way. Once his hand was free, he took out the pins and stuck his tongue out at me, wincing as he flexed his face. "I don't want to get soap on my pants, okay?"

"Yeah, it's great. You look…. Manly." I laughed again

"Ok, funny guy. You want me to come up there?"

"Why? Need help tying your apron strings?" Renewed laughter roared through me.

"Ha ha ha. You are hilarious. To answer your question, I have some plastic sheeting in the shed, but not much. How large are the areas that need to be covered?"

"Not big; maybe two feet of plastic all together would cover it. Can you grab it for me, or do I need to come get that? I know that you are a very busy washer-woman."

"You are not nearly as cute as you think you are, you know," Duke grumbled as he went around to the shed. He appeared a few minutes later, apron missing, with a roll of black plastic in hand. "Better?" he asked as he handed it up to me.

"Well, I can see your manliness better this way," I said, waggling my eyebrows at him.

He chuckled as he went back to his laundry chore. This guy was the light of my life. I marveled at how much he had become to me in such a short time.

The sun was hot on my back as the afternoon wore on. I pulled off old wooden shingle slats, laid new plastic, and nailed new ones in place. Sweat dripped down my face, stinging the gash in my side before I was content with my work. I climbed down and joined Duke to fold up the freshly dried clothes. He still wasn't wearing his shirt, and I blushed when he caught me staring.

"You know, you don't have to be embarrassed by me, Noah," he said and gave me a playful nudge.

I smiled and dropped my eyes. "I know, it's just… I don't know. You were a faceless regular at the bar; then you were this pushy cop, then you were this heroic savior, and now… "

"Now I am your drop-dead gorgeous husband? Arm Candy? Sugar daddy?"

I laughed. "Forget it. I'm just being weird."

"Noah, I get it," he said, taking the shirt from my hand and tossing it back over the clothesline. "Things have not been normal in a long time. And now you are wondering if you made a mistake by marrying me, that it was a rash decision made out of fear and loneliness."

"It's not that I don't love you. I am just worried that we rushed into it and that you won't like me after a while. That I will get comfortable with you, begin to plan the rest of our lives, and then… you will leave."

He pulled me close, our sweat mingling. "Noah, I am not going anywhere. I chose you. I chose to get you the day of the Fall. I chose to stay when things got hairy. I chose to marry you. Noah, I don't know who left you, but I will not leave you as long as God lets me be here with you."

He pulled my chin up to look into his eyes. "Are you… Sure?"

"Forever and always, my Noah." He kissed me and ran his hand through my hair. I sighed into his kiss and wrapped my arms around him, too. "So, you wanna get out of here?" he winked at me.

"I do," I said, letting my hands linger on his skin. "But we should probably finish the laundry first."

He groaned. "Fine. But I am not wearing the apron anymore." He laughed as we finished up and brought the fresh clothes to the cabin to put away. The sun was beginning to sink into the sky, and there was still more to be done before we could check out for the day.

I called for Bob as we headed into the woods to check on the new trap. We had caught some kind of critter that Duke identified as a fisher. It looked more like a ferret to me, but we took our kill and reset the trap. Bob started barking and snarling as we turned to head back home. I looked around as I drew my gun. I didn't see anything, but Bob had never been wrong about the Rovers being close. Well, not yet, anyway.

Duke took his position behind me, the ferret-like critter tossed over his shoulder, gun at the ready. "Where is it, Bob? Where's the Rover?" Bob's hackles were up, and he snarled towards the west. Deep in the shadows, I could see movement and glittering eyes.

"Warning shots?" I asked, scanning the rest of the surrounding area for more Rovers.

"No, better save the ammo. Let's just get moving towards the clearing. Bob, come."

We moved with practiced ease, a dance of spins and back steps, our eyes ever watching the shadows that seemed to darken by the moment. There was a clicking to the left, and Duke jerked toward it, with me matching his movement in the opposite direction. Two shots rang out, making me jump. There was a thump and a strange gurgling sound, accompanied by a sickening suction noise and scuttling in the leaf litter.

"I missed the head. He's off," Duke warned, his tone level and professional. We continued our dance for about a quarter mile before entering the clearing again. Duke scanned the area while I watched our backs. It all seemed clear, so we scuttled double time to the cabin door. Once inside, we set to work preparing the fisher and began making supper. It felt so odd doing a task so mundane after the shooting of a Rover, but what else was there to do? We chatted about going to the river the next day as we sat down to our meal of canned beans, fried assorted roots, and some of the fisher. It wasn't bad, but it had been a while since I had eaten any meat other than rabbit or fish. We worked together to wash up the dishes and fed the remaining food to Bob. He wolfed it down happily. He was adjusting to apocalypse food better than I thought he would.

"You want to shower first, or should I go?" Duke asked as we put the last of the dishes back.

"You can go first. I want to get a fire going and do a couple of things out here first," I said.

"Sounds good. I won't be long," he said, heading into the bathroom and shutting the door. I got the fire going pretty quickly using the coals from the kitchen stove.

I took a deep breath and talked some courage into me. It was time. Tonight, I was going to be a wife. I put the kettle on and walked to the bathroom door, taking another deep breath before quietly opening the door. Duke was behind the bear and moose-themed shower curtain and couldn't see me. I stripped off my clothes, walked over, and pulled back the curtain just enough to peek in. Duke had his pack to me, and I took a half moment to appreciate his posterior.

"You need help getting your back?" I asked softly.

Duke jumped and shrieked like a little girl in a haunted house. "Noah! Don't do that to me!

What are you even doing here?"

"Well," I said, climbing in to join him. "Saving water?" He smiled at me and handed me a washcloth.

"I would love some help," he said, dropping his eyes for a moment, then looking up at the ceiling quickly. It took all my self-control not to cover myself. He took a deep breath and added, "It's a good thing this shower only lasts so long."

After we were both properly cleaned, we dressed in comfy clothes and drank tea by the fireplace. It was warm and cheerful. I snuggled into Duke as he played with my hair. "We were a good team out there today," I said, running fingers idly over his arm.

"We are the best team," he said. "We are doing great. Massive injuries and all."

I smiled, looking up at his wounded face. "We are." I looked back into the fire and sighed contentedly. "And we are just getting better."

Duke finished his tea, took my cup, and stood up. "Come on. Let's get to bed." He took my hand to help me up and deposited the mugs in the sink. We walked hand and hand into the bedroom.

Bob got up from the couch to follow. Duke turned to him and said, "Sorry, boy. You have to sleep out here tonight. Three is a crowd, and I just got married yesterday." He winked at Bob, shut the door, and we headed to bed.

CHAPTER 14

The sun streamed warmly through the window, bathing me in a comfortable glow. I smiled and sighed, smelling coffee and hearing Duke whistling to himself as he prepared breakfast. I rolled over and hugged his pillow, absorbing his scent and basking in the morning glow.

Too bad reality sucked, and the warm feelings couldn't last. Rolling out of bed, I pulled on some freshly laundered clothes. The memory of Duke in the frilly apron made me snort and laugh as I joined him in the kitchen.

"Good morning, lovely," he said over his shoulder as I wrapped my arms around his waist.

"Yes, it is," I replied into his back. "Did you sleep well?"

"Yes, I did," he responded in a cocky voice. "And I know you did."

"Meh, it was okay," I teased, grinning.

He turned with a mock-offended expression and then cracked a grin. "Well, at least the coffee is good, huh?"

"That you are definitely good at," I said with a smile, grabbing a mug. We had sardines and eggs with some late-season apples we'd found nearby in the forest, giggling as we shared our homely repast.

The bright morning promised a day filled with peace, hard work, good company, and pride in our new-found way of life.

If only I could get it right just once, that would be great.

We finished eating and cleaned up, stealing, kisses and hand-feeding Bob, who was feeling rather put out by our lack of attention on him. Having planned a trip to the river, we loaded up with packed lunch, fishing poles, a hand trowel for digging worms for bait, a bucket for fish, a few knives, and our guns.

"You want to take the lead, or you want to follow?" Duke asked me.

"Do you trust me not to get us lost? It is a way to the river, and I don't know these woods like you do," I responded.

"No, I don't, but I like to watch you when you get confused. Your nose gets this little wrinkle to it and…" Duke's voice trailed off as we walked around the front of the cabin from the shed.

"What is it?" I asked, following his gaze.

There was a very large bear less than twenty yards away, lumbering in our direction.

"Noah, stay behind me and get on the roof," he said, using that steady cop voice that always made me more nervous.

"The roof? Why not in the cabin or the truck?" I asked.

"We won't make the truck door before that big boy decides to charge, and I don't know that the front door can withstand a bear attack."

"What about Bob?" I asked, trying to keep my panic out of my voice. I know a headshot of the Rovers took them out, but a 9-mm bullet to a full-grown bear would really do nothing but make it mad.

"You get up there, and I will hand him up to you."

"Where is he?" I asked, suddenly fearing the worst.

Great, NOW I get to be right.

Bob ran out from the other side of the cabin and charged toward the bear at full speed, barking and growling like a rabid beast, challenging the huge animal.

"Bob! No! Bag dog! Get back here! Bob!"

He ignored me and met the bear head-on. There was a mass of golden, silky fur and deep brown, matted fur mixed with angry sounds, teeth, blood, and wicked claws. Bob was a brave dog and had fought off some pretty tough adversaries before, but he was no match for this creature. The bear tore at him with chef's knife-sized claws, wicked, blood-stained teeth, and a temper that made me look coy.

Duke ran toward the melee, firing into the air above the bear to try to spook it, but it was in full-on battle mode. Bob yelped in pain, and I screamed, covering my mouth, terror coursing through me. *Not again,* I thought to myself. *Not Bob again. He can't take another surgery.*

A clicking sound behind me almost went unnoticed as I was so focused on the fight before me. Something deep inside urged me to divert my attention from the fight to the noise. I glanced over my shoulder just in time to see a clawed hand large enough to remove my appendix and spleen at the same time come swinging at me. I shrieked again, ducked, and rolled to the right, away from the cabin. I tried to draw my gun, but it was stuck in the holster.

"Really?!" I yelled at the thing, tugging it again, but I had to dodge another attack from the Rover that was trying to kill me. I felt the stitches in my side rip free, and I tumbled farther from the cabin. I grabbed one of the Rover claw knives from my belt and hurled it at the beast, which flicked it away as if it were a mere fly.

I could hear the bear ripping apart my best friend, my husband was running off heroically to try to save the day, and I was going to be eaten by a giant toad with a yucky little soccer ball head held on by a penis.

Seriously, could we ever have a normal day?

"Duke? I could use a little help over here!" I yelled out, risking a glance at the fight taking place to the left.

The monster jumped onto me and began chewing on my arm.

When I say that I screamed in agony, I really don't mean the kind of agony that you feel when you stub your toe on something, or when you get something sharp in your eye, or when you choke on a potato chip, and it gets lodged in your throat that leaves you unable to speak properly for the rest of the day. This was the agony of setting your hair on fire and having your fingernails ripped out all at the same time. This was like being covered in a thousand paper cuts, doused in lemon juice, and then shoved down all the stairs in the Empire State Building.

This was the agony of an early 2000s Justin Bieber/Mylie Cyrus playlist on repeat.

Its teeth were like little razors, and each seemed to rotate back-and-forth in a sawing motion, taking less than a minute to reach the bone. I screamed and beat at the creature with my free arm. I tried again for the gun in my holster, but the stupid thing wouldn't budge. I used my thumb to gouge at one of its eyes, eliciting a chorus of clicking sounds and wails, but the large mouth continued its gruesome work.

It's odd how, in moments of pure terror, the most ridiculous thoughts spring to mind. I was about to die, and the only thing I could think of, other than *Get this thing off me,* was, *Well, shoot. I was so excited to try to find the river on my own this time*.

Suddenly, the monster on top of me grew immensely heavy. I felt like I was going to pop. I could feel the blood shooting out from an opening in my side, and my breath was being pushed from my body. *Woah, not even going to be chewed to death. Weird. I really never thought I would die by being flattened by a toad monster.*

Then I heard the bear—snarling, roaring, grunting. It was so close I could smell it. By the way, bears really stink.

The razor-wire-like teeth ripped out of my arm, and the Rover lifted off of me. I sucked in a breath and let it out again in a ragged squawk. The bear and the Rover were fighting over my carcass like a couple of vultures. I sat watching for a moment, too shocked to do anything, too hurt to move, too squished to care, and too apathetic about dying to consider that I could get away while they were distracted.

Then, a thought broke into my mind, tearing through the fog of shock. Where were Duke and Bob?

I rolled to my side, cradling my ruined arm, blood soaking the ground around me. How much blood can a person lose before they need to either get a transfusion or die? I'm not sure, but I was pretty sure my body was trying to set some kind of sick record. I looked toward where the fight had occurred before and saw Bob standing over Duke, snarling toward the beasts, his face covered in blood, dripping from his teeth. If I didn't know any better, I would say that Bob ate Duke.

He wouldn't, right?

I took a steeling breath and began to army crawl away from the gladiators, killing each other over the top of me. I made it about three feet before I heard a shot ring out. *Yay! I did it! I got my gun loose!* I told myself. Then I realized that I was still crawling through my own blood and sobbing like a snot-covered kitten who just wanted her milk. I did not shoot.

Duke was lying on his stomach under Bob, with his gun held in front of him, and he, too, was covered in blood. Why was there so much blood everywhere? I felt a giggle bubble out of my mouth as

I hollered in my best Papa Ray voice, "Git all that blood offa my yard, d'ya hear me?!"

Duke looked at me with the most confused expression ever, making me giggle all the more.

"Honey, look! A giant monster beast death match!" I yelled at him. He closed his eyes and shook his head.

Which just made me giggle more. I could feel my blood slipping out of me rapidly, and I feared any minute, one of the big guys was going to win and come to eat me. Suddenly, I felt very cold and wanted a blanket. I pushed myself off the ground, Duke began yelling something, Bob ran at me, more shots rang out, and then I found myself face down in the grass. It was itchy, and I'm pretty sure an ant crawled up my nose.

"Bob, can you get this ant off your old papa bear's nose?" I asked, feeling a little delirious.

"Missy, you best not move too much. We got them big, bad boys shot dead, but it looks like they tried to dead you first, huh?"

I giggled yet again. "Duke, you sound like Papa Ray," I twisted my neck and looked up to see the weathered face smiling, the old arms cradling Bessy. "Wow. You have impelicable timing. Implimental. Imipicible."

"Ray, thank God you are here! She is hurt badly. They came out of nowhere! We saw the bear, and I was going after Bob, I have no idea when the Rover came. I didn't hear anything until the bear took off from attacking us to go after the Rover! What did it do to her?

Can you help me?" I had never heard Duke sound so frantic before, and it scared me. I tried to look at him, and my eyes just wouldn't focus.

"Course, Sonny. Let's get your little missus inside and get her all patched up. Looks like you and Bob could use a little TLC, too, huh?"

"What? No, we are fine. Minor stuff. I shot the bear enough times to get him off of us before he did too much damage."

There was more talking, but I couldn't really hear it anymore. Everything turned black and silent. Maybe I died, maybe I fell asleep. Was there even a difference in this new world?

CHAPTER 15

Before I could open my eyes, I felt the pain. My head felt like it was trying to lift off my shoulders from the pressure, my arm felt like it had gone through a sawmill, and my insides seemed to be trying to escape through my side with dull steak knives.

I was incredibly thirsty, more than I had ever been in my life. I wanted to climb into a river and just open my mouth to the flow. Actually, a nice cold river sounded great for my torn-up body. I could hear voices softly chatting around me as my eyelids fought under the weight of an elephant to open.

"She's awake," a voice said. "Noah? Noah, can you hear me?"

"Wa-wa." Even I didn't understand that one. Let's try that again. "Wa-tah." Yeah, much better.

"Water? Here you go." Someone gently lifted my head and placed a glass of water on my lips. I slurped greedily, draining the glass. "Slow down. You need to pace yourself."

I opened my eyes to see the face of Daisy, the guard looking at me. "How are you feeling? Can you talk?"

"Duke?" I asked.

"He is okay. Papa patched him up, and they headed back to the station to prepare for an excursion into the pits to find supplies."

He… he left me?

“Bob?” I asked instead.

“Right here, on your feet. Hasn’t left you for more than going to relieve himself since the fight.”

I heard footsteps leaving the room and turned to see who else was there. My attention was drawn to the window. It was dark. How long had it been? It was morning when the bear had come, it must be after ten now.

“How long?” I croaked out, gesturing for more water.

“You have been out for five days. We didn’t think you were going to make it for the first two.

Lost your pulse a few times, but your husband got you back. He was by your side for three days before Papa said they had to get moving for the raid. He was torn over leaving. Ricky and I were left here to take care of you and Bob.”

I closed my eyes. *Five days? Really?* I couldn’t quite wrap my head around that. No wonder I was so thirsty. Daisy lifted the glass back to my lips and let me drain it again.

“I’m so cold. Did it snow?” I managed.

“Nope. We are having a nice little Indian summer. Been sticking right around 70 most days. Only dropped to maybe 50 at night. I will grab you another blanket.”

Daisy rose and walked over to the closet. I froze. Sitting in the living room, on my couch, was the guard that grabbed me. He looked my way, smirked, and turned back to the fire. Maybe Duke had warned him not to get within five feet of me? I shivered as Daisy threw another blanket over me. “Here ya go. You try to get some more sleep now, okay?”

“When will Duke be home?”

Daisy stood to leave. “Either tomorrow or the next day. Depends on where they find their opening to get in and what they are getting. Some raids last overnight.”

I shuddered. The thought of Duke spending the night in a dark pit filled with ruined humanity and monsters miles away from me made me more scared than the bear had. Daisy’s military-like empathy made me halt my questions and simply nod. She seemed about as sympathetic as a cactus, but I guessed she was a good guard, or Duke would have never agreed to leave her here with me.

“Thank you,” I managed and dropped my head back onto the pillow. She froze for a moment, then placed a hand awkwardly on mine.

“There, there. It’s going to be… fine… and stuff…”

I smiled up at her. She was as uncomfortable being here as I was having strangers watch over so while I healed. That was somewhat comforting. “Thank you,” I said again, more genuinely.

She smiled back, sort of. “I got you, girl.” Then she turned her back and left, taking the oil lamp with her. The door clicked, and I felt so terribly lonely. I wanted Duke here with me. I called Bob up to my pillows and snuggled into his thick, freshly washed fur. He must have gotten pretty beat up by the bear as he had many bandages wrapped all over his body. He whined just a little and licked my face. I love my Bob. I fell asleep with tears on my cheeks and Bob's nasty dog breath on my face.

CHAPTER 16

I don't know how long I slept, but it was still dark when I came back to this side of the void. Bob was gone, and I couldn't see much in the pale light of the half-moon coming through the window. I was in pain everywhere, but that wasn't what woke me. There was something wrong. I couldn't really tell what it was, but something bad was happening. I tried to roll over and felt a rough hand cover my mouth and the other pin me down by my good arm. My eyes shot open as sparks of bright white pain blazed through me. There was someone on top of me.

I tried to scream, but no sound came out. I tried to move, but all the bandages and wounds made me mostly immobile. I tried to kick with my legs, only to have my legs pressed together by larger, more powerful legs than mine. Who was attacking me? What did they want? Where was I? Thoughts raced through me as my heart tried to tear out of my chest.

A voice accompanied by foul, rotting breath drifted into my ear.

"I told you there was more where that came from."

I froze in terror; everything came back in a moment: the station, the guard, the voice, the dirty feeling.

I tried to bite his hand. I tried to roll over. I sobbed into the pillow, and he held me down. He released my arm to pull at my pants. I kicked with all my might but to no avail. He was too big, too strong. He kept one hand on my face, holding me down and keeping me quiet, while the other hand revealed my backside to him. He slapped it hard. Tears shot out of my eyes, and panic gripped my heart. He was going to rape me, and I was helpless.

God, please help me! Please send help! Please send someone! I prayed desperately in my floundering mind.

"Oh, relax, baby. I promise to be gentle," the man's hoarse whisper in my ear was nearly as bad as his rough hands squeezing my stitched-up side. I whimpered in pain. Everything was pain and darkness.

"Bob!" I yelled around his hand. "Bob!" I knew my muffled voice wouldn't make it far, but dogs have great hearing. Maybe Bob would hear and come to the rescue.

The man's hand left my side painfully as he began undoing his own pants. "Don't worry, baby. We won't be disturbed. That stupid, clumsy brute Daisy could sleep through a hurricane, and your mutt is locked out with the monsters. It's just you and me." I fought with every fiber I had left. This was not going to happen to me. Was it?

I heard barking in the distance. Bob had heard me and was too far away. Duke was who knows where. I was alone. I pinched my legs together as he forced himself on me. He dug his fingers into my side, and I gasped for breath.

"See? I'm not so bad, huh?"

"Worse than I thought you were, Sonny."

Light flooded the room, Bob barked from close by, and the weight of the man was pulled off me.

"No one touches my wife!" Duke's face was a mask of murder and rage and was brimming with darkness. His fists flew, pounding the man over and over. Bob went to work with teeth of fury at the man's arms.

I sucked in a breath and sobbed it out.

"There there, missy. You take a deep breath. We men are gunna take care of this here, coward." Papa Ray pulled my pants up and covered me with a blanket. He sat next to me, resting his hand gently on my back, rubbing soothingly, watching Duke and Bob beat the ever-living-snot out of Ricky. "Duke, I don't want to tell you how to do your job, but I do believe you missed one of his ribs on that left side there."

Ricky sobbed out, "I'm sorry! I'm sorry! I thought she wanted it! She was leading me on! She invited me in here!" He looked at Ray sitting on the bed. "Uncle Ray! Help me! I didn't do anything wrong!"

"Oh, sonny, you certainly did. You never touch a lady in violence, and else you are gunna get some violence your way. I thought you were a good man. Even vouched for you on guard duty for this little lady here. You deserve every bit you get here," Papa Ray said calmly, watching as Duke delivered blow after blow while Bob chewed the man up unapologetically.

After Duke expended all his energy, he kicked the bloodied and sobbing lump once more. "Bob, that's enough. This weasel has learned his lesson. And if I ever even see your filthy little face again, Ricky, I will use bullets in place of fists. Now get out of my home."

One final kick sent the miserable Ricky speeding out the bedroom door.

Duke turned to me and fell to his knees. The anger was replaced by anguish. Tears filled his eyes. "Noah, I'm sorry. I'm so sorry. This is all my fault. I should have never left you here with that man. I thought…"

His voice trailed off as a sob stole its way out of him.

"Not your fault," I managed to whisper. "Glad you're home."

"I'm gunna go see to my nephew. I'll leave you two to it now." Papa Ray stood, then leaned down to plant a kiss on my head. "I am sorely sorry, Noah. I had no idea that boy was so much trouble." His steps receded by closing the door. Bob climbed gingerly onto the bed and lay his head on me. Duke ran his hands over my face.

"Do you want some water? Pain killers?" I nodded as much as I could muster. Duke poured some water from the bedside basin into the cup and reached into his pocket. He pulled out a pack of pills. "I got some really good meds for you. I know that is not much of a consolation, but it will help with the pain." He fumbled with the packaging, his hands swollen and bloody, his eye glistening. Somehow, I knew it wasn't from the pain in his hands.

"Go wash up. Bob has me," I croaked.

Duke looked at me, tears staining his cheeks. “I will never leave you again, Noah. I’m so sorry.”

He stood and walked to the door, looking back one last time. Bob snuggled up to me and whined. Duke nodded to him and walked out the door. I let out a croaky laugh. “He left me again, Bob.” He lifted his head and gave a deep woof. “That’s what I thought.”

I closed my eyes as the adrenaline rush from the attack wore off. *I thought there were only monster-monsters to deal with.* I shuddered, then began crying anew. I was racked with sobs, making the stitches hurt all over again, and my head thumped with agony. Bob growled deeply. I tried to sit up to get my own water, but Bob laid a paw on my chest. He looked at me with his big brown eyes and whined.

“Water,” I croaked. He responded with a whine and laid his head over the top of my face. I smiled, burying my tears in his silky coat.

It was a few minutes before I heard Duke coming out of the bathroom. I nudged Bob off my head and looked towards Duke. His eyes were locked on something in the kitchen area. He took a few seconds to wrap his busted-up knuckles with some cloth, maintaining eye contact with whomever he was staring at, then turned to me, closing the door behind him.

Without a word, he knelt beside the bed and helped me to sit up. He gave me water, tore open a pill packet, tipped the pills in my mouth, gave me more water, and then lifted my shirt to examine my side. Angry purple bruises had begun to form around the stitches, and blood was seeping from the wound. He stood, walked out of the room, and closed the door behind him. He returned a moment later with a bowl, the med kit, and Papa Ray.

"Noah, can I please show Ray your side while I clean it?"

I looked from one concerned face to the other. I felt like a child being asked for permission for something that was going to be done either way. I hated the tears that bloomed in my eyes again. I hated being a victim. I hated needing to be saved again.

But hate doesn't solve anything.

I gave a small nod and turned away. Papa Ray knelt beside the bed where Duke had just been and looked at my side as Duke lifted the now-bloodied shirt. He sucked in a breath, shook his head, and placed a hand on my cheek.

"Sweet little Noah," he said, tears misting his old, wizened eyes, "I will never let that boy near you nor another lady as long as I have breath in me. If he weren't my late sister's child, I might take him out back and shoot him myself. I'm not sure I won't let Duke do it later if he fancies it. But I vow to you right now your pain will not be forgotten nor go unpunished. Duke, you take good care o' this treasure you got here. I will come back in a few days to check on the two of you. I think it would be best if I take Daisy and a soon-to-be-castrated-or-imprisoned Ricky back to the compound tonight."

Duke nodded silently and began working on cleaning my reopened stitches. Papa Ray stood and gave Bob a scratch behind the ears. He turned and walked out of the room. I could hear low voices as Duke tended to me.

"Noah, this is all my fault," he said, dabbing at the bruises and blood with the cold cloth.

"No, Duke. You couldn't have known." I replied, setting down the water glass, now able to speak, and covered his hand with mine.

"I should have stayed. I should not have let that man stay here with you. I should have known better than to trust some guy named Ricky."

I cocked an eyebrow at him. "The name should have told you not to trust him? Is that supercop-spidey-sense?"

He cracked a half-hearted grin and set the bowl aside. "Italian mobsters are named Ricky."

"Would that be racial profiling or name profiling? I can't make up my mind."

He smiled genuinely this time. It didn't last, though.

"Noah did he…."

I looked at him, wanting to keep joking and avoid talking about the assault, but his gray eyes were stormy. Fear filled my heart for a new reason. Would he even want me anymore? Was I damaged goods?

And would he believe me when I told him the truth?

"No, you got here just in time. A few seconds later and…" My voice trailed off as I looked away. Shame flooded over me as new thoughts poured in unbidden. *Had* I led Ricky on somehow? *Was* this all my fault?

"Do you think you can tell me everything you remember?" Duke asked, keeping his voice low and even.

"Who is asking? The cop or the husband?" I couldn't meet his eyes.

Duke climbed up to sit beside me on the bed, wrapping his arms around me and pulling me to his chest.

"This is not your fault, Noah. You did nothing wrong. Talking about it is going to be hard, but you need to get it out and not hold it. Holding assault inside is how trauma owns you. You cannot let it own you."

I nodded and pulled back. Taking a deep breath, I began to relay all I remembered about the attack. Every sentence felt like a stitch being pulled out—painful yet freeing. I did not deserve what happened to me, and I was not going to let it own me, so I pressed on. The narrative took only a few minutes, and by the time it was done, I felt like going and shooting that coward myself.

Perhaps therapists are onto something.

Duke inhaled sharply and wiped the tears from his face. "You are incredible."

I looked at him questioningly. I was bleeding, had a likely ruined arm, had nearly been raped in our own bed, and was exhausted after sleeping for five days. I didn't feel very incredible.

"Noah, you were uprooted at the drop of a hat and thrived. You have learned and embraced survival like a queen, and you always have a smile and a joke. You have faced down more dangers than I ever did on the beat. You are stronger than I will ever be. You are… incredible."

He intertwined his fingers with mine and kissed each one, lingering on the ring finger. "Someday, I will put a proper ring there."

I smiled. "Yeah, from the Rings-R-Us down the block?"

He smiled back. "I love you, Noah. Will you marry me again?"

"Every day."

"Good. Now, let's see how that arm is doing."

I groaned. I had not been looking forward to this. What would it look like? A section of the arm with no flesh, just the bone? Were maggots eating at the wound? Gangrene? I turned the best I could to give him access to the well-wrapped left arm.

He began slowly taking off the bandages, and my nerves started jumping again. The pain meds had not taken effect yet and everything hurt, though not as bad as it should have in the arm area, which was concerning. He reached to the bloodiest layer and gingerly pulled it off, using a cloth dampened with cool water to loosen it as he proceeded.

If I had eaten anything in the past few days, I would have thrown it up. My arm resembled ground beef.

Skin hung about the wound at odd intervals, most of my forearm muscle appeared to be missing, and there were a few spots where I thought I could actually see bone. I gulped and looked away. “Well, it looks so much better already,” Duke said. My face drained of all color as I thought about how bad it must have been before. He looked back at my face.

“I knew I could lose those last few pounds if I tried hard enough,” I said, feeling nauseous.

“That’s my girl,” he said with a smile. He slathered on some creams and ointments generously, added layers of bandages, and chatted to distract me from the shock of my arm’s condition. After he finished, he kissed my head and helped me lie back down. I was so tired I thought I could sleep for another five days and still wanted an afternoon nap. I closed my eyes as Duke cleaned up the medical supplies and refilled the water basin. I was half asleep when he came back and sat next to me.

“Noah, are you okay with me sleeping with you tonight?”

I opened my eyes as fear grabbed me unbidden. I looked up at him. His eyes were soft and full of worry. He was afraid of hurting my already wounded mind. I thanked God for his compassion. “Please do,” I told him. This night had been full of fear; it was time for some peace. He undressed and laid down beside me, gently wrapping arms around my broken body, kissing my shoulder, and caressing my hand. Bob took sentry at my other side and lay over my legs. Our bed was crowded, but we were all together, safe, and very tired. It didn't take long for sleep to take hold of me as I listened to Duke whispering prayers of safety over us and our home.

CHAPTER 17

"I told you there was more where that came from." The voice came out of the dark, and fear gripped my heart. A heavy body was on top of me, pushing all the air out of my lungs. I looked all around the clearing to find Duke. He had just been here!

The Rover that was lying on me turned its weird little head to face me while its huge, bloodied mouth chewed on my arm, tearing it to shreds. The face was Ricky's but still, with four eyes and covered in blood. "I'll be gentle, baby," he said, then clicked and barked. Duke appeared at my side.

"I lost the river. We better look for a new one," he said.

I looked at the beast trying to eat me and then back to Duke.

"As soon as I feed Bob. I think he's hungry."

awoke with a start. "Bob's hungry!" I yelled. Duke was leaning over me, apparently trying to wake me.

"Bob's okay, Noah. Are you okay? You were crying out in your sleep."

I looked around the room in panic. A dream. It was just a dream. A weird dream, but harmless nonetheless.

"I'm fine," I said, trying to sit up. Pain shot up my arm, and my head throbbed like crazy. "Water and drugs?" I asked, laying back down.

"Right here, love." Duke had pills and a water glass ready for me before I had even opened my eyes. He was great.

Duke helped me sit up and fed me the pills. I drank deeply and laid back down, closing my eyes again. "You need to eat something today," Duke said. "I can make some soup. Do you want to try to get out of bed today? I can get the water going for a bath?"

I groaned. "That sounds amazing, Duke. You are too good to me."

"No, I am making up for my failures. But I will take it," he smiled as he stood. "Bob, come here. Keep an eye on Mommy, got it?" Duke scratched Bob behind the ears and winked at me. Bob hopped up on the bed, causing a shockwave of pain through my body. I groaned again, but more hurtly. He drooped his ears and whined. Duke gave him a severe look, then turned to leave the room.

"Duke?" I called after him.

"Yeah?" He leaned on the doorframe and faced me.

"I'm glad you didn't lose the river."

He looked at me, cocking an eyebrow. "Me, too?"

I laughed a little, and he smiled and walked back to the bed. He leaned down and kissed me. "You are so strange, Noah." He turned and left the room, then returned quickly with a paperback. "Here, keep your brain moving while I get a bath going."

Duke helped me undress and climb in the tub. I leaned back in the hot water and sighed happily. I had to keep my left arm out, but it was still heavenly. Duke came back into the bathroom after a while. Keeping his eyes on the floor, he knelt by the tub and asked if I needed any help washing up.

I laughed. "What are you doing?"

"Asking if you need any help. You are down half an arm, and your stitches are a mess. I can do it without staring."

"Duke? Um… We are married. We have had sex. We sleep in the same bed. I'm pretty sure I don't care if you see me in the bathtub."

He glanced at me, cheeks flushed a little, then dropped his eyes again. "I know, but that was in the dark. And we sleep at least partially dressed."

"And I recall that I climbed into the shower with you? Not terribly long ago?"

"I kept my eyes to myself."

"I thought you said you had a rather long belt full of notches? What is with the shyness now?"

He glanced at me and blushed. This time, he actually blushed. "I was lying. Trinity was my first lover ever, and she was a big fan of privacy. I'm not really… that… I guess I was trying to impress you? I mean, young cops have a reputation to uphold."

I reached my ruined arm out to him, taking his face in my hand. "Duke, you are impressive enough just being yourself. There is no lie on this planet that would make me think more of you. Besides, that whole 'chicks dig players' thing is a total myth. Most of us actually don't find that attractive at all; we find it more off-putting than anything else."

Duke looked into my eyes, a strange look flicking across his features. It looked like shame or anger, but as soon as it was there, it was gone. He flicked a glance at my body, then looked away again, blushing deeper. I laughed again.

"Tell me about the excursion. I will try to keep my frightening feminine body from scaring you," I teased.

"I'm not scared of you! I just want to be…. You know, respectful and chivalrous and all that."

"You are all of those things and more," I leaned over to kiss him. He kissed me gently, touching my face with almost reverent lightness.

"Now help me wash up, and we can go eat some soup together. I might even let you see my elbows." I winked at him, making him laugh and blush all the more.

He was gentle, washing my hair, cleaning around my stitches, and helping me move around. The water was pretty cold by the time I was done, and he helped me out, stealing a glance at me before wrapping me up in a towel. I winked at him again. "You scoundrel."

He kissed me and helped me into the bedroom. He had put on fresh bedding and pulled the covers back for me to lay down. "I thought we were going to eat?" I asked, laying back on the pillows.

"I think I need some husband lessons first," he said, shooing Bob out and shutting the door. I smiled as he walked back and sat beside me.

I smiled at him. "You want to start with ankles? Or get really freaky with the shoulders?" I giggled as he leaned in to kiss me.

"I would rather start here," he said, kissing me gently.

CHAPTER 18

By the time we got around to the soup, it was very cold. The fire in the stove was out. Duke rekindled it and began the heating process again, then got the fire in the living room going. We sat together on the couch, holding hands and talking. I took a moment to really look at his face. The gash down the left side was closed, and the stitches had been removed. It looked more like a scar than a gash. I felt a pang of guilt looking at it. I wasn't there to remove the stitches; I hadn't been taking care of it for him. I know that was irrational, but since when was love rational? I reached out and touched the side of his face. He leaned into my hand and smiled warmly at me.

"I'm sorry I haven't been able to take care of you."

"Well, to be fair, you were unconscious," he said, kissing my hand.

"I know. I still feel bad. Who took out the stitches?"

"Daisy. She apparently was an EMT before things went south. Papa Ray says she has been an invaluable asset at the compound. He also said her bedside manner left something to be desired, but she gets the job done."

I laughed a little, thinking back to waking up and her awkward reassurances. "Well, he's not wrong," I said. "Can you tell me about the excursion? What was it like? Where did you go?"

He took a deep breath, held it for a moment and blew it out through pursed lips. "You sure you want to hear about that? It was…rough."

"Of course I do. If you ever plan to go again, we will be going together. I'm not being left out of all the adventure."

He looked grim, his smokey eyes hazy around the edges with unshed tears and his face sunk. "Noah, if I can help it, you will never go on an excursion. It was more dangerous than I thought possible. We lost some good people."

The smile fell from my face instantly. Had I been close to losing him? "Tell me the story," I said softly.

He nodded and leaned back on the couch, looking at the ceiling.

"It started with the bear attack. I was trying to get the bear off of Bob when the Rover came. I had no idea it was there until the bear left us to go after what it must have perceived as a threat. It lumbered off while I tried to help Bob, not even realizing that you hadn't gotten to the roof. Once I saw the Rover attack the bear, I saw you on the ground covered in blood. I panicked. I emptied my clip into the beasts. Probably didn't hit either one. You yelled something about getting blood on the grass, then something about a monster death battle. You were so covered in blood, torn up, panicked, and yet you just had to try to make a joke. You are a freak, by the way." He smiled appreciatively at me.

"Papa Ray and Daisy had come to tell us about the upcoming raid and happened to arrive right in time to save the day. You passed out, and I carried you in. Daisy worked on your arm the best she could, but there wasn't much she could do but clip off some of the more jagged parts that might hinder cleaning and healing. She was cool the whole time. I was a mess.

"Papa Ray had me go out and help him with the bear and the Rover. Both were dead, and the bear alone would be a good resource for meat, fur, and even tools from the bones and sinew. It took my mind off of things while Daisy got you patched up and in bed. As soon as she gave me the go-ahead, I washed up and sat with you. I cried a lot. I kept thinking that I was going to lose you. When Trinity was killed, I was helpless by not being there. Here I was again, helpless, being here. It didn't seem fair.

"Your pulse was weak. You had lost a lot of blood, and even between me and Daisy, we weren't certain you were going to pull through."

"Daisy said that you lost my heartbeat a few times, and you brought me back?" I asked. Part of me didn't want to know, but more of me needed to know.

He sighed and closed his eyes. A tear ran down his cheek. "Yeah. I lost you. Four times. The last time, Daisy was the one who got you back. I was exhausted, and my chest compressions weren't strong enough to do any good. After the second day, you stabilized and started talking in your sleep a little. That made me feel better. You talk in your sleep often, so it was a comfort to hear."

"I do?"

He laughed a sad little laugh, weakly but seemingly composed. “Yes, Noah, you do. It gave me some hope, which I desperately needed.

“Papa Ray was a blessing. He sat with me, prayed with me, and read you Bible passages while you were out. He really helped me through the first day before he had to head back to the station. When he returned, he brought Ricky, his nephew, whom he vouched for. Said Ricky was a solid young man who would be happy to stay and help Daisy take care of you if I still wanted to go on the excursion.

“I weighed the options for an entire day. I didn’t want to leave you, but there was so much that I could do to help the group that was going. That, and there would be supplies not readily available that I could have a first go at. It was a hard decision to make, but ultimately, you were out of the woods and going would be the most good I could do for everyone, so I agreed. We left the following morning. I rode in the bed of Ray’s old pickup truck with Bessie. He even kissed it before handing the rifle over. Guess that meant he trusted me.

“When we got to the station, there was already a group preparing to go. It was a team of 12. There was David, a doctor; Nilla, a young farmer; the army twins Bert and Bruce; Johnny, a skinny little nerd of a kid; Damien, the fireman; Maudie, a very accomplished thief and con artist; Leonard, the driver; Marsh and Davies, the sharpshooters; Phillipe, an experienced mountain climber, and myself. We spent the day making preparations, mapping the route and alternate escape routes, packing light supplies, and getting to know the team.

"Everyone had a job on the crew. David and Damien were the medical support, with Nilla as a fallback. She had a variety of animals on her farm that she was practiced in caring for, so she had a little knowledge to fall back on in a crisis; plus, she was strong and great with a shotgun. Bert, Bruce, Marsh, and Davies were the big guns. Two took point, the sharps taking high ground one at a time, leap-frogging to cover the crew from above and give advance warning of attack. Maudie, who has escaped from two different county jails and a federal prison, plotted our paths: in, out, alternates, and emergency escapes.

She also had a lock picking kit and a few other handy burgling supplies."

I grinned at him. "I bet the cop in you had a really hard time dealing with her, huh?"

"Actually, she was a riot. We shared a few stories and had a few laughs. You would have had fun with her. No, the hardest one to deal with on the team was Johnny, the tech guy. He was in charge of walkies, batteries, and this handy gadget that detected body heat and vibrations from up to 100 yards and through concrete. He was as smart as Einstein but had the common sense and social grace of a wombat. Weird kid. Next, we had Phillipe, the mountain climbing expert. He trained those who didn't know how to tie knots, use a grapple, and how to climb up and down ropes safely. Just a crash course, really, but it was the best that could be done in the time frame. Then was Leonard, the driver. He was an ex-military tank driver who turned trucker, so he knew how to handle big rigs. Papa Ray had this old camper that would be our transport. It seemed like a silly choice, but it had cargo space for goods, and he had souped it up with a bigger motor and some beefy tires, so it was the best option. Lastly was me. As this was my first excursion in the pits, my main jobs were defense, learning, and mule. I got the impression that they did not like newcomers in their group, but the gash across my face must have been a good resume. Maudie seemed intrigued by how I got it. Once I told her it was a Rover battle and my wife saved me, she winked and said that you were a lucky lady."

"I wasn't your wife when it happened, though."

"Yeah, she didn't need to know that part.

"The plan was as simple as it could be: drive to the shopping center on the outskirts of Carlton, get into the pits, enter the mall, gather as much as we could, and get out fast. If we were able to make a second or even third trip, we would discuss it after everyone was back on the transport. If we did not all agree, we headed home. Simple.

"We had maps of the layout of the mall before the Fall and a rough idea of what the path was once we were in the pits. There were markings of locations of Rover attacks from previous missions, showing likely places we could get hit, as well as targets marking which stores had not been looted yet. Well, by our groups, anyway. The pit we were going to was only about 30 feet deep, which was pretty shallow compared to some of the other pits. The shopping center had been about 30 square acres, and it all had been taken down in a single sinkhole, so we mostly just needed to drop in and climb into a broken door. It was largely intact; it just dropped down and shattered a bit.

"The plan once we got into the mall was to break into two teams. One medical person, one shooter, one muscle, and then two others to help fulfill the duty of that team. The sharpshooters were to stay high and keep their eyes open. Each person had a dog whistle to help repel the Rovers. My team was team med and food, focusing on hitting the two pharmacies, food court, and grocery store. The others were team winter gear. They were to hit up the camping and outdoor stores for anything and everything that would be needed once the snow flew. Each person had a backpack and duffel in which to gather as much as they could, except the muscles. They each had a few bags. Bert and Bruce were trying to one-up each other and making bets on who would bring back more.

"My team was made up of David, Nilla, Bruce, Maudie, and myself. The other was Damien, Bert, Johnny, and Phillipe. Leonard was to stay with the vehicle to guard from Rovers and people alike, and Marsh and Davies were our cover. We loaded up and got a few hours of sleep at the station and then headed out before dawn. The drive was pretty smooth, all things considered. When we were about ten minutes out from the shopping center, we double-checked equipment, counted rounds for all weapons, and went over plans for smooth sailing in case of trouble. We had to stop almost a full mile from the sinkhole that took the mall. We all grabbed our gear and headed out.

"We made it to the edge before the first Rovers appeared. There was a big one that seemed to be organizing the others. The things are not close to human intellect, but there are a few mice on their wheels. The first four Rovers came at us from the sides, and while we were focused on that, four more came out of the pit, the big one taking up the rear. They attacked in a pattern, always two at a time and on opposite sides of us, trying to find a weak spot. Davies got a shot through the big one, and the others went crazy. They began attacking savagely, randomly, with no logic beyond hunger; even though we blew the whistles, they fought through their dislike of the sound. We took out a few, and the rest fled, but we knew there would be more. Phillipe had done the most study of the things and said that vibrations attracted them as much as sounds and motion. We stood totally still for about thirty minutes. The few more passed by us in the pit and above on solid ground, never paying any attention to us. After enough time had passed for us to continue on, we got some ropes anchored and repelled into the pit.

"Davies and Marsh took turns following us down, then performed their protection leap-frog, always one ahead of us, stationary, and the leaper covering rearguard. There were a few straggling Rovers that came at us, but between all the guns, we took them out pretty fast.

"Once we reached the mall itself, things got a little trickier. While the mall was technically still mostly together, the entrance was sitting at about a 20-degree angle. It was… other-worldly. The black and white tile floors were cracked and jagged, random benches, still intact, were sitting at odd angles, large potted plants were tipped over and had begun growing in new directions, and there was a wishing well fountain with three angels that used to squirt water, now just broken bodies and mildew. I must have looked a bit shocked. Phillipe gave me a gentle nudge and said that I would get used to it. I don't think that I ever would.

"We got in and split the teams. Marsh would go with us and keep high eyes, and Davies, the other team. Each team leader, the medics, took out their maps, and we made our way to our destinations. There were scattered remains here and there, and every so often, we would come across a Rover carcass half-eaten, usually just the larger female body. It smelled terrible.

"Once we reached the pharmacy, we loaded up everything we could carry. Pills, glasses, bandages, condoms - you name it, we grabbed it. Maudie made quick work of locked cabinets, and we were able to fill-up. It had not been raided yet by the teams that met at Papa Ray's, so it was a gold mine."

"I'm sorry, you guys grabbed condoms?" I gave Duke a somewhat exasperated look. "I mean, was that really a necessity?"

"Not really, but we were there. And, frankly, bringing a baby into the world right now might be the cruelest thing anyone could do to another human being. There are monsters everywhere trying to eat everyone."

I stood and walked to the kitchen to get our hot soup. "There have always been monsters. Why not bring up warriors to fight the evil rather than stop their existence?"

Duke smiled as he took his soup. The thrill of his storytelling now engrossed him. "Well, I guess I will bring them back the next time I go down there."

"I'm not saying that it wasn't a good idea, just that it was not maybe a necessity?"

"I bow to your thought-provoking, if not cheesy, ideals. May I continue?"

"I digress."

Duke smiled and sipped his soup. "Once we had emptied the pharmacy as much as we could into our backpacks, we regrouped our team and headed to the food court area. Chances were good there would not be anything useful there, but it was right by the grocery area, so we gave it a try. As we got closer, we could hear the Rovers clicking, buzzing, and making odd sounds. It was not exactly loud, but we could tell there were a few of them, and they had to be close. We all got our whistles in our mouths, ready to use as we rounded the corner and were shocked by what we saw.

"Walking into that food court was like walking into a nightmare. There were dozens of Rovers, odd mounds made of anything lying around, like clothes, manakin parts, human bones and hair, with what had to be nests built into them. There were males and females free of each other, the males scuttling around and the females lumbering blindly. Some males sat in the nests, others were lying on the floor being eaten by something that looked like giant black slugs, but was probably the larva of the Rovers. There were a few females that appeared to be laying eggs in a very large communal nest in the center of the food court on top of tables that had been pushed together. When one was done, a male would scuddle up, scoop out as many eggs as he could carry and head off to an empty nest.

"We froze and barely dared to breathe. I was behind Bruce and before Maudie, Nilla, and David. I whispered to Bruce that we had not been spotted. We could edge back the way we came and find a new route. I saw his eyes dart to the grocery at the other end and shake his head slightly.

"'We can make it if we move along the edge and slowly,' he said.

"I tried to grab the back of his shirt as he moved forward, closer to the colony of Rovers, but I missed. I tried to call him back, but he just kept edging forward. Nilla gave a strangled croak and sobbed. Maudie shushed her a little harshly, causing Nilla to sob a little more. It was enough to draw the attention of a few Rovers at the edge of the colony. A female body turned in a few circles, giant mouth opening and closing, searching for what made the sounds. A male climbed up its body and attached itself to its female counterpart. It was like watching a robot boot up. All of a sudden, it was aggressive and turned to face the direction it heard us coming from. We stood as still as we could, not even daring to breathe lest we give away our position. Bruce was a good ten feet closer to the Rovers, but I could see the tension in his body. He was scared. I watched as he raised his gun, inch by inch.

“The shot that rang out made us all jump. The Rover colony froze in silence and turned to watch the lifeless body of the one who had watched us slip to the floor with a squelch and a thump. No one moved for a few minutes. I don’t think we even breathed. Bruce had his gun still held up, though it was not his shot that killed the Rover. Davies must have been nearby watching. Slowly, the Rovers returned to their lives; a few close ones to the body began tearing into it, and a nest full of slug babies slid onto it and began devouring.

“Then Maudie sneezed. It was loud and echoed throughout the court and probably through the entire mall. Hundreds of eyes fell on us. We stood as still as we could in the silence that followed.

“Two Rovers that already had linked with partners took a few steps in our direction, little black eyes flicking around. The large lower body of one leaned over enough to lay its claws flat on the ground. I breathed deeply and prepared to grab for my gun, still in its holster. Someone behind me, I don’t know who, shuffled their feet slightly. The Rover with claws on the ground let out a wet, crackling sound from the lower mouth, followed by a loud clicking from the top; then, all hell broke loose. Bruce raised his gun and shot the talkative Rover while at least fifteen more let out howls and clicks and shrieks of rage, charging at us with lightning speed. I blasted my whistle, then drew and began firing, yelling to the team to retreat. Bruce screamed out a battle cry as the beasts overtook him. I froze in horror as the Rovers ripped his head clean off his body, a fountain of blood erupting to shower the beasts in red, hot ichor, his gun firing off a dozen more shots before falling to the ground. I have seen some pretty terrible things as a cop. I have never seen anything that horrific before.

"I drove the rest of the team back. Nilla was in shock, but I was able to shove her back. The Rovers were occupied with consuming Bruce's body, buying us a few precious seconds to slip around the bend and make a break for the cover of a small baby clothing boutique. We leaped behind the counter and crouched low. Nilla began to cry, and I couldn't get her to calm down. David tried to get her to focus on him, but she was hysterical.

"'Shut her up! I can hear them coming!' I told him.

"I was about ready to knock her out when Maudie jabbed her in the leg with a syringe. We started blankly at her as she calmly leaned Nilla's head onto her shoulder.

"'Sorry about the sneeze. Allergies.' We would have asked her more, but the Rovers had arrived.

"David was about to blast his whistle when I stopped him.

"'It will give away our position,' I whispered.

"He nodded in agreement. I could hear a few of them enter the shop, clicking loudly, feet sliding on the polished floor. We had our backs to the wall behind the counter, facing the shop. I ejected the mag from my gun as quietly as I could, sliding a fresh one in. The click, as it snapped into place, got the Rovers' attention, and they dropped into silence. Maudie calmly drew her gun. David pulled his as well, though it was shaking. We sat facing the top of the counter, guns pointed out, as two Rovers curiously wandered over, eyes scanning. They paused when they looked at us. We knew they couldn't see us clearly as long as we were still, but it was still terrifying. Their breath stunk from both mouths. One had fresh blood running down its chin and along its ribs. My stomach turned over as I thought about how that blood had been part of my teammate not five minutes before.

"The Rovers scanned around and moved on, wandering off to search another part of the shop. I let out my breath slowly, gesturing to David and Maudie to stay low. I rose as slowly as I could to peer over the counter. There were four Rovers in the shop in total. One stood at the door, blocking any chance of escape, while the other three searched for movement. I froze and one of the searcher's heads whipped around 180 degrees, clicked a few times, and rotated the rest of the way around to face the front again. I lowered myself smoothly and sat back.

"'We wait,' I mouthed to the others.

"Then I pointed to Nilla. 'How long?'

"Maudie shrugged and flashed all ten fingers three times. Thirty minutes.

"We heard shots ring out in another part of the mall, both automatic and semi, so the other team had met some adversaries as well. The Rovers hunting us clicked excitedly and ran off. We sat still for a few minutes more to make sure they were gone before David took a relieved breath and stood up.

"A Rover grabbed him from the other side of the counter and pulled him over, clicking and squealing. Maudie and I jumped up and grabbed his legs, trying to pull him back. I shot the Rover a few times, and it released him. He was still alive but messed up. Maudie jumped the counter to put it down with a few more shots and keep eyes open for more while I worked on the doctor. He walked me through what to do. His shoulder was practically gone, the arm hanging limply, bones sticking out at frightening angles. He kept his head while he took a good look at it.

"'You have to take the arm,' he said.

"I tried to argue with him that we could do it; we could get him stitched up. He pointed to a few places and said some medical stuff that I couldn't get my head around, but it came down to 'the arm was dead at this point and keeping it attached by the lingering muscle and tissue would slow us down and just lead to infection later on.'

"I agreed to do it. I opened up my bag from what we raided at the pharmacy and dumped it out. I had mostly gotten the pills, so I needed Maudie's bag. She had raided the bandages and alcohol. David had some antiseptic in his med bag and a couple of scalpels. I opened a fresh water bottle and cleaned the area the best I could while David took as many pain pills as he dared. I dumped antiseptic on the area and my hands. David bit down hard on his leather belt as I began slicing through the layers of tissue that still held the arm in place. There wasn't much left, but it still took a few minutes to get through it all cleanly; he tried to stay as quiet as possible and bit through the belt completely. I had Maudie come back over and dump more water and antiseptic over the wound while I cleaned my hands. David walked me through cauterizing the artery with a lighter. He said it was not ideal, but in a pinch, it would keep him from bleeding out. As I did it, he bit through the belt again.

"I got him wrapped up in gauze as tightly as I could, and Nilla began to stir. For opening her eyes to a gory mess and a freshly amputated arm, she handled it, well, like a farmer. She sat up and asked how she could help. I laughed a little at that. She had been in a panicked frenzy from being hunted by monsters, injected with Lord knows what, then woke up to a bloody arm lying next to her, and she was ready to jump in like nothing happened. I was a little skeptical about bringing a random farmer with us, but she was a boss when the monsters weren't around.

"She took over the wrapping process, though she was still groggy from the injection Maudie gave her. David was fading, and we would either have to get out then or plan to stay for a while as David rested. We opted for the second, but we would need to get ahold of the other team. The walkies were just for emergency contact, but this was an emergency.

"I called the other team, but there was no response. I radioed Leonard and got a hold of him. He hadn't heard anything from the other team, either. We also hadn't heard shots in a while. Maudie and I were in the best shape for search and rescue, so we decided that we would go find them and bring back anyone still alive. We left the backpacks but brought the empty duffels in case we had an opportunity to grab anything vital. David insisted I bring his arm to use as a distraction in case we were attacked. I tried to argue with him about it, telling him that it would just slow me down and the smell would be a beacon for the Rovers, but he just gave me a sober look and told me that arm had helped him save a lot of lives, and if it could save a few more, he would be grateful for the chance. That won. I strapped it to my back, checked that I had enough ammo and loaded mags, and we set out."

CHAPTER 19

Maudie was practically silent as a shadow as we made our way across the mall toward the outdoor store where the other team was supposed to be. It took us a while to get there as we had to stick to the shadowed storefronts and leapfrog to watch each other's backs. There were a few times when we came upon Rovers, but we were able to avoid them.

"We reached the outdoor store to a massacre. There were bodies everywhere, human and Rover alike. The problem was we didn't recognize the humans. We crept along the side of the store against the wall, giving a two-tone whistle—our predesignated signal. A faint whistle echoed back. Maudie and I smiled at each other as we made our way to the sound. We arrived in the hunting section, which had been picked over of all firearms, but there was still some ammo on the shelves. We piled as much into our duffels as we dared try to carry. David's arm was heavy on my back, and his hand kept touching my butt, which was weird. I blew the dog whistle as we crept on, not seeing any signs of life. Once we hit the camping section, we found the other team barricaded in an alcove with large smokers and mannequins. It seemed a strange option for protection, but it seemed to be working, so why question it?

"Johnny was unharmed. He sat with their team's walkie in his lap, trying to fix the bullet hole in it with a screwdriver. Damien had gauze over one eye and was working on Phillipe's back, which looked like he had narrowly missed being someone's lunch. Bert was sitting in a lawn chair that was made for a 90-pound lady, scrubbing blood off of a lap full of guns. I don't think he had brought that many with him.

"Damien looked at us, then at the arm on my back, and took a deep breath. 'So, rough day, huh?' he said. I asked how they were doing and that we were happy to see them all alive. He told us about their trek into the outdoors store and how they met opposition not from Rovers but from squatters. There was a militant-like group that had taken up in the store. They tried to ambush our guys, but Johnny had seen them coming on his gadget, so they were able to get to defensive positions first. Damien had negotiated with their leader about needing supplies and being able to help each other, but the man pulled his gun and shot. Good thing Marsh was already in position and took him out before he could raise his gun all the way, or we would have lost our other medical guy. The shots attracted Rovers, and an all-out firefight took place. Our guys managed to slip away in the chaos, although a Rover got a good swipe on Phillipe before Marsh took him out. Bert was able to grab some guns off the floor that had been dropped. Johnny was the one who suggested the faux human barricade using mannequins to disguise their presence. A few Rovers had gone by, checked out the mannequins, and moved on. They had been sitting tight since; they hadn't even had a chance to raid anything yet.

"I told them what had happened to us and broke the news to Bert about his twin. He grunted and returned his attention to cleaning his guns. He was either in denial or they hadn't been that close. I was leaning more toward the first. I let them know about the bodies out in the entrance and that we didn't see anything alive on our way in, so we could post a couple of sentries, and they could fill their bags, but we needed to regroup. We whistled to get Marsh's attention, and he joined us. We stayed as a group and made our way through the store. There were a few guns that had been missed behind the counter, so we grabbed those. The team loaded up their duffels with all the coats, boots, clothes, lighters, propane and everything else we could carry. Bert insisted on taking the arm, which was really beginning to get heavy, so I let him take it.

"Once the team had filled their bags, we began to make our way back to the boutique. Maudie had warned everyone that we had stumbled into a Rover colony and to keep as quiet as we could on the way back. It took about ten minutes to make the return trek to the rest of the team, and once we got there, we had a hurried conversation about trying to get to the grocery end of the mall. While Maudie was certain she could get us a safe route, I said that we had lost enough. Bert grunted and said we had better get everything we came for, or his brother's loss would be for nothing. I couldn't argue with that, but I also couldn't ask anyone to try to get past that death trap colony. Maudie insisted that she had a way, so I asked who wanted to go and who wanted to wait for us. Nilla said she would stay behind and take care of things. David and Johnny wanted to stay and fix the walkie, while Davies would keep cover for them.

That left Damien, Maudie, Phillipe, Bert, and myself, with Marsh giving cover for us. I was worried about the group being too large to make it, but no one wanted to back out. I should have insisted more strongly.

“Maudie pulled out one of the maps and showed us a path we could take along the second level. The plan was just to go above the heads of the Rovers and sneak both ways unseen. We wouldn’t have easy access since the stairs were piles of unstable rubble, and the elevators were, obviously, toast. There were some escalators off to the side of the colony that we could try to make it to, but none of us felt that was a great option either. Phillipe suggested that we use the climbing ropes just outside the boutique, and keep close to the rest in case we needed cover. We all agreed that was the best option.

“We grabbed all the empty bags and said our goodbyes to the ones staying behind. Even with a gash in his back, Phillipe was an amazing climber. He found the smallest cracks and crevices to put weight on and scaled what looked like a flat wall in seconds. Once he was on the second floor, he secured the rope and gave the whistle. Maudie was next, and she climbed that wall almost as quickly as Phillipe. Then came Bert, who was by far the largest in this part of the journey. He took to the wall like it was nothing. Army training is not for the faint of heart. Damien insisted I go next, which I will admit stung my pride a little. It seemed a little like he wasn’t sure I would make it. We practiced with the rope and wall in training, so I made short work of it, but I did need a little help getting over the railing. Damien, being a firefighter and all-around beefcake, didn't even use the wall. Just went arm over arm all the way to the top."

"Did you call him a show-off when he got to the top?" I asked, grinning at Duke's embarrassment over the ordeal.

"You bet I did!" he smiled back. "He just grinned and said the ladies love it when he does that. Maudie rolled her eyes at him and called him a name that I would not repeat in the presence of a lady.

"Marsh was last up the rope. Phillipe pulled up the rope and left it tied off so we wouldn't have to search for our drop zone when we returned. Marsh took the rear guard as Damien took point. We filed in a single file along the mall's upper-level walkway. There were no Rovers that we could see, but we had to check every shop we passed. The food court had a huge skylight, which helped us immensely as we trekked on, searching high, low, and around corners, always remaining as silent as possible. We were about to the halfway point when we spotted the first Rover. It was one of the larger ones. Damien held up his fist to signal us all to freeze as soon as he spotted it, though it seemed to be asleep. All four of its eyes were closed, and its rattling was steady. I crept up and whispered to him that I would keep watching it while the team went by. He agreed and waved the rest forward.

"Maudie, Bert, and Phillipe made it by before its eyes snapped open. I didn't move, but Marsh was walking past when it awoke, letting out a wail of shrieks and clicks that echoed around us, bouncing around the acoustical ceiling of the food court and calling the beasts below us into battle. I put a round through the creature's head and grabbed Marsh's arm. We ran like lightning, but our little legs were no match for a Rover's. They were upon us in seconds. Dog whistles blaring, and shots ringing out, we tried our best to find cover."

Duke took a deep breath, which shuttered out of him slowly. "I don't know if I can do this, Noah," he said, looking at me with misty eyes. I breathed out the breath I had been holding.

"Do you want to pick it up tomorrow?" I asked. "I know this can't be easy, but you need to get it out as much as I did. Trauma is trauma. And holding it in…"

"I know," he sighed, taking my hand. "I know it is, I just…"

"Would it help to finish tomorrow?" I asked, looking into his eyes and giving his hand a gentle squeeze. He glanced down at my bandaged arm and bit his lip.

"No, I can finish. They all deserve to have their stories told," he asserted. He rubbed his jaw and winced as his hand brushed against his wound. Taking another deep breath, Duke continued.

CHAPTER 20

Marsh was the first to go. We had multiple Rovers coming from behind, and he couldn't stop them all. A smaller one was barreling down on him when he shot at it. He hit the body but not the head. As the female fell, the male launched itself, using the momentum to fly at Marsh. It landed on his face and started eating his eyes. While he was trying to free himself, another came up and started ripping into his torso, pulling muscle and organs out and shoving them into the female's mouth. I shot at it. I missed… The… the bullet…. I don't know if he was alive or not when the bullet hit, but it tore through his head. I watched in what felt like slow motion as a fine, red mist covered everything around him. And then he fell. A few more joined in eating his body.

"I don't know how long I stared at the gory scene, but someone grabbed my arm and hauled me off into a punk rock supplies store. I puked all over the floor while someone shushed me. Maudie slapped me clean across the face, thankfully the not ruined side, and I came back to reality. Damien was firing two guns at the Rovers as they cleared the railing in a single jump from the colony below. Bert was still outside the shop, firing everywhere he could. I checked my mag and reloaded, then went out to join the fray. I took out two Rovers that were coming up on Damien's blind side. Bert pulled the arm off his back and yelled out to us that as soon as he gave the signal, we needed to run to the grocery store and take cover. None of us knew what he had in mind. We kept firing as fast as we could at every moving threat.

“Then we got the signal. Bert took the arm and heaved it with all his might over the edge into the colony, then jumped after it, screaming at the monsters. The Rovers all jumped down after him, leaving a clear path for us to run.

“I heard the cracking of bones as he landed. He shouted loud and clear, ‘For Bruce! I would do it again! For Bruce!’

“He shouted and fired, the clicking and wild sounds of the colony tearing him to pieces, slowly covering him, drowning out his final words.

“Damien stared at the place where Bert had gone over, glanced at the blood slick where Marsh had been eaten, and then dropped his eyes to the feasting monsters below us. We all watched him, waiting to see what he would have us do. He lifted his head, raised his weapon, and waved us forward toward the grocery store. We followed close behind; I took up the rear guard.

“We made it to the safety of the grocery store and were hit by the stench of rotting food. With freezers full of meat, produce decomposing, and the stench of Rovers and dead bodies, added together with the bloody battle we had just witnessed, we all were retching. Phillipe and Maudie vomited.

“The store was dark, not having sky lights. We had a brief discussion in the dark about our plan now that we were there.

Maudie and I were going to hit up all the dry foods we could possibly carry and Phillipe and Damien were going to load up on canned goods. We were to stay together in our pairs no matter what. We would use the two-tone whistle to communicate trouble and reverse it when we were loaded and ready to get out. One hundred twenty seconds. That was our goal."

I looked at Duke with surprise and asked, "120 seconds to raid a two-story grocery mart?"

"We needed to be in and out before the Rovers remembered we were there and came looking for more. If it came to it and we had to sit tight for a while, we would go out to see if we could gather more, but the plan was to hit hard and fast.

"Maudie had a lanyard-like rope with clips on both sides. She clipped one side to her belt and the other side to mine. Damien and Phillipe used a length of rope that they looped around their arms so no one got lost in the dark store. We all clasped hands, gave a grim nod, and set out with the clocks ticking. We didn't have flashlights, so we just did the best we could in the dimness that surrounded us. It was like being in a basement with tiny ground-level windows.

"We found our way to the baking aisle and started grabbing. Flour and sugar are heavy, but it was worth it as they are staples that can help a lot of people. We grabbed the oil and moved on. Boxed foods were next. We loaded Maudie's bag with the contents of boxed meals. We tore them open as quickly as we could and dumped the contents into her bag to save space.

"We heard shots ring out. We weren't sure where they were coming from as the place was like a cave with echoes. We were not supposed to go chasing after the other team, but I couldn't leave them in a tight spot if it was them. We ran as fast as the darkness allowed us through the maze of aisles. Another shot rang out, closer this time. We turned a corner and ran face-first into the back of a Rover. I was quicker to draw than Maudie and put a round through its head. It fell, revealing a blood bath. Two dead Rovers and a human leg were being eaten by three of the monsters. They hardly looked up from their feast as the one I shot fell. Maudie and I slowly backed away, rounding a corner for cover. We had a whispered conversation, trying to decide our next step. Run with what we had gathered? Try to get around the gory scene and find out if either man is alive? I blew the two-tone whistle, hoping for a reply. Silence. I blew it again, praying for a reply. Nothing came back.

"Maudie was desperate to get out of that place, but I couldn't leave not knowing for sure. I handed her the bags and told her to run, get back to the group, give me twenty minutes to return, and then get out of the mall. She didn't want to split up, but the supplies we gathered could mean life for someone on the surface. I unhooked my side of the lanyard and told her to get moving.

"Once she was safely away, I had to get around the Rovers. I gave them a wide berth, zig-zagging down aisles to find the safest path. One of the team's bags lay in the aisle ahead of me, full of canned goods and splattered with blood. I swept past it, keeping my gun ready. As I approached the next corner, I heard the crunching and clicking of feasting Rovers. I didn't want to look, but I knew I had to know for sure. I peeked around the corner. Damien was sitting against the shelves, Phillipe's decapitated head in his lap. He glanced up at me and waved me to go. I tried to take it all in the gloomy light of the store but couldn't see much. I crept up as quietly as I could to find out why he didn't just run. The Rovers were a few yards away, with their backs to us. As I got closer, I saw why he didn't move.

"Damien had a Rover claw lodged in his torso. He looked me in the eyes and whispered, 'I'm done. Get the goods and get out. Tell Maudie… Just tell her…'

"'Tell her yourself,' I told him. I crouched down next to him and slid my arm behind his back. The Rovers were making enough noise, eating each other and Phillipe, that we managed to get him standing and hobbling alongside me. He wanted to bring Phillipe's head, but I knew that neither of us could afford the extra weight. We grabbed the bag of canned goods and made our way out of the store.

"The stink of the Rover colony was mild compared to the grocery store, which was a relief. We still had to make it along the entire side without the Rovers below realizing we were there. We crept as slowly and silently as we could, with Damien growing weaker by the minute from blood loss ."

"Did you get the Rover claw out?" I asked.

"Couldn't. If I took it out, he would have bled out in minutes. It was corking the blood loss."

"Good call," I said, acknowledging his quick thinking under pressure.

"We made it back to the drop zone rope, where the rope was hanging down, giving me hope that Maudie had made it back. I gave the two-tone whistle, hoping and praying that they hadn't left yet. Maudie and Nilla stuck their heads out of the storefront, looking up at us with relief spreading across their faces. I lowered the bag to them; then, we had the task of figuring out how to get Damien down. We were both slick with blood, exhausted from the day's event, and dehydrated. Nilla shimmied up the rope to assist us. She did something fancy with loops and made a slip, knowing that we could tie around Damien's hips to help him down. We got him over the edge and began the task of lowering his rather heavy body. He was halfway down when a Rover spotted us from the upper level. It rattled and clicked excitedly. Nilla and I froze, not daring to move. We could hear Damien grunting in pain as he dangled, our hands burning from the weight.

"The Rover got closer, clicking and scanning around us, trying to focus on what movement it had seen. It was within feet of us, the smell from its breath so foul that it made me want to vomit and run away at the same time. Nilla was frozen in fear, not even breathing.

"It felt like an hour had passed. My muscles were screaming in pain. I was ready to drop the rope and jump over the side when the Rover lost interest and turned away. We stayed still until it dropped back down to the colony.

"Nilla let out her breath in a ragged sob and let the rope slide farther down. We lowered Damien the rest of the way and rappelled down ourselves.

"We regrouped with the remainder of the team and made our escape plan. Nilla took out the claw from Damien's abdomen, and she and David worked together to patch him up. Maudie, Davies, Johnny and I planned our route out of the mall. As we were four men and an arm short of coming in, everyone was going to have to carry more than we had accounted for. Davies was still our main cover out, and we radioed Leonard to get as close to the rim as he dared to provide high-ground cover for us upon the signal. Everyone else loaded up with as much as we dared to carry. We managed all the bags we brought, but moving was slow due to wounded, overloading, and watching for Rovers. We made it back to the pharmacy we first hit and took a rest. David talked Maudie through what medications we had left the first time through and what to give him and Damien to help prevent infection later on. Everyone loaded pockets and hoods and stuffed more pills in every crevice we would find. The need for medications seemed more urgent on the way out than it had on the way in.

"He radioed Leonard and returned to our initial drop point. Maudie was the first to scale back up to help the wounded at the top end. Damien was next to go. I climbed directly behind him to help support his weight. He definitely wasn't showing off this climb. It took us a good ten minutes to get to the top. I got him into the camper and we began hauling up the goods. He stashed bags as they came in while Maudie and I took turns hauling bags up the rope.

"We had hauled all the goods up when Johnny gave us a warning that there were bodies approaching. We were making too much noise. A dozen Rovers came at the group still down from behind. Johnny threw what I can only call a grenade and took two out, Leonard got headshots on two more, and Davies managed to hit a few, but they were nasty fast. They overtook the group."

CHAPTER 21

uke rested his face in his hands and took a deep breath. "Did they make it out?" I asked, tears fighting their way out.

He rubbed his eyes and sat back. "We shot the Rovers, but there was already a lot of damage done. David was okay, but Johnny, Nilla, and Davies took some hits. Nilla looks like she will pull through, but Davies is in rough shape and…. Johnny bled out on the way back."

Duke took another deep breath. He had tears staining his cheeks. "When we got back to the compound, we buried Johnny. We made head stones for the others. We divvied up the loot and had a meal together. Papa Ray has banned all future excursions to that mall from the station. The losses were… they were too much.

"After we ate, I asked him if he would drive me home. I missed my wife. I was worried sick, and I just needed to feel you being alive and see you okay. When we pulled up, and saw Bob was outside alone, I knew something was wrong. On Papa Ray's request, we came in as quietly as we could.

"There are no words for the rage, hatred, disgust, and murder I felt walking in to see that coward assaulting the last pure thing in this God-forsaken world."

His eyes burned. I swear I could hear his heart burning. The pain of the past weeks—the close calls, the losses, the darkness, the death, all of it had stacked up into exhausting torment. No wonder he had nearly beaten Ricky to death.

I took his bruised, broken hand in mine and gingerly kissed it. He looked off into the middle distance. “So many good people lost, so many brave people dead. And for what? A few coats and some pills? Noah, I may have murdered a teammate.”

“No. Do not,” I said.

He turned to me, his gaze falling to our clasped hands, and shook his head. “I have no idea if my shot is the one that ended Marsh’s life. He was alive, then I shot him.”

“Duke, you will drive yourself into madness trying to solve that. There is and never will be a way to know for sure, but you have to know that if he was still alive, you ended his pain quickly. You have to know and accept that.”

“How can I ever trust my aim again? How can I take aim at a Rover charging my wife or our dog and trust that I will not be murdering you?”

“Because you are a great cop, you are a straight-laced man with his head on his shoulders, and I trust you. Bob trusts you. We know that you will make the shot when the time comes.”

Duke just stared numbly at our hands. Bob made his way over to us, placed his paw on top of ours, and leaned in to lick Duke’s arms. A small, sad smile tugged at Duke's cheeks. "We are a pretty decent team, huh?"

"Decent? We kick booty," I grinned at him. *Woof!* "See? Bob agrees."

Duke chuckled, then laughed, and soon, our little, broken, hurting, damaged family was rolling with peals of laughter.

We took the rest of the day to rest, recover and unpack the blood-stained bounty over which my husband had nearly died. He unloaded lots of pills in paper parcels with really messy scrawling on them. David had lost his right arm and now had to write with his left, so his already scratchy doctor's handwriting looked like that of a cross-eyed gorilla. He showed me the bags of flour and sugar he was able to get, lots of canned goods, a few bags of pasta dinners, and two cans of cherry pie filling. I kissed him when he showed me those.

He had gotten coats for both of us and a pair of boots for me. He had even grabbed a small sewing kit from the pharmacy to add to the few needles and thread that we had. He pulled out eight boxes of 9mm rounds and a light blue SIG Sauer that he had picked up from the counter in the outdoor store. "You will look so hunky using that bad boy," I winked at him.

"I can tuck it in my apron pocket for when I am doing laundry." We laughed all over again.

After a light dinner, re-cleaning all the wounds, and a cup of tea, we decided the day had been long enough. As we lay down to go to sleep, Duke reached out and gently touched my stitch-up side. "I'm sorry I wasn't there to protect you."

"You were, Duke. As soon as I needed you, as soon as the monsters were here, you showed up, and you saved the day. You did protect me. I'm sorry I wasn't there to protect YOU."

He sighed. "You were there with me. I could see your smile every time I closed my eyes. I could hear you call my name every time I listened close enough. I carried you every step of the way with me. Thinking of you and how you needed the medicines that I would bring to you, the coat, the boots, all of it—that was what kept me going. I wanted to die down there, Noah. Watching good men torn to pieces, sacrificing themselves…." His voice trailed off in the darkness of our room.

"Promise you will always come home to me?" I whispered.

"There will never be a need. I will never leave you again."

We lay in silence, each lost in our own thoughts. The steady rhythm of his breathing slowed and

I knew he had fallen asleep. I leaned forward in the dark and kissed his nose. "Dream sweet."

CHAPTER 22

Everything was dark and smelled like rotting flesh. I couldn't find the right direction to go. There was blood everywhere. I felt hands touching me, caressing me, then slapping and scratching me. Something in the gloom pulled my hair.

"I'll be gentle," a voice whispered in my ear. My side felt like it was on fire. Then, there was a huge weight on me, forcing the air out of my lungs and pushing my legs apart.

"No!" I screamed. "Get off me!"

Duke appeared, but he had Ricky's face. His breath was hot and putrid. "I'll take it over and over again, rag doll."

I fought with everything I had. He was forcing himself on me, trying to get inside me. I bit and clawed at his eyes, but two more appeared, taking their places. I screamed.

 screamed. Duke was on the floor holding something down, yelling in the dark. Bob was barking like mad. I screamed again, confused and angry.

It took a moment for everyone to fall into silence in the predawn darkness. Duke sighed and stood up. "Well, that pillow is going to think twice before trying to wake me up again," he said, climbing onto the bed next to me. "You okay?"

I could feel sweat rolling down my face and my heart still hammering in my chest. "Yeah, yeah, I'm good," I lied. "Bad dream?"

"Yeah," he said, laying back down. "Can we try to get some more sleep, or are you awake now?"

I laid my head down, not sure if I would ever sleep well again. "Yeah, I'm fine. Just startled."

I don't know how long we laid there pretending to be fine before we actually fell asleep, but rest assured, it was a long time.

When I opened my eyes again, the sun was peeking in the window. Duke was still asleep next to me. I tried to climb over him as quietly as I could to get to the bathroom, but my head was still swimming from trauma, my ribs were still massively bruised, and my ruined arm was throbbing, so I ended up falling practically on top of him. He grinned. "Nice of you to drop by," he smirked.

I rolled my eyes and grumbled about needing to pee. He helped me up and gave my butt a gentle pat as I walked away. My breath caught in my throat, and I froze for half a beat, then carried on my way. When I returned, he was sitting on the side of the bed. "I'm sorry, Noah. I didn't know that would trigger you."

I shrugged it off. "Oh, no, it's all fine. I just had a thought and then lost it. You didn't do anything," I lied again. He didn't look like he believed me, so I opted for a sudden subject change. "So, I was thinking that I would like to try to make a bunny skin hat and mittens today. What do you think?"

"I think that was the worst segue I have ever heard in my life," he retorted. "And you should face your demons when they come to ruin you."

"Nope, I am going to move on and not let it get me. Let's make bunny hats today. I will make yours extra fluffy with a little bunny tail on it."

He sighed and shook his head. "Ok, bunny hats it is. Let's please start with coffee, though. I, for one, can admit that I fought demons in my sleep and need a pick-me-up."

He set about making coffee while I tried my best to make the bed one-armed. I hoped that the damage was not so bad that I would lose all use of the arm, as it was tricky doing that simple task with only one useful limb; I couldn't imagine how hard it would be to, say, set a trap or sight in a shot. The future of my arm looked bleak.

We had breakfast outside in the fresh fall sunshine, with the horrors of the past week almost forgotten as the wind kissed our cheeks and the sun smiled down on us. Bob was enjoying the freedom of running wild and we were enjoying not being attacked.

Once we had our fill of food, though never of sunshine, we cleaned up and set to work on the furs we had in the shed. Hats, mittens, and indoor slippers would be our biggest needs in a few weeks when the sun came to see us less frequently and the bitter cold began to make its way into the world. I had never sewn a hat before, but my mother was an accomplished seamstress, so I had seen it done many times. I tried to piece together the parts in my mind and failed. Duke sat patiently, watching me flip the skin over and over, talking gibberish to myself for a while before gently suggesting we draw it out on paper and make a pattern. I just about slapped myself. It seemed so obvious, yet I forgot that was how it was done.

Pulling out a legal pad and sketching the shapes out make all the difference. Soon, the ideas were sewing themselves together in my mind, creating a durable, warm bunny hat. By lunchtime, we had pieces cut and were taking turns stitching. Between my arm and his hands, we were a bit slow. After lunch, we continued sewing, and by dinner, we had managed to make a rabbit skin hat. I tried it on, and it made me feel like a queen. Well, like a wild rabbit queen of the faeries in some weird author's novel, but a queen nonetheless. Duke kissed my nose. "You, my love, are the warmest little bunny I have ever beheld."

I scrunch my nose at him with what I thought would be a fierce expression. It was clearly not as ferocious as I thought as he laughed and kissed my nose again. "I could poke you in the face wound, you know."

CHAPTER 23

week went by. We were both battling nightmares and pretending we didn't know that the other was. As long as we didn't have to talk about the traumas, we were fine. We had gotten it out, talked about it, and now we had to let our thick skins do what clams do—turn those intrusive, dirty thoughts into beautiful pearls. Layer by layer, day by day, we trudged on, healing inside and out.

The mornings had begun to leave a kiss of frost for us to awaken to, and the leaves all around were bathing the already serene landscape in blushes of auburn and tangerine. Life was beginning to feel almost cozy. My arm was keeping the infection at bay, and I had regained some use of the limb. Duke and I stock piled wood for the winter months, hoping it would hold us out until spring. We fished every few days and dried what we could, knowing that this might be our best source of protein for a while. Papa Ray came to check on us and shared the good news about Nilla and Davies. They both made it through the woods. Nilla would limp for the rest of her life, but Davies would hardly carry a scar, which was amazing considering what damage had been done to him.

"Now the next news isn't quite so cheerful," Papa Ray said. "That sneakin' nephew of mine slunk off 'a few nights ago and took some o' the best supplies we had with 'im. I wanted to let you folks know in case he comes round here lookin' for more trouble."

Duke took my hand in his. "Thank you for the warning. We will be ready for anything. What was taken? Anything I can help with?"

"Well, he took quite a bit of gas, lots 'o ammo, and a good bit o' food. Not much can be done about that at this point."

I took a deep breath. Ammo. Is it for protection?

Or revenge?

I cleared my throat and opted for a subject change over a mental breakdown. "Have you eaten?

Would you like to have dinner with us?"

Papa Ray smiled and shook his head. "That is mighty fine of you, young lady, but I have to get back to the station. We have another group comin' in from a raid, and I need to be there for them. You folks have a good night now."

"G'night," we said in unison.

We prepared dinner and ate in silence, both deep in thought. Bob gave my hand a gentle lick as I stared into space. "Are we going to be okay?" I asked, seeking comfort in Duke's eyes.

"Noah, there is nothing on this Earth that could stop me from protecting you," he replied, leaning over the table and touching my cheek. "Nothing can stop this love. Our team is going to win the day.

You and me."

Bark!

"And Bob."

I smiled gently. My eyes drifted to the scar that ran along his face. It was a brute of a wound, marring his strong cheekbone line. Somehow, it just made him even more handsome. "You know, I really love it when you tell me things like that."

"Why do you think I say them?" he said, winking at me.

We cleaned up, lit a fire, and cuddled on the couch. It was a peaceful moment—man, wife, and dog, by a roaring fire, a cozy life. I looked up at Duke. His face was full of concern, haunted. "Hey, you okay?"

He snapped back and kissed my forehead. "Yeah, all good. Just thinking."

"Anything you would like to share?"

"No, just some…. Mistakes I've made. Things I would love to be able to undo."

"We all have our demons. What happened in the mall was horrible, but you did the best you

could."

He chuckled a little. "I wish that was all to the story."

"What do you mean?" I asked.

He shook his head. "Nothing. Just thinking. You going to be up for setting traps tomorrow? We need to do as much as we can before the snow flies."

While I was curious about what he meant, I let it go and followed along with the subject change.

“Yeah, of course. Any thoughts on where we will set them?”

We chatted for a time while as the logs turned to embers and evening turned into night. As we lay down to sleep, my thoughts began to drift. I thought of my mother. Was she even alive? What did the rest of the world look like? Was it just North America? How long was this going to last? Was anyone working to save the world? Tears burned their way out of my eyes as I lay in the dark, lost in thinking. Duke always seemed to know when I was upset. He pulled me close and let me bury my face in his chest to cry.

He didn't say anything and didn’t try to make me stop or offer empty comfort. He was just there. No matter what skeletons and mistakes he had, I was certain that he was a good man. In a world where certainty was scarce, that certainty was a blessing.

CHAPTER 24

few weeks later, the morning was cold and windy. We enjoyed our breakfast by the fire and talked about what our day would look like. We were about to get going when Bob suddenly started barking madly.

Quickly, we took up our firearms and positioned ourselves with our backs against the wall on either side of the door. Duke leaned over to steal a glimpse through the tiny window on the door. "Truck. Older model. Too dirty to see in the windshield. Single occupant." Duke was back in cop mode, which made me nervous. It had been a while since he was in cop mode around me.

I nodded at him and chambered a round. "Shoot first, ask questions later?"

"No," he replied. "It could be someone else from the station."

I took a deep breath and whispered, looking to the floor, "That's what I'm afraid of."

"I've got you, love. I will go out first, you cover me from the doorway. If it looks like trouble, go for a warning shot at the ground beyond, not the driver."

"Got it," I said, swallowing again.

Duke reached over and squeezed my hand. “Hey. I’ve got you,” he reassured me. I looked up into his eyes. Somehow, it didn’t make me feel safer this time. I bit my lip and gave a curt nod.

Duke pulled open the door and strode boldly out to face our unexpected guest. He took a couple of steps to the left so I would have a clear shot at the truck if needed. “Hey, there. You mind stepping out and letting us see your face?” he called out.

The door opened, and a slim figure stepped out. “Tasha?!” Duke exclaimed, his tone a mix of surprise and anger.

The woman looked terribly familiar. I couldn’t place her face, but her long blond hair, slim build, and high cheekbones, everything about her seemed so… familiar. “Hey, Tim. Long time no see, huh?” I felt a pang of insecurity. She was beautiful, tall, fit, and seemed quite familiar with my husband.

“Stand down, Noah. I’ll handle this. Just stay inside.” He gave me a sharp look, and I closed the door, happy for an excuse to get away from the uncomfortable feelings that were taking over my mind at warp speed. I walked over to the fireplace and sat down. What was that feeling? Where had I seen her before? I don’t think she was a regular at the bar. Library? Gym? Church? I couldn’t put my finger on it.

I sat for a few minutes, then decided that she was obviously not dangerous, so I should go back to my husband, right? That seemed the right thing to do. And not because I was curious about who she was and where I had seen her before. I walked back to the door and put my ear against it, just to know what I was stepping out into. I could not make out the words, no matter how hard I tried. Well, it looked like I was going in blind. I peeked out the window. Duke and the woman were talking rather closely together. She kept reaching for his arms and leaning in toward him as if she was waiting for a kiss. Okay. That's enough.

I opened the door boldly and stepped out into the chilly morning. Duke turned to me and pointed. "Back in the house, Noah. I mean it."

"Excuse me? I will not leave my HUSBAND out here to be grabbed and slobbered all over by some random ex. Anything you have to say to her, you can say in front of me."

"Husband? Are you serious?" she said, looking shocked. "Is she serious? You said that you had a friend staying here for a while, and there wouldn't be room!"

I turned to Duke. "What do you mean, room? Who even is she? Is she planning on staying here?

How does she even know where it is?!"

"Does she seriously not know who I am?"

"Enough, both of you!" Duke roared. I raised my eyebrows at him.

"Timothy Duke, you have one minute to explain what the heck is going on before I begin asking her questions," I stated.

He looked like a deer caught in the headlights. Or more accurately, like a man caught in his lies. What was I missing?

"Look, Noah, I made some mistakes in the past. Some things that I wanted to take back and fix, but it doesn't work that way."

"Fix?!" the woman interjected. "Mistake?! You want to say that we were a mistake?"

"Tasha, we were never a we! We had some laughs, but-"

She held up a hand in his face. "Don't you even. Do not cheapen what we had."

Duke shoved her hand away. "You need to leave and never come back."

She gave a puff of laughter and turned to climb into the old truck. She pulled herself in and turned back to us one last time. "Enjoy the wedding pictures." She slammed the door and peeled out, leaving a trail of dust in her wake.

Duke turned on his heels and stalked back to the cabin. I took a breath of the cold air and suddenly felt a chill that I didn't know if I would ever recover from. The wedding pictures.

She was the woman in the wedding pictures.

CHAPTER 25

DUKE

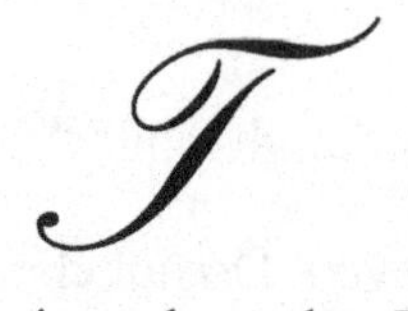

he dirty, dingey bar that I liked to hang out in was crowded. The drunks pressed in tight, pushing me from behind as I sat at the bar, nursing a beer that I hated the taste of. The juke was too loud for me to really focus on the book I had been reading on my phone. It wasn't the best book ever, but it had some great characters. The bartenders were rushing around, filling orders, mixing drinks, and chatting up the customers like they always did. Everyone but Noah. She was different.

I knew that she was a reader. I saw her getting books out of the little box library in front of the station downtown all the time. That was the reason I started sitting at the bar with a book in front of me as often as I knew she would be working. I know it seems like a long shot, but maybe we could bond over our love of reading. Either that or some other chance would open up. That night, my chance sat down three stools over from me, dressed as a drunk guy with an agenda for the evening. He started the usual "Hey, girlie" crap that all the other guys that sat at the bar tried, but Noah was too smart for that. I sat and listened to the conversation, knowing the moment was close. I smiled to myself as the drunk began to tease her using the name on her name tag.

Without looking up, I loudly spoke up. "That's her name, your jerk. It's a pretty name for a pretty girl. She is single, but she won't go home with you. Try Molly by the Juke over there. She likes her martinis dirty."

The drunk took a little too long to come up with something, which turned out to be the dumbest thing I could have ever thought up. "This nice little thing and I are having a little A-B conversation, so why don't you see your way out of it?"

I wanted to punch that guy just for being an idiot, but he was giving me an in with Noah, so I had to play along. "Are you in 5th grade, Bro? Trust me when I say that you are out of your league here, both with Noah and with me, so why don't you just do yourself a favor, order your drinks, and let the lady work."

I glanced sideways at the guy and gave him a subtle nod. He understood; this was my girl. He ordered a couple of drinks and made his way over to Molly, the owner's daughter and the police department's favorite prostitute. The sheriff knew that she was whored out against her will, but he got a nice slice of pie for his silence. Most of the department knew about it and simply looked the other way, many joining in as customers. I tried to inquire about it but was threatened with losing my job, so I, too, looked the other way with the rest. Damn, it felt terrible, but I excused it with the thought that she could just run away if she really hated it, right?

"Thanks. I appreciate the preemptive stupid question answers."

Noah approached me and handed me a fresh beer. “Mm-hm,” I hummed, trying to feign indifference. When I stole a glance at Noah again, she had moved on to the next customers, away from me. That was fine; the seed had been planted. Now, it was time to let it grow.

I left forty bucks on the bar and left a while later. The bar was still hours from being closed, so I

had some time. I drove home, jumped in the shower, brushed my teeth, and did the work. Just in case, ya know?

I don’t really know when my obsession with her started. I started seeing her out the window of the sheriff’s department every few days, and it took off from there. She wasn’t traditionally beautiful, but that didn’t dull her shine. She was a little heavier than I liked; she didn’t wear a lot of makeup, didn’t wear the tight little leggings that showed off her booty, didn’t flirt, and didn’t go home with guys, but somehow that made her so appealing, so refreshing. I started to watch her.

Suddenly, other girls didn’t look right, didn’t smell right, didn’t feel right. Whenever I went home with a woman, I couldn’t stop thinking of Noah the entire time. It felt like all food turned to grass in my mouth as if the sunshine was not as warm, and like the feel of a woman’s touch was just another bump from a stranger on a bus.

She haunted me.

I did some background research on her at work and used that to help me out. I figured if I looked into her a bit, she would lose her appeal, and the opposite happened.

She was from a small town, she liked cows, her father had died of cancer when she was 12, and she was an only child. She sent money to her mother every week to help her with expenses. She was just so… pure, so wholesome. I found myself furious at everything I discovered about her. She was an honor roll student in high school and on the Dean's list in college. She volunteered her free time at the humane society, where she had adopted her dog. She had no parking tickets, no skeletons, nothing! She was clean and pure and righteous. Everything I read made me hate her more, love her more, and desire her more. She was a puzzle box that I felt compelled to figure out.

A timer on my phone told me that it was 1 AM. The bar would be closing, and I would need to be in my truck, ready to give the lady a ride home. I hopped into my truck and headed back to the bar parking lot, parked in view of the employee exit, and pulled my book back out. The lights went out; the door opened, the kitchen staff lit their cigarettes and Noah—my perfect little church girl Noah came out and began her walk home. I waited until she was out of the lot and a bit down the street before making my move. I pulled out of the lot and cruised up slowly, giving a quick toot of the horn. She turned like a deer caught in the headlights and reached for the gun she kept in the small of her back. She was a smart girl.

I rolled down the window and leaned out.

"Hey, Noah. Want a ride?"

"Hey…. Guy. Nah, I'm good. The walk is a nice way to wind down."

Introduction time. "It's Duke, actually. And I'm fine. I only had three beers, and that was over a few hours. If that is what you're worried about. If you think I might be a serial killer luring young ladies to my dungeon, then I can assure you, I am probably not."

She laughed a little. "Duke? Like Prince? Earl? Baron?"

"Those are my brothers, actually. And the whole serial killer bit doesn't spook you?"

"I mean, really, what are the chances of us both being serial killers?"

I grinned at her. She had balls; I'll give her that. She smiled back, and I could see her wheels turning. I leaned my head just a bit into the light to make my eyes shine. That trick worked on girls all the time. But this one was not the normal kind. I had to keep it smooth and genuine.

"Thanks for the offer, and it was nice to actually meet you, Duke. I really am fine and enjoy the walk. Get yourself home safe. G'night."

I smiled at her. I was in; she just didn't know it yet. "You got it. I don't suppose I could talk you into texting me when you get home so I know you made it safe?"

"Not a chance," she said, smiling sweetly back. Why did I want her so bad? What was her appeal?

Grinning, I nodded once before my thoughts betrayed my face. "You got it, killer." I drove off.

I felt frustrated but remained patient. I knew she would take some time. I thought about her all the way back to my house. I barely got out of my truck when my phone rang.

" Sup, chief?" I asked.

"Hey, Duke. I need you to get down to the station. We are having a briefing in 20. Big deal, lots of chaos about to ensue."

I sighed. Probably another riot over something stupid. "I'll be there."

I climbed back in my truck and headed downtown, which was really only about two miles away. I was lucky to get a place so close to the station. The neighborhoods were peaceful, and it was a drive I could make in my sleep. Well, most nights. Tonight, not so much. Halfway there, I turned onto a side street and almost choked on my stomach. I slammed on the brakes just in time to stop my truck from falling into a huge pothole as wide as an entire lane.

I cursed and leaned out my window. What I had thought was a mere pothole was actually a huge pit, deep enough that I couldn't see the bottom in the dark of the night. I pulled out my phone to call the chief, taking a deep breath. That was a close call.

"Sturgeon," the chief's rough voice answered.

"Hey, Duke here. There's a huge sinkhole in the middle of the road. I almost drove into it. Can we send someone to block it off? Down Highland, between 8th and 9th."

"Damnit, they made it here, too. Yeah, just get to the station. No one is going to be out driving this late to fall into it. I'll send a couple guys to block it off."

"They, sir?"

"Just get here. I'm starting the briefing with or without you." He hung up.

My mind was racing. Who? And what? And what?!

CHAPTER 26

I drove around the gaping hole and sped the rest of the way. I walked into some pretty grim faces. No one was strutting, not one complaining about the girl they had to leave in bed, no one talking about kids' latest accomplishments, just silent, solemn stares toward the TV beside which the chief was standing. On the screen was what I could only guess was a prop from a weird sci-fi movie. It was a huge, greenish body with a mouth that slashed across what I would assume was the chest. It had no eyes and long arms that reached the floor. The Chief nodded to acknowledge that I was in and began.

"This is a Rover. They were developed by the military over the past few years to be a weapon against our foreign enemies. They are big, they are fast, and they got out."

A roar went up from the department. Every man and woman, myself included, jumped to their feet, shouting. "What? Are they dangerous? Are we getting help from the military since it is their mess?"

"Shut up!" Chief Sturgeon roared. The chief was a large, beefy guy who looked like he belonged to the local chapter of Hell's Angels. He wore a handlebar mustache and a black bandana. He had a booming voice that could echo in a room with carpeted walls. When he yelled, even the junkies, too stoned to know their names, listened up. We all obliged. “If you will be so kind as to let me finish this briefing, I will answer all your questions.

“As I was saying, these bad boys were developed by the military to be totally controllable and expendable soldiers. They were created and kept in a large underground cavern in Kentucky near Mammoth Cave National Park. They were initially designed with a few fail safes set in place, but they are still dangerous.

“This video I am going to show you now was a top-secret file until a week ago. As soon as I watched it, I called the briefing. This is something that cannot wait until morning. Just to warn you, it is hard to watch. If anyone needs to step out, feel free to do so.”

He tapped a few buttons on his laptop, and the image on the screen began moving. The Rover they were testing was huge, at least eight feet tall, if the lab rats working with them were of average height. It was hard to tell in those white coveralls. The Rover was standing on the floor in the center of a cave that had all kinds of machinery built into the walls. The camera angle showed a glass panel with lots of brass standing behind it. It must have been a test for the big guys.

A woman’s voice came from somewhere that I couldn’t discern. “Good afternoon, ladies and gentlemen. Thank you for coming to see us demonstrate our Rovers. The specimen we will be showing you today is called Lima 42 and is made up of 2 separate parts. The part that we have on display currently is called Sarah 66. This is the strength part of the body. Its legs,” a figure in white motioned to the massively long legs accordion-folded beneath the body, "are designed with multiple knee joints, giving it the ability to jump up to 30 feet from a standstill. With a running start, it can easily do 80."

The brass behind the glass nodded in approval, a few golf clapping.

Two individuals in white suits approached the thing and picked up its arms at what would be the wrist, holding them out at full extension. "The arms are designed extra-long to give it a reach of 25 feet, wingtip to wingtip. At the end of each arm, we have hands that grow claws at multiple angles, creating a perfect weapon for grabbing ahold of fugitives that have wriggled into tight spaces."

More nodding.

The lab rats set the arms down and stood to the side of the Rover, pulling at the mouth to reveal rows of sharp teeth. "In the mouth, we have four rows of serrated teeth on a jaw that is hinged between each row. This allows the Rover to create a sawing motion with the rows, giving it the ability to saw through bone in as little as two minutes."

A voice came through what must have been a speaker by the glass overlook. "How is it that you are able to handle this thing the way you are if it is indeed so dangerous?"

"Excellent question. The two Rover parts are perfectly harmless on their own. It is one of the fail-safes we built into them. We currently have 100 female components and 100 male components. The male and female together create a full Rover. The female body is the powerhouse, and the male is the brain. Sarah 88 here couldn't attack me even if she wanted to. She has just enough brain power to keep her vital organs going and eat when she is fed directly into her mouth, like this." The white suit turned and pulled a bloody glob of something out of a bin, opened the thing's mouth again, and deposited the bloody goo into it. The jaws began to move slowly, sawing back and forth. Some blood trickled down the front of the thing, which another white suit wiped up, sprayed with something from a spray bottle and wiped again. "She is designed with tiny ears over here," the speaker pointed. "And here, they are very sensitive, but only to certain frequencies. I could blast a tuba right next to her and she wouldn't hear it, merely feel the vibrations. However, if I blew a dog whistle, she would recoil and try to escape it. The males as well."

The main white suit pulled a step ladder next to the thing and climbed to the top, pointing as she spoke. "If I could direct your attention to the top of this specimen, you will see a small indent. This is where the second part fits. This is what would be considered the sexual organ, or the 'Bridge Point,' as we call it, where the male part attaches."

Another voice came through the speaker: "These things breed? How do you keep the population under control?"

"These specimens cannot reproduce. We have them built with sexual organs that are non-functioning other than for joining the two. We intend to add the ability to breed later to certain specimens to keep costs of replacement down."

More nods came from behind the glass.

"Now," the woman said as she descended the ladder, "I would like to introduce you to Quincy 8."

Another voice came through the speaker: "How do you come up with the names? Is there a reason or are you tender-hearted lab rats in here getting attached to the weaponry?"

The white suit didn't respond to the jab, simply answered the question. "The specimens have designations, not names, based on what trial they were from. The first sets of full Rovers were the Alphas, then the Bravos, Charlies, Deltas, and so on. This is the 12th trial set, so Lima. This Bridging is the 42nd of the trial, so Lima 42. The individual components are separated by traditionally gender-specific names and then numbered based on their activation date. It took longer to get the female component right, so the names made it to Sarah. This specimen is 66th in her trial. The males have fewer parts but more complex brains, so it still took a while to get it right, thus Quincy. We give each specimen its own designation, so we can keep notes on each individually, and a separate designation for the bridged pair."

"So if this female is bridged with a different male, does that change the designation?"

"Yes, though we keep each specimen restricted to only three bridging partners. We gave them multiple partners in the beginning and found they were more likely to die in the separation process the more partners they take."

Another white suit came through a door in the cave wall, holding a large cat carrier.

"Ah, here he is. This is Quincey 8." She opened up the kennel door and took out a bowling ball-sized creature. It was the same color of mottled green and black as the female half. It would have been far less disturbing if it looked like a head, but instead, it looked like a deformed version of the green monster from that kids' movie. It had spindly legs that hung seemingly uselessly beneath it, along with a disproportionately sized sex organ. Its face had four large eyes and a narrow slit of a mouth. It was making a rattling sound as its eyes scanned the room. Its bald head was too round, too shiny. It was grotesque.

"Quincey 8 is a strong specimen as far as the males go. His intelligence is comparable to a gorilla and he has been taught to do a few minor tasks on his own without being bridged. His four eyes work to create a 3D image in his mind of his surroundings, though the strongest sense that they have is feel. A bridged pair can detect the movements of a mouse over a stone from 100 yards. Their vision is motion-based, so while it is able to track movement with complete accuracy, it is not in its strongest sense. As these have been designed to hunt in the dark, they do not rely on vision to get around, hunt, or track a target.

"We designed them to attach at the sex organs, which create a bond of approximately 150 Newtons of suction force between the components. If they are released voluntarily, neither is harmed. If they are forced, the female often dies as she stops using what little brain power she has while attached to the male, allowing him to guide her, feed her, and even keep her breathing. We designed them this way so, once bridged and aggressive, a shot to the male will terminate both specimens."

Another voice called out from the speaker, a woman this time: "How much do each of these components cost? Are you just killing investments that get a little out of control?"

"Absolutely not. The only time that termination is used is when human lives are in danger. Each bridged pair costs roughly $180,000 now that we have the process streamlined. And now, Jeff, if you will do the honors…"

Another white suit came from off-camera and began looping straps over the female component. As he worked, the main speaker filled the space. "Jeff Phelps is our security chief who does all the restraining when a bridging is to take place. He has studied the skeletal structure of the Rovers and knows the best locations for restraints to keep them controllable. These straps each have a breakpoint of three tons, so as you see, we are in no danger at all once it becomes aggressive."

Jeff finished up, and another lab rat came along to double-check all his attachments. When they all seemed satisfied, the main white coat said, "And now, without further ado, I give you Lima 42."

She climbed back up the ladder with the wriggling bowling ball-like creature in tow. A sick feeling rose in my gut as I knew that this would be a disaster. If the chief said it was hard to watch, it had to be gruesome.

It was as if someone had flipped a switch. The large female body opened its enormous mouth and began making a grinding, rattling noise that was so off-putting it made me shift positions. It pulled at the restraints, arms fighting to get free, teeth gnashing, legs beneath it bracing against the bonds. All staff members were outside of a red line on the floor at least ten feet from it and still, they looked a little nervous. The main speaker came around the back to the side with a goat on a leash. "Now, to demonstrate the power of this predator-"

The lights flickered a little, and a red light on the wall began spinning, a whining siren calling out, causing the rats to scatter and the goat to kick wildly. The only one who didn't seem alarmed was the Rover, who was suddenly very quiet and very still.

"Ladies and gentlemen, that would be our breach alarm. We have components out of containment and need to evacuate immediately. If you would please use the exit to—"

Then chaos ensued. Four bridged Rovers tore through the door, clicking and rattling, the too-long arms reaching out and slicing the speaker clean in half. There was screaming and running, guns firing, Rovers calling to each other. One of the smaller specimens began chewing the ropes that held Lima 42, freeing it in less than a minute. It pounced on the body of the main speaker as fast as thought and began ripping her apart, limb by limb, and shoving the parts into its huge, gaping maw. Every now and again, the female part would tear off a chunk of flesh or rip out an organ and feed it to the male head.

The screen went black.

"I think we have all seen enough of that," Chief said.

No one moved. I don't even know if anyone breathed for over a full minute. Finally, a sob broke out from the back of the room, shattering the deafening silence; then, every officer present was on their feet, shouting questions, swearing, and just plain being loud.

Chief Sturgeon shouted above the roar, trying to restore some order. "There's more! Shut up! SHUT UP!!"

The shouting calmed, fading into a pensive hush. How could there possibly be more? Then, it dawned on me: the road collapsed. He said "they" had made it this far.

"I know you are all scared. I'm scared, too. But we have to think clearly. There is more information that you need to know." He picked up a manila envelope and pulled out a stack of papers, flipping through them until he found what he was looking for. He took a deep breath and let it out slowly. "This is the report that I received for briefing my men. Everything that is known about these things is in this. There is more about their design and their weaknesses. Each of you will be getting a copy of this to help you along."

He began reading from the document. "' June 11. The initial breakout of the Rovers from the

McDonough Research Facility was on May 3rd at 1435 local time. There has been no contact with the Rovers for over 40 days, and while a search was conducted, it is assumed that all 112 missing assets are deceased, as the specimens that remained in holding died within 36 hours of the initial event. While thirteen lives were lost, including all nine scientists present and four members of the military panel, it was considered within the reasonable limits of acceptable loss for a failed experiment though the project was barred from further research and experimentation.' Well, good to know the government considers us expendable."

We all murmured in agreement as he flipped a few pages and continued. "June 30. A sinkhole in a rural town in Indiana has been discovered with reports of large monsters climbing out. Military personnel were dispatched. A small band of surviving Rovers were discovered and captured. The project manager for the operation took control of the Rovers and brought them to another facility for further study. Questions about the intelligence level of the assets are being answered. Fourteen civilians were killed in the incursion. No military personnel lost.'

"'July 14. Rovers were discovered in 18 different locations from Chicago to Houston. Over 200 complete specimens have been captured or killed, indicating that the Rovers have indeed developed the ability to breed at a rapid rate, and their physical development is beyond that which was observed in a lab setting. The death toll has reached 127 civilians, 42 military and local police. Military keeping wraps on the Rovers to prevent a media outcry and public panic. Emergency meeting with the president is scheduled.'

"'July 23. Rovers were discovered to have been traveling by underground caves and tunnel networks far below the Earth's surface. They break through the rock using the female components' jaws and claws, opening up new tunnels, connecting caves and creating a huge network under the surface. Teams have been sent down to eradicate nests as they are found, but casualties are high. The Rovers plan coordinated attacks, set traps and use weaker specimens as bait. The death toll has broken 1000. The media has been asked to hold the story until a plan of eradication can be implemented. The reach of the Rovers is growing every day. The worst of the damage had been in larger cities. The vibrations of traffic and city life attracted them, and they set up their colonies in subways and sewers. Local authorities are being advised to watch for sinkholes opening up without warning and to contact their state's governor for local protocols.'

"August 7. God save us all. They are here. Tell Beth that I love her.' And that is the end of communication out of the Pentagon."

Silence had overtaken us again. I took a deep breath and cleared my throat. "Chief?"

"Yeah, Duke?"

"That sinkhole I almost drove into on the way here?"

"Most likely."

"So, what do we do?"

The chief took a deep breath and looked at the ceiling. "We need to evacuate the town. Thankfully, we are a small enough community that we have not attracted too much attention, but it looks like they are here now, and we need to act quickly. Once we have the town cleared out, get yourselves and your families safe. Stay in the rural areas—go to your cabins and lake homes and remote Air BnBs. We are to tell the population officially that there is a terrorist organization that has been tunneling around the country, targeting larger cities and moving to smaller ones. That should be enough. Everyone needs to grab only the essentials and get out of town. To avoid traffic attracting the Rovers to us, we will work in a grid through town and get smaller groups preparing at a time. I have created a list for the evac that I want you all to follow as closely as you can. Get the civilians out, get yourselves out, and stay alive.

"Prepare for war, people. It might be one."

He looked from one face to another. "Collect your instruction packets here and head down to the armory." We lined up and began approaching the desk, each one grabbing a packet and quickly flipping through it.

Tasha Barkley, a friend and sometimes lover, turned to me. "You said that a sinkhole opened up?

In town?"

I just nodded. "Did you see any of them?"

"No. I damn near drove into it but didn't see any of the Rover things."

"What are we going to do?"

I shrugged. "Follow the chief's orders, then get out of town. Who knows how long this is going to last?"

Tasha came closer. "Are you going to your cabin? Can I come with you?"

I shook my head. "I sold it. It wasn't panning out, so I cut ties."

"After all the work we did on it? I loved that place."

We had reached the desk and collected our packets, so I directed her out into the hall. "Seriously, this is what you want to talk about right now? No, you can't come with me anywhere. I am getting in my truck and driving away from this place."

She looked a little hurt. We had been friends and even lovers for a long time. I sighed. "Look, I didn't sell the cabin. It's still mine, but I just don't think that it would be a good idea for you to have to be stuck there with me. We would kill each other within a week. Tiny water heater? No TV? You would hate it."

She smiled wistfully. "I know. I just thought that maybe you were ready for more from me. And the world falling apart might be a good chance for us to build something more. I mean, we already did fake wedding pictures," she added with a halfhearted grin.

I took her hand gently. "Tasha, I will come back for you. Give me some time to get it set up to have a lady there for more than a night or two. Okay? I'll come back for you."

She nodded, and a tear slipped down her cheek—poor sap.

I pulled my hand away, and I turned to head to the armory. “Duke?” she asked, hopefully.

I turned to face her again. “Yeah?”

“I love you.”

I took a breath and forced a smile. “I’ll be back for you.” I turned and walked out of the room. Tasha had been a lot less clingy when she helped me set up my cabin to look like a broken-hearted man’s shattered dreams. We had fun. We painted, she cross-stitched, and we made a photo album of our fake wedding pictures. When did she start with the real stuff? Probably just the terror talking.

I collected what ammo I could, a couple of dog whistles from the K9 department and some body armor from the armory, and then headed out to my truck. I climbed in and looked at the packet in my hands. This couldn’t be real, right? This was all just a big hoax. A Hollywood stunt, maybe? I took a deep breath, letting it out slowly. My coffee threatened to come back up. All of a sudden, I thought of Noah.

I would have to save her; I would have to take her with me. I could plan my takeover of her heart when this was all done, but for today, she would have to be my priority.

I wiped the tears that were trying to escape my eyes and ripped open the envelope.

CHAPTER 27

The hours flew by as I knocked on doors, loaded kids and boxes into cars, and hugged crying people. For many, this was the worst day of their lives, and they needed strong, caring men. I gave my town 110% of me. It was fulfilling, in a way, knowing that these people would possibly live because I helped them. It was pretty great to think about, yet Noah kept creeping into the foreground of my mind. She would be sleeping still. If all worked the way I hoped, we could get the town cleared out and moved on before I had to go to awaken her and take her away with me.

By noon, I was ready to go and collect my own belongings. The section of town that I was given was cleared out, and I was free to find my own way. I got to my house and began rifling through the cupboards. I filled bags and boxes with whatever food and bottled water I could grab. Next was clothing. I stuffed my gym bag with pants, shirts, underwear, and socks. Since I already had some clothes in the cabin, I kept that light. After grabbing a few toiletries, I hurried back in my truck to go get to Noah. I still had most of a tank of gas, so we should be fine to get there. It only took me a few minutes to get to her house, and then I hopped out and banged on her door. "Noah! Noah, you home?!"

She opened the door faster than I expected, and I stumbled into the doorway, catching myself a moment before embarrassment.

"How do you know where I live?" she asked. I would have to ignore that question.

"We have to get out of here, now!"

"Not until you answer my question," she insisted.

I took a breath and let it out in a puff. "Seriously, Noah, it is on your mailbox. You have a huge dog that everyone knows. You live a straight mile from the bar you work at. And I happen to be a police deputy. Nancy's husband is my boss. He called me on my radio to check on you. Any other stupid questions, or can we get moving?"

She took a moment and blinked at me. Shaking her head, she said, "What's going on? I just saw the news! And then I lost contact with my mother. She lives in Ashlan. That's outside of-"

"I know where that is. We don't have time. Can we please talk while you get some essentials?" I asked, pushing her in the direction of what I assumed was her bedroom. Her dog, however, was not happy with me. He didn't like seeing my hands on Noah, or maybe he just knew I wasn't much of a dog person. Either way, he bit me. I gave out a manly roar of frustration while Noah pulled the huge dog off me.

"Bob! No, Bob! Let him go!" she yelled, tugging at the huge dog.

Before I could stop myself, my temper found the better of me. "Control your animal!" I roared, holding the arms, feeling for punctures.

"Excuse me," she sassed right back. "You pounded down my door and shoved me in my own home! You control YOUR animal!"

I was taken aback for a moment, and I realized she was right. I was in the wrong. Man, I hate being wrong. I swallowed hard and gave the best apology I could muster. "Sorry. It's hard to turn it off. Good boy, Bob." I said, pausing a moment and contemplating the oddness of that sentence. "Seriously, who names their dog Bob?"

"Can we please focus here? This whole thing feels like a vaudeville routine. Packing, walking, talking, m'kay?" She led me to her bedroom, where she went straight for the closet, looking for a luggage bag, duffel, or anything she might have handy. "Duke, talk. What is going on."

I had a decision to make: Do I tell her everything? Do I tell her part of it? Do I lie entirely? I decided on a half-truth. I mean, I didn't want to scare her too badly, and keeping a little something in my back pocket was a good way to keep her needing me, right?

"Three months ago, sinkholes began springing up in random places all over the US. No one is certain what caused them or why they began, but terrorists are suspected."

I fed her a few lines that sounded scientific, which seemed to sustain her. I would tell her the full truth later. She looked at me and said something that hit me off guard. "Duke, what are you doing here?"

I was a bit confused. Hadn't I already told her? "To warn you? I told you, my boss is Nancy's-"

“Duke, why are you here instead of getting your friends and family ready?”

I felt my cheeks flush. I wanted to tell her a huge lie about how they were all safe and sound, but instead, the truth came out before I could stop it. “I don’t… have… anyone.”

“Oh,” she said, a little blush touching her own cheeks. “So where are you going? Any suggestions on which way I should go? I just…. I’ve never been in an apocalypse before and have no idea what to do.”

I hated the way her blushing and gentleness made me feel. “We could go together? I mean, if you want to. I’m not trying to…. I just meant…”

She cracked a grin. “Duke? If you are worried that I think you are trying to flirt or get lucky while the world is literally falling apart around us, you are insane. I have my car, but it does make sense to just go in one if you don’t mind. It’s only for a few days, right? The government will figure out safe zones and get everyone back home. Right? That’s the plan?”

“Officially, yes.”

“I am really beginning to hate that word.”

We loaded everything into my pickup's bed and climbed in. Bob made sure to sit between us and growled when I tried to pet him. We chatted lightly, which I think helped us both calm our nerves. I couldn’t believe that she came with me so willingly. I was expecting more of a fight from her, but she was scared and I am a big, strong man. It just seemed right to her, I guess.

We got to the Quick Mart at the edge of town to find the doors shattered. My adrenalin spiked as my cop instincts took over.

"Well, might as well see if there is anything useful left," I said as I began to climb out of the truck. "You want to wait here with Bob or come see what we can find?"

"I'll help," Noah said, hopping lithely from the passenger door. I tried not to think about how much more athletic she was. "Wait here, Bob. I'll be right back," she told the dog.

I looked her in the eyes, hoping she understood the seriousness of what I was saying. "Stay behind me until I make sure the coast is clear."

"Seriously? What are you expecting? Pirates?"

I held a hand up to stop her. "Noah, desperate people do desperate things. Behind me, please?"

"Okay, Duke. I will follow you. That way, you can get shot, and I can be the hero that pulls you to saf-"

PAH! PAH! PAH!

Red hot pain ripped through the flesh of my bicep as shock tried to subdue me. I tried to fight it back, but my mind burrowed into it, leaving me feeling cold, desperate, scared. I had been shot before, but I was expecting those; they were firefight situations. This came out of the blue, and I wasn't ready for it. I tried to breathe, but my chest was so tight from the pain that I just choked out a bit of air.

Then, a voice emerged from the fog. "Cease fire!" I blinked as my mind reeled, trying to place the voice. My mind swam through a sea of misty confusion and dull lighting. "Cease fire!" the voice called out again, this time pulling me back to the reality of the situation. I groaned and tried to roll over. My heart roared in my ears; my mind began shouting at me to get up.

I managed to turn my head in time to see Noah. She seemed to gleam with the bright sunlight flooding in the broken glass door. She was poised behind a shelf with her gun drawn; she breathed heavily. My eyes caught hers, and I saw the fear in her eyes. Something inside me broke free. I had to get to her. I had to protect her.

She broke her eyes away from mine and flipped around the shelf. She shot off a round, which blew through a rack of chips, then leaped over to me. She threw herself over me. "Duke, I got you! I gave us some cover!"

The moment caught up with me as I heard the back door slam shut.

The pain roared in my arm, my blood was sticky under my body, and I began to laugh. It hurt, but I laughed anyway.

"Noah, you shot a bag of chips. The bad guys ran out the back. And one shot is not how you cover somebody."

"No, I did it! I shot, and now they… And you…. Shoot. Where are you hit?"

"Left arm. Through and through."

"You got hit twice?!"

"What? No, that's what you call it when… Oh, never mind. Just help me up."

Noah helped me sit up. I could feel her shaking. She was a strong woman, but this day was beyond anything else.

"Let's just go," she said. I finished getting to my feet and took a deep breath.

"No, I didn't get shot for nothing. You grab, and I will keep watch. Keep your gun easily accessible, though I hope not to see you shoot it ever again. That was ugly."

"Hey, I was scared, ok? I have never been shot at before, never had someone shot in front of me. This is a day of firsts for me!"

"I'm just teasing," I said, grinning at her innocence and charm. "You were very brave. Now, help me tie this thing off. I don't need to lose any more blood." She pulled the bandana from her hair and tied it nicely and tight around my arm. I groaned, to which she peeked up to my face. Her eyes were glossy with tears, so I gave her a slight nod. She nodded back.

"I will cover you from here." She started running through the store, searching aisles for anything and everything that could be helpful. She dropped an armload of items next to me on the counter. "Paper, please," she said with a sweet grin, then turned and dashed back for more. I smirked as I began shoving everything she brought up into bags. After a few minutes, I could hear sounds coming from the back of the store. Not wanting to frighten her more, I called out to her. “Noah, hurry up. We have to get out of here.”

She nodded and brought her armload to the front. “Ok, that should do it, I think. Can you carry some of this? I’ll pay.”

“Are you serious right now, Noah?!”

“I am no thief!” I could have left her to the monsters at that moment if more shots didn’t come for us.

POW POW!

“Never mind!” she shouted as we grabbed it all, tossing it in the bed and hopping back into the truck.

“I’ll drive, you patch,” I told her as I pulled the door shut. Being my left arm that was shot, it hurt like crazy to even do that.

“Is that a good idea? You lost quite a bit of blood.”

“No kidding? Did you remember the French-Fried Onions for our baked potatoes later?!”

“I said we should have just left after you got shot!”

POW POW! I peeled out of the parking lot and almost launched my coffee back up between the pain, the fear, the adrenaline, and the frustration at this woman.

“Defensive pirates! I was even going to pay you!”

Exasperated, I yelled, “Noah! Can you please help patch up this gun wound instead of yelling at the nice pirate man?!”

"He is not nice!"

"I changed my mind. Can I apocalypse with someone less crazy?"

"Oh, you big baby. Give me your arm."

She pushed Bob into the back of the truck and then turned her attention to me. "I can't reach your left arm very well, Duke. Could you have been shot somewhere else?" She flipped around, folding her legs under her so quickly and gracefully that I had to think about getting shot for a second. I mean, yes, we had been through a lot already today, but I'm still a red-blooded man. I pushed the feeling aside and returned her sass.

"Next time, I will ask the nice pirate to shoot me in the other arm, okay?" She tried to hide her smirk, but I caught it. It was adorable, and I needed to think about my gunshot wound again. I slowed to get around a car that was halfway on the road—someone must have run out of gas during the evacuation.

I had half a second to react to the cracks surrounding the car and lurched the truck to the side, throwing Noah into the seat back face first. "Hang on!" I yelled a moment too late.

"Hang on to what?!" she yelled back. She grew solemn as she watched the road collapse behind us out the back window.

"Let's just get a little way out of town and pull over. I don't think I can take any more of your driving backward."

I swallowed hard and took a shaky breath. There was too much going on, and I could feel my mind getting foggy from all the blood loss. "We can do that. There is a pull-off a few miles down."

"Good. It would probably be best for me to get you out of your shirt anyways."

I used all of my cop-self-control to keep my eyes on the road and not respond with something suggestive.

"You know what I mean!" Noah said quickly. She harrumphed and pulled Bob back up to the front between us, sneaking a glance at me. I met her gaze and gently raised an eyebrow. She looked back to the road and blushed.

A few miles down the road, we came to a small pull-off that I used for speed traps and rendezvous with women. Noah opened her door and hopped out to grab the medical bag while I scanned the area for movement. The thought of the Rovers still floated in the back of my mind. I knew they had made it this far, though I hadn't seen any in the flesh, thankfully.

She opened my door and the first aid kit, setting it on my lap.

"Okay, you big baby, let's see this wound of yours," she said. She untied the bloodied bandana from my arm and pulled off my shirt. I groaned as pain flooded my mind, pulsing through my arm and head. I grimaced and let out a jagged breath as my stomach threatened yet again to expel anything that I still had in it. I pushed it down as Noah gasped, seeing the gunshot wound for the first time. "Duke, this is…" she started to say as her eyes filled with tears.

At that moment, I wanted nothing more than to stop her tears. "It's really not that bad. I've had worse. Just do what I tell you. We have to clean it first, get all the extra blood off." I handed her a bottle of water. She looked at me with eyes filled with tears.

"Duke, I am so sorry. This is my fault. I should have just listened to you and let you focus. I… got you shot. I'm-"

"Noah, it is not your fault. I'm a cop. I have been shot twice before, and both were worse than this. If anything, you saved me by being there and helping me get out before they came back." She looked away, and I reached over with my right hand and lifted her chin. Her face was a picture of innocence, shame, fear, and something else I couldn't quite put my finger on. "Noah, this is not your fault."

She took a deep breath and nodded.

"Now, let's get this cleaned."

She was a good nurse. She followed my instructions and only almost threw up once. A few times, I had to bite my tongue to keep from screaming in pain. She did a great job and had gentle hands, but I mean, it's still a gunshot wound.

By the time she had it tied off nice and tight, we were both covered in my blood. It gave me a primal sense of pride, like she was marked with my scent or something. I focused back on the pain. She rinsed and sanitized her hands and offered to drive for a while.

"Probably a good idea. I need to take some painkillers and rest. I lost a lot of blood." And I really wanted a little time to rest as I had been up for over 30 hours.

"Where do you want me to head?"

"North. I have a friend who owns a remote cabin a couple hours from here. We should be able to make it before dinner time."

Her eyes sparkled at the mention of dinner. "Let's grab something now. I'm starving." I walked to the bed of the truck and pulled out a bag of food, picking out some nuts and fruit along with the freshwater bottles. A good high-protein snack would be about all I could handle for the moment. I popped a couple of painkillers and climbed back into the truck. Then, we were on the road again.

I spent the next few hours in quiet contemplation. I was feeling new things and I didn't like it. While I was glad to have the chance to get closer to Noah, I didn't feel good about it. I was confused about why her tears made me want to cry and why the fear in her eyes made me want to fight dragons. I had wanted her for a while now, obsessed over her even, yet now that I was here with her, it was.... Not what I imagined. I.... I actually liked her. I wanted to see her smile and know that I was the one that made it happen. I had bled for her, and I found myself feeling that I would do it again without question.

After who knows how long, Noah's voice broke the silence.

"Hey, Duke?"

"Mmm?" I mumbled, my eyes still shut.

"Are you awake?"

Even her silly questions made me want to smile and be playful. "Nope. This is the Pope using

Duke's mouth. What a handsome little puppet."

"I'm serious. When was the last time you saw a car? I mean, a moving car?"

I opened my eyes and sat up, snapping out of my thoughts and coming alert.

"You know, I don't think we have seen a car since we got out of town. That is odd."

"Where do you think everyone is?"

"Hopefully, somewhere safe. We can't really worry about that now. Let's just get to our destination."

I jumped as Bob barked a deep boom from the back of the truck. I had momentarily forgotten that he was back there. "Woah, buddy, it's ok! We will get out soon. You're okay," Noah said, reaching an arm out to pet the big dog. "Hey, Buddy. It's okay."

I turned to look at Bob for a moment and then back to the road. "Look out!" I yelled, grabbing the support bar on the roof of the truck. A Rover was on the road in front of us in all its nasty, slimy glory. It was even freakier than they had looked in the video.

Noah slammed the brakes, sending the truck into a fishtail. Before I could even draw my weapon, it was gone.

Noah stammered out in shock, "What… What was…. Did you see…"

"Noah, please tell me with as much detail as you can what you just saw." I came to another crossroads: do I tell her about the Rovers now or act as shocked as she?

"It… Was tall. I think it was a giant toad. On two legs. With a mouth on its chest."

"Good. Good," I said. "I am certain that we are both hallucinating the same thing." Shame filled me for a moment as I realized how easy it was to lie to her.

"What should we do? Keep moving?" she asked.

"I think so. I am not sure what just happened, but I do know that it can't be good."

Goosebumps pricked my skin as I heard an unearthly rattling sound. Noah sucked in a quick breath and whispered, "Duke, don't look now, but our hallucination is watching us."

I scanned the mirrors and spotted the thing behind us. I gently reached for my sidearm and pulled it from its place on my hip. "Noah, I need you to cock this for me slowly and hand it back. Then put the track in gear and slam the gas like it owes you money," I said gently. I raised the gun to hand it to her.

Noah seemed to be frozen in time. She didn't even breathe. Her eyes were locked on her mirror at the beast. I gave her a gentle nudge to bring her back to reality. She gasped, grabbed the gun, cocked it and practically tossed it to me.

She slammed the truck in gear and peeled out, screaming out her adrenalin. The truck roared as she pushed it on, gaining speed rapidly, but I knew the Rover was going to have no problems keeping up.

However, there is a huge difference between reading a report and seeing it on a TV screen and watching it catch up to your truck as you drive away at 60.

"What is that thing?" Noah screamed.

"Just drive! Drive! Keep moving forward!"

I rolled down my window and spun around the best I could, leaning out enough to get off a few shots. One of them hit the target somewhere, and it went down. Noah made a weird squawking snort sound when she saw it fall. I spun back around and groaned. My arm was burning, and I just wanted to sleep, but I needed to be strong. "Well, that was… something," I said.

"Duke, in case we die by getting eaten by a weird black frog monster, I just wanted you to know something. I just have to get this off my chest."

My heart began to race. I prepared to act shocked at her admission of affection for me. "Yeah?"

"Your name is Deputy Duke. Seriously, who is named Deputy Duke?"

I took a deep breath and let it out slowly. That was not at all what I had expected. “Yes, that is correct.”

“I just wanted to make sure that you were made fun of for it. You know, before we die later today,” she said.

I smirked a little. She was something else. “Thank you, Noah. I can die humiliated now. You are the yin to my ego’s yang.”

“I do what I can.”

Then she burst into tears. As she sobbed, she curled her body up as she let loose what were probably enough emotions to fill a high school. I reached over and grabbed her hand on the wheel, partially to steady the truck and partially to steady her. “Noah, pull over. I can drive for a while. We will be getting off the main road soon anyways.”

She pulled over without a word and climbed out. I scanned the tree line for movement and then pulled her in for a hug. She clung to me, shuddering breaths escaping every now and then. Part of me was thrilled to have her in my arms, finally, after all the seeds I had planted and all the work I had done to get her to this point. The other part of me hated myself for lying to her. She was so scared; she was so alone. She had just lost everything important to her, and I was taking advantage of her vulnerability. I took a breath and scanned the tree line over her head again.

“I’m sorry. I don’t know where that came from,” she said, avoiding my eyes and pulling out of my arms.

"Hey," I said, catching her chin in my hands. I needed to tell the truth. She deserved that. At least a little bit of the truth. I locked eyes with her and took a breath to begin. She cut me off with a kiss.

I froze, unable to process what was happening. A million thoughts shot through my mind at warp speed, filling my head with a buzzing that seemed to shake every cell in my body. I knew she was kissing me out of fear, but I didn't care. I kissed her back hard, and her hands were touching me all over as I slipped mine around the small of her back, pulling her closer. The part of my mind that wanted to tell her the truth melted away, and the primal man who wanted to drag her to my cave took over. A small moan escaped her as she kissed me, and I was gone. There was nothing on this planet that mattered at that moment.

She pulled away gently, and I came back to the world, fire in my belly, ready for anything.

Anything but the look on her face. Her beautiful, innocent face shone with terror. I would do anything to protect her. "Noah, we are not going to die today."

"How can you know that?" she asked, tears welling in her eyes.

I took her hands in mine and looked into her eyes. "I will not let you die today. I don't know what is going on, where the sinkholes are from, what that monster was, or what to do other than drive far away, but I do know this: When a beautiful woman kisses you out of terror… you count your lucky stars because she is never going to do it again."

She laughed and fell into my arms again, letting me hold her a moment longer.

"I still don't really like you, just so you know," she said.

I smiled, smelling her hair and feeling her pressed against me. "I would expect nothing less. Now, we need to keep moving. It's about another 100 miles to my friend's cabin, so we should make it before dark. Hop in, take a deep breath, and keep watch in case there are more of those things around. Can you do that?"

"Yes," she said, putting on a brave face.

"Good. Let's get moving, Killer." I began to turn, and she squeezed my hand.

"Thank you, Duke. For everything. I don't know what today would have looked like if it weren't for you."

I turned and looked at her. I leaned over and kissed the top of her head. "What can I say? I love a damsel in distress."

"You are a chauvinist," she faux-pouted.

"I like to think of myself as a knight, actually. You know, brave, handsome, heroic saves the girl and slays the dragon."

"As I recall, I was the one who saved you in the shootout," she retorted, climbing back in the truck.

"I know," I said in my most condescending voice. "Those chips didn't see what hit them."

We passed another abandoned car on the side of the road. Noah looked at it, and her face turned pale.

"Keep watching. There might be more of them around here," I told her. I didn't want to scare her, but let's be real. This was a scary situation, no matter what.

"Duke?"

"Yeah?"

"I am scared."

"Me, too, Noah. But we have a pretty good team here. We are going to be ok." I glanced at her again, and she looked terrified. I grabbed her hand and gave it a gentle squeeze. "So, what is your favorite type of book to read?"

"Really? You want to talk about books? Right now? As we avoid man-eating-monster-toads?"

"Well, we could talk about the toads, or we could pass the time a little more cheerfully. Up to you."

She was silent for a moment. I wasn't sure if she was deciding if she wanted to answer or thinking about her answer. "I really love a good murder mystery. Suspense, danger, who-done-it, spy versus spy, gripping, thrilling roller coaster of a read. How about you?"

I couldn't resist messing with her at this point. "Well, if I could read every romance novel out there, I would be a happy man."

She sat in shocked silence for a few seconds before replying. "Well, that's… cool. I kind of figured you for a sci-fi guy."

"Oh, man, I read this amazing book once about this woman who falls in love with an alien, and the alien takes her back to his home planet to meet his people, and she meets his old alien girlfriend, and the woman thinks that he is still in love with the other woman, but he kissed her and…"

I looked at her and burst out laughing. Her face was more terrified than when we saw the Rover. "I'm sorry, I can't keep that up. No, I don't read romance novels. I am more of a historical fiction and suspense guy. Wow, the look on your face was priceless."

We laughed and entered into a comfortable time of light chatting. It eased both our minds.

When we reached the outskirts of Carlton, the forest was thicker and made it more difficult to watch for Rovers, though I saw them every few miles. Noah sucked in a quick breath and said, "I think I just saw another one."

"You did. We have passed three in the past few miles. We should be able to stop safely for gas if there is a station in the open at the edge of town. Then it's a road change and cabin, but on smaller side roads, so we will have to be extra cautious, keeping both guns out and at the ready."

"What if we can't find gas? Will we still get there?"

I looked at the dwindling tank and decided it was better not to lie this time, so I kept my mouth shut.

We reached Carlson, and the blood drained from my face. I knew the town well; it was the closest town to my cabin. The little shops, the restaurants, the sights, the sounds. The people. All were just. Gone.

There were huge, gaping craters with some flooding from broken water mains. I swallowed the bile that shot to my throat and almost lost the battle nausea as I spotted the Rover. There must have been hundreds of them. They were crawling out of the holes, dragging human carcasses, ripping into them, feasting in a twisted orgy of blood and gore.

Noah opened the door and spewed violently. I handed her a bottle of water and said, "We need to keep moving."

She sobbed, "Duke, we need to stop this. They are eating…"

"I know. But there is nothing we can do right now. Let's get safe and make a plan. We are low on gas and vastly outnumbered. Even if we weren't, we can't spend our ammo this way."

She slowly nodded. "Let's get gas and get to the cabin. Can you figure out an alternate route, as we can't get through Carlston?"

"Sure thing. We will get back on the main road and-" Bob cut me off, barking and snarling out the window. Then I saw what he did. "Grab your gun!" I shouted, slamming the truck into gear and speeding off down the road.

Three Rovers were in hot pursuit of us and gaining. Noah pulled her gun and flipped around, her back on the dash, rolling down the window, trying to get a good shot with her left side facing the opening. "This would be way easier if you had a sunroof in this thing," she grumbled.

"Yeah, I should have thought about that when I was looking for a reliable vehicle. How will this sucker do in a roadway shootout? Is it going to work well in all end-of-the-world scenarios? What is the monster-proofing on the body like?"

"I know, right? Who taught you to shop for cars?"

Thank God the Rovers decided that we were not worth the trouble. They turned and ran back to their gut-wrenching meal.

We drove the rest of the way in silence around Carlston. Noah was looking around us like a deer during November.

CHAPTER 28

We arrived at the little gas station that was down the road from the cabin. "Do you want to see if they have any more supplies left? Water, bullets, maps, the works," I asked her.

"Sure," she said, unbuckling her seatbelt and stepping out of the truck.

She took a few steps away from the truck and raised a hand to the old man sitting on the porch of the station. I recognized him from my many trips out here, though I doubted that he would remember me. Without warning, he stood up, lifted his rifle and fired at my Noah. She fell without a sound.

I died inside; a fear that I had never felt before gripped me. We had made it this far, and she was killed right in front of me by the gas station guy.

I flew out of the truck and screamed her name.

"Noah! Noah! Can you hear me?" I ran to her side and threw myself next to her, scanning her body for the blood.

Noah blinked at me. "I think I just died. Did I get shot in the head by an old guy with a rifle?"

"Who you callen' an old guy, little missy?"

I was on the verge of losing it. I wanted to pull my gun on this old guy and shoot him as he walked up to us. I wanted to pistol whip him and knock every remaining tooth he had left out of his face. Instead, I just yelled at him.

"What the hell is wrong with you? You almost killed her? That was-"

"Hold up, sonny. No need to get uptight. There was one of them beasties over yonder in the trees, by that big ol' pine tree. S'prolly is still there if you care to take a look. I been keepin' my eyes out for the rascals so folk can load up on what I have left. S'not much, but if it helps keep 'em going 'til they can find safety, then it's worth it. I'm Papa Ray; this here is Bessy." His eyes glanced meaningfully at the gun in his arm. "Now, I am terribly sorry to cause such a fright to a pretty little thing like your wife here, but them things are fast. Not much time for small talk when they get close."

I took a deep breath, reaching down to touch Noah's beautiful, very intact face. I blinked back a tear that wanted to escape and cleared my throat.

I reached out to take Pap Ray's hand. "I'm Duke. Nice to meet you, sir. This is Noah. We are in need of gas. And ammo if you carry it? We have plenty of cash. Not sure what your prices look like right about now."

"Oh, Duke, I can't take yer money anymore that I can take yer lady's life. We are all human beans here and needin' to work together as much we can. Come on in and have a look around when yer done fillin' yer tank."

"We appreciate it, though a word of caution to people before you open fire on them might help with your roadside manner," Noah said, sitting up and double-checking that she indeed did not get shot.

"My apologies, little missy. I will certainly give a holler before I shoot at you again. Deal?"

She gave a slight nod as I helped her up and dusted her off. I may have spent a little more time on the back of her pants because, well, I am still a man. Bob hopped out of the truck and before I could warn Ray about how he can be a little vicious, he climbed up on the old man, showering him with licks and tail wags. I wanted to shoot the dog.

"What… did… Is he… Oh, never mind," I mumbled as we climbed back into the truck to pull up to the pump. Papa Ray seemed to love Bob, and they wandered off together. I started pumping gas as thoughts began to crawl through my head. I thought of the briefing, the file I had stored in my bag, and the benefits of seeing the enemy up close filled my mind. Now, to convince Noah.

"Noah, I need to ask you something."

"No, I will not marry you," she replied as snarkily as she could.

Man, this woman. Without even meaning to, I smiled at her and replied, "I can work on that later. For now, I need you to think open-mindedly and listen carefully." I steeled myself, took a deep breath and blew it out. "I want to bring that body with us."

I watched as the shadows of a thousand thoughts raced past her eyes.

"I'm sorry, what?"

"Noah, if we can learn about these things, we can see if they have any weaknesses. We can study it up close; we can see how it is put together so we can see how best to take them down."

"Duke, are you crazy?! What if they carry diseases? What if it rots and fills everything with a smell that we can never get rid of? What if it comes back to life and eats our faces?!"

"I know that it sounds terrible, but think about it from a greater good standpoint. We have no idea how long these things will be around, where they came from, anything about them really. A chance to get one dead to look at, cut open and learn about—it might just save our lives and many others. That is worth the smell haunting us, right?" By now, I had lost count of times I had lied to her. Would I ever find my way out of this web? I buried the thought and tried to focus on immediate survival.

"I super hate you right now, Duke. You know that, right?"

"I do, yes." She made a face as the pump ticked, signaling me it was done. I turned to unhook it, scanning our surroundings for possible threats. In all my time as a cop, I learned a lot of lessons about desperate and scared people. I returned the pump and turned back to face Noah. "Just think about it for a few minutes while I talk to Ray. Are you okay to drive the truck and park it over there so the next cars can get in?"

She sighed. "Yes, I can move the truck, and maybe I will think about the corpse absconding. Good enough?"

"Good enough." Impulsively, almost subconsciously, I leaned over and pressed my lips to her head, inhaling the scent of her hair, her essence. She was fierce, strong, beautiful, deep. In a moment, right before my eyes, I thought she had been ripped from me. "I thought I lost you," I whispered. I wasn't sure if she heard me or not, but I turned and strode away without looking at her.

There was too much going on. I felt like I was on the verge of panic. My arm was in so much pain I almost lost the woman who had been haunting my thoughts for over a year. The world was swarming with murderous science fair projects. I was exhausted, and I needed to focus on what good I could do.

I strode up the porch steps to talk to Ray. He nodded genially at me. "Hey, sonny. I am frightfully sorry about the scare I gave yer wife. Is she gon' be okay?"

"She is tough. She will be fine. I'm just thankful that you were on guard. Have you seen many of them here?"

"Yeah, them buggers seems to be comin' outta the woodwork."

"I have some information that will be helpful for you. I'm a cop-out of Lincoln. We were briefed before being dismissed to get to safety." I gave a look around to make sure there were not too many ears close by. As much as I wanted to help the public, panicked, angry people looking for someone to blame are even more dangerous than good old scared people. Sadly, we cops were always fair game in the blame game. Papa Ray seemed to understand my meaning.

"Let me show you some things I have available inside."

He stood up and led me into the general store. While I had stopped for gas here many times, I had never been inside. It resembled every mom-and-pop Shop along every roadway, crowded with souvenirs, salty snacks, and items for minor car issues. Papa Ray led me behind the counter and leaned against the window frame.

"Anything you can tell me to help these people will be greatly appreciated, son."

"Okay, in a nutshell, these things were a failed government experiment. They are designed to tunnel underground, hunt, and kill terrorists. They were being tested in a secret facility when they broke out, killing all of the scientists and most of the military personnel in said facility. They have a few weaknesses, though they seem to be adapting and changing at an alarming rate.

"First of all, they are built of two separate creatures. The head is the male, and the body is the female. They can be separated, but they have to choose to. The males can be removed from a dead female, but not a female from a dead male; a headshot kills them both.

"Secondly, they are sensitive to certain sound frequencies, namely from a dog whistle. It repels them, so if you can have a couple on hand, it will help you out greatly.

"Lastly, they are attracted to vibrations through the ground. Carlston was hit and practically destroyed. I am sure you heard, so they are definitely underground in this area, so if you can find a way to limit vibrations or create a sound barrier of some kind, you should be able to hold them off for a while.

"Also, if you could keep the government involvement to yourself, I would appreciate it. They will face the music when the time comes, but for now, we need to band together as much as we can."

Papa Ray stared thoughtfully at the floor, his hand resting on his wizened face while he listened for me to finish. He gave a slow nod, absorbing the information. "I thank you, my boy. This could be the difference betwixt life and death for many a folk. I would certainly suggest, however," his bright eyes jumped to mine in a flash. "You had better think twice about why yer holdin' this information from your lady."

I looked at him dumbfounded for a moment. How could he possibly know something like that? I wanted to deny it, ask him how he could accuse me of something like that, to get angry. I couldn't. I lowered my eyes. "I feel like it's too late for that. Can you please just keep that… quiet?"

He nodded and quickly returned to his cheerful demeanor. "Well, we best head out and get you and the missus on the way."

We walked out the door together when a ruckus caught my ear. There was a group of people gathered around a car at the pump. Noah was barely visible, sitting on the ground in the middle of it all.

I froze on the spot. Was she okay? She caught my eyes, with desperation, fear, and grief etched on her face. She was holding a weeping woman, who gripped her tightly, howling out in agony. What had happened? I began to run toward them when Noah's voice rose above the din.

"Hey! Stop that! Someone, stop them! Duke! Duke!" I spun around to see where she was pointing behind me. Three men were raiding the truck bed, two inside tossing our precious supplies to another man who was throwing them into the open door of an awaiting van.

I didn't even have time to take off in their direction before they jumped out and climbed into the car, throwing up dust and gravel as they sped off. Our survival was in there. Our hope for the future. Our only chance at making it.

Without a second thought, I drew my sidearm and lined up for the tires. After three shots, the van careened wildly toward the side of the parking lot and then came to a stop.

I ran toward the van with my gun still raised. They would have to face me for this. They tried the wrong truck. "Freeze!" The three men climbed out sheepishly. They knew they were caught. They raised their hands and looked my way.

Then, one bolted straight for the tree line. "I said FREEZE!" I shouted again. I walked over to the men and glared at them before stepping closer to the woods. Noah appeared at my side, her weapon out as well, her face streaked with dust. I was about to tell her to pull up the truck to reload our supplies when we heard it—the clicking noise from the video of the Rovers. I sucked in a sharp breath and held steady. The man's voice rang out, a savage, primal howl of terror, turning into a wet gurgle and repulsive crunch. I extended my arm out to support Noah, who seemed like she was about to faint. My mind was reeling. What was happening to humanity? "He didn't have to run. I just wanted our supplies back. It wasn't worth his life." I sighed as Noah reached out, placing her hand on my arm, and looked up at me sadly.

The sound of tires on gravel coming behind us quickly pulled me back to the moment. The minivan, beside which Noah had been sitting, was being driven directly at us by the woman who had been on the ground, though now she was looking angry rather than grief-stricken. I grabbed Noah as well as I could with my wounded arm and pulled her out of the way. The van barely slowed as the remaining two thieves jumped in, and they took off down the road.

This day, man. Seriously.

"Duke, can we go now? This is the worst pit stop I have ever made in my life, and I have driven across Montana."

Her humor somehow made everything seem like I could handle it. I chuckled and pulled her in for a quick hug. "Yeah, let's get out of here. Papa Ray has some supplies left that we can take a look through, if you are up to it?"

"Yeah, I think I can handle that, but we should leave Bob to watch the truck."

"Agreed."

As we walked back to the truck, I shook my head. That man had just died, and his team took off without even a thought for him. No honor among thieves?

Noah got Bob settled in the bed of the truck with some fresh water and gave him a kiss—lucky dog.

Where's my kiss? I allowed myself a small grin as we headed inside the general store.

Papa Ray was watching the abandoned van as we walked in. "Well, that sure was quite the performance, huh?" he asked, shaking his head. "Had a few dishonest folk come through today to try that kinda garbage. Makes me feel like there ain't any reason to care 'bout 'em."

"I hear you there, Ray. Been a cop for about six years now and there are more people that need to be saved from themselves than you would believe."

"Oh, I sure do believe it," Papa Ray said, shaking his head sadly.

"Mind if we take a look at what supplies you have left?"

"Yeah, come on, kids." For the next ten minutes or so, Papa Ray helped us find some supplies that would help us out that we didn't already have. He led us up and down the aisles, handing us packages. He was so pleasant, kind, and so intuitive.

I led Noah back to the truck and opened the door for her as she brought Bob up from the truck bed. She climbed in and settled into her seat, seemingly shell-shocked from the long day's events.

I looked at her and thought about what the old man had said. She deserved the truth. I would tell her when we got to the cabin. For now, I would offer the man a parting gift.

"This will help you keep your place safe," I said, handing over my small dog whistle. "Thank you for your generosity, friend."

"You take care of that lady of yours. I am sure you have your reasons for your choices, and I ain't one to judge nobody, but I feel like you needed to hear that. The good Lord wanted you to hear that."

I smiled and shook his old hand. "See you around."

Climbing back into the truck, I took a deep breath. I was tired, and my arm hurt like crazy. Papa Ray was right.

We pulled up next to the thieves' van and began to reload our belongings. There was more inside than what they had stolen from us. They must have been at it for hours. No wonder the other driver looked so pissed.

"I'll tell Ray to get this stuff in his store for those who need it. You sit tight." I walked back over to the porch where Ray was once again seated, his rifle cradled in his lap.

"There are more supplies in that van that the pirates had loaded up. I'm sure there are some goodies in there that can help out more than a few desperate people."

"Well, thank you for your honesty, Duke. Most folk would just load it all up and not say a peep about it. Glad to see good folk like you are still out there even durin' this crazy time. As terrible the whole situation was, I am mighty glad it was you who was here and not some helpless young 'un. I'll be keepin' a closer watch for them bad fellers now that I saw 'em in action."

I smiled at the kind old man. "Glad to have you out here, Papa Ray. You have a bug-out plan in place?"

"Oh, no, sonny. My place is here helpin' the weary travelers and shootin' them Rover buggers."

"Well, if you find yourself needing a safe place, my cabin is not far, and we would welcome you happily if you needed it. Ten minutes down the road, take a right on Celtic Sparrow Lane, about two miles, then another right onto the little dirt road by the boulder. We are at the end of that little dirt road."

"I sure do appreciate it. I will keep that in mind, though I sure don't mind if the Lord calls me home doing what I love: helpin' people."

I nodded and shook the old man's hand once again. "Take care." I turned and began the trek across the parking lot to the truck.

I groaned as I climbed back into the truck; the pain meds had worn off by then. "Ray is going to keep his eyes open for more road pirates, warn people as they stop. I gave him directions to the cabin in case he needed a safe place. He just laughed at me and said his place was here, where he could do the most good. Why can't the world be full of Papa Ray's?"

"I was just thinking that," she replied, giving a small shiver and pulling Bob closer. "I really don't want to bring the body of that monster with us, but I think it would be best if we did to learn as much about it as we can so that we don't have to get eaten and can hopefully learn the best way to kill them."

I looked at her and shook my head. "Noah, as much as I was hoping you would say that, I think we should just get out of here and get to the cabin. Once we are safe and have a routine, we can come back and look for a fresh one. I do think we need to do this. I don't think we should do it now."

"Oh, I am so glad to hear you say that!" She impulsively grabbed my hand and squeezed it.

"Well, Wifey, shall we be off?" She quickly let go as I grinned wearily at her.

"Okay, you did correct him, right? Papa Ray?"

"Nah, why would I do that?"

She looked at Bob. “Can you believe this guy? I don’t even like him. Who does he think he is?” she mumbled. “How far to the cabin?” she asked, turning to me.

“About 20 minutes from here, so close enough that we could come back for supplies as we need them if Ray can stay alive and keep the looters at bay.”

“I hope he does. I like him, even though he almost shot me.”

“Yeah, that was off-putting, but he shore do grow on ya, hey missy?” Noah’s musical laughter filled the cab of the truck as we pulled out of the lot. I had been shot, seen people being eaten by monsters from a nightmare, been looted by thieves, not to mention facing the threat against all of humanity, but in that moment, I wouldn’t change a thing. All that horror brought me to the moment when I was rewarded by the ringing of her laughter, and it was beautiful.

CHAPTER 29

I love my cabin. When I first bought the property, it was just a shed with a well. Some DIY enthusiasts thought they would turn it into their summer home. Either the money or the motivation ran out, and they just wanted it gone. I got it for a steal.

It took me a year's worth of weekends and holidays to build the cabin. I had just put in the water heater and mounted the solar panels on the roof a year ago. It was so simple and homey. I thought it was perfect. When I had some buddies out for a long weekend, I met Tasha. She had just joined the force and was looking to make friends. We knew it would never be more than casual sex, but we had a good time together. She came up with the idea for the phony wedding pictures. I wish I could blame her for the idea of using them to gain sympathy from women, but I came up with that one all by myself.

When we arrived, I spent some time contemplating what I would be telling Noah if she asked. She thought the cabin belonged to a heartbroken friend of mine, and the loving touches scattered around were glaring, angry reminders of the lies I had already begun to spin. After we ate and had a moment to sit together in the quiet, she broached the subject. "So. Tim?"

I took a moment before answering. I couldn't tell her the tale I had concocted about the cabin. The heartbreaking story of love and loss. I couldn't be that shallow as to weave that tangled web of a story around her when everything was already so bad.

Then again, how else would I explain the décor, the photo albums, and the family feel of the place? If I told her the truth about it, I would seem like a total dick. Maybe I was a total dick.

I delved into the story, adding passion and anger at just the right moments. The drama of the narrative was exactly what I needed to really get her sympathy working, which would help me as I pursued her down the road. The man meets the woman, and they fall in love. They create a life together and build a future, then tragedy strikes and the life is snuffed out, leaving the man broken.

As I reached the end, I was sick with myself. I wanted to go back and tell her that I was just kidding. That none of it happened and it was all just a story.

But what kind of monster made up stories like that? The dirty reality of the words that I spun her eclipsed the thought of any advantage that the tale may have given me. I couldn't sit near her. I had to get up. I offered her a warm beer and finished the story with fire in my heart. Not fire for the heartbroken man but for a truth-breaking one who was manipulating the woman he was supposed to love.

What was I doing?

I needed to think. I needed a shower. I stripped down and let cold water rush over me as I leaned against the wall of the shower. *Liar.* The word popped into my head as a whisper. *Liar. Liar. Pant on. Fire.* The words grew louder.

I hit the shower wall. I had never had a problem lying to women before. What was wrong with me now? Maybe it was the fact that the world was ending, or maybe it was the way I felt when I saw fear in her eyes, but I knew I had to come clean. I had to tell her the truth. I quickly scrubbed up, climbed out, and wrapped a towel around my waist. Maybe some naked, wet man muscles would smooth out the wrinkles I had created.

When I opened the bathroom door, Noah was standing close by with fear on her face. It took me a minute to hear the sounds that came, but I heard them all right—scratching, scratching. The sound made my teeth want to fall out. I pulled Noah closer to me, then guided her behind me and into the bedroom.

Noah climbed into bed and invited me to join her, but I couldn't. I just couldn't. I didn't deserve to. I would never deserve to.

CHAPTER 30

The sun was just beginning to tint the sky golden outside the small bedroom window when I woke in a cold sweat, the remnants of the nightmare ripping its claws into my heart. I took a deep breath and looked at Noah. She was sleeping with her face smashed into the pillow, a small puddle of drool gently dripping down. I smiled, pushed the hair off her forehead, and leaned over from my spot on the floor to kiss her softly. She smiled and mumbled something about Bob.

I got up and headed to the kitchen. I needed coffee and a pain reliever. While I was thankful my gunshot wound was not serious, it still seriously hurt. Bob followed me out and sat nicely by the door.

"Just give me a minute, buddy."

I got the water heating and took Bob out for some fresh air. Together, we relieved ourselves in the early morning light and ran a few laps around the clearing. I always ran in the mornings. It gave me a morning boost, cleared my mind, and jump-started my heart. We started off with a nice, slow jog, always listening for the rattle from the forest.

My mind wandered, and the frustration from the previous day's events tumbled through me. How many of my brothers and sisters in blue made it out? How many were gone?

Would I ever see my home again, or had it been into the earth like the entire city of Carlston?

I was so thankful that I had Noah with me, but how long could I protect her? Would we be overrun in a week? A day? Having some prior knowledge of the Rovers could help us, but would it be enough? How long would we be able to survive?

And if we survived, to what end?

Would I ever be able to backtrack and tell her the truth about how much I knew? Would she understand? Would I be able to explain it to her? How far into the lie would I allow myself to go?

The more my mind raced, the harder I ran. My heart was thundering in my chest, my lungs screaming for air, but I couldn't stop. I had to get the anger out. And so I ran on, with Bob at my side, just happy to be out, oblivious to the rage I was pounding out.

By the time I collapsed into the grass, the sun had risen. I lay in the cool, wet grass, feeling the earth beneath me, the air above me, and the life in my chest.

A sob tore out of me; it was too much. I could barely breathe. My stomach clenched, caught between anguish and stitches. I was about to scream out to God to just drop a Rover on me when Bob lay down next to me. He laid his head on my chest, his brown eyes looking up into mine. "I know. Pull it together. I'm trying, Bob. Everything just feels so hopeless."

He lifted his head, looked toward the cabin and whined. "I know. I have to hold on for Noah. I have to protect her, to make sure she makes it through. I'm just not sure what is on the other side of this tunnel. Is there light? Or is everything collapsed?"

Bob tilted his head and grunted. "I'm trying. It is all just so unbelievable that I'm not even sure I know the right thing to do. And, to make it all worse, I'm talking to a dog!"

Bob gave a small woof and nudged me with his nose. "I know. I'm heading back in. Noah will be up soon, I suppose, and I need to pull myself together before she is, right?"

Woof! I smiled at Bob and scratched his ears. "Thanks for the pep talk."

CHAPTER 31

Then Bob began to bark.

My heart leaped into my throat. I glanced at Noah, drew my pistol, and handed it to her. "Cock this; my arm isn't ready to." She chambered a round, handed it back, drew her own weapon and got into the ready stance I had shown her earlier that day. She whispered Bob's name a few times and was met with silence.

"Bob?" she called out louder. I could hear the worry in her voice.

"Bob!" I yelled. "Bob! Here, boy!" The sounds of what could only be a Rover and a dog fighting floated toward us. I should have sent Noah back to the cabin, but I knew she wouldn't go. "Noah, stay behind me and watch my back. We will get to Bob."

"10-4," she whispered. I would have smiled at how cute she was if the situation was not as terrifying as it was.

"Ok, with me," I whispered instead, starting the silent walk toward the sounds. They grew louder and louder, and as they did, I became more and more certain that Bob would not be walking away from this. The sounds crescendoed into a pain-filled yelp and a sickening wet rattle. Noah sobbed behind me, causing a pause from the monster we were hunting. She was going to get us all killed. I had to send her back. "Noah, listen to me. Walk back to the cabin. I am going to cover your back. Straight to the cabin," I whispered.

"Bob?"

"It's too late. Back to the cabin now. We have to get-"

Before I could finish my sentence, she pivoted around me and drove headlong into a raspberry thicket, letting off shots along with an ear-splitting war cry. Her voice shifted from a crazed shout to a shocked scream without even a breath in between.

I scanned the area and watched as the male head of the Rover skittered away into the underbrush. I shot off a few rounds after it for good measure, but it was gone.

Noah continued to scream, a throaty, heart-breaking, soul-shattering sound. I could hear her anguish and terror like grenades tearing through the air around us. I looked at Bob and knew I had to get her out of there. He was gone, blood pooling from an open wound on his abdomen, his eyes misty and full of fear. I was amazed when I heard a small whimper from him.

"Hi, baby," Noah said, cradling his face. "Hey, look at mommy. Good boy. Bob is the best boy." His tail trembled as he tried to wag it. I watched in horror as more blood poured out of him, and I was pretty sure I could see organs peeking out among the gore.

"Noah, we have to get out of here," I urged. There was no way Bob would make it out of this alive. I could only save Noah.

"Not without Bob. We have to get him home and patched up." She smiled at him, and I realized that she was in shock. I could hear more Rovers in the distance, attracted to the smell of the fresh blood. "Noah, listen to me. We have to go now." She kept smiling, her eyes growing misty.

"Noah!" I tried to pull her off of the ground, but she resisted, turning and throwing a punch. I was not prepared, and it hit me square in the jaw, making my head ring. I could hear the Rovers getting closer. I stood tall and fired off a few warning rounds, hoping to scare them away, but they kept coming. When I could get a clear shot, I took out the middle one with a clean shot through the male head, dropping the thing to the forest floor. The other two stopped running and turned to look at their fallen Rover. I watched as they turned and started to cannibalize the carcass. Bile rose in my throat as they feasted.

I needed to somehow get Noah in her shocked state back to the cabin. I pulled her up from the ground and tugged her through the raspberry bushes. As I shifted her weight to account for the pain in my shoulder, I heard Bob. His whimper was neither scared nor begging, just soft, like a goodnight kiss or… a peaceful goodbye.

I sucked in a deep breath and turned back. He lifted his head to look at me, then set it gently down again.

I pulled off my shirt and watched the feasting Rovers for a moment to ensure they were still content with their gory meal before kneeling down by Bob's side.

"I'll get you home, buddy. I won't leave you for the monsters."

His eyes were glassy, and his breathing was labored. I tore the shirt as quietly as I could, then wrapped it tightly around Bob's middle. It would have to suffice until we got back home.

I heaved the huge dog over my injured shoulder, the pain searing through, causing me to stumble. Pain is terrible, but it is still just pain. Once I regained my sure footing, I carried Bob over to Noah. She lay on the forest floor, mumbling, shock fully set in. "Come on, Noah," I said quietly. "I have to get you two home. I need you to help me. I need you to walk."

She nodded. It took a few attempts to get her to move, but eventually, we began our slow walk back to the cabin.

I set Bob down on the table, my shoulder screaming in pain. Noah stood still, eyes forward, unable to process anything. I faced so many problems.

One thing at a time. One thing at a time. One thing at a time.

I locked the door and grabbed some pain meds. I popped a few and crushed some up, sprinkling them on Bob's tongue. He was going to die, but at least I could make it a little less horrible for him.

I guided Noah to the bedroom, laid her down, and pulled the quilt over her body. She pulled the covers up and rolled over, not saying a word. I planted a gentle kiss on her head. "I'm so sorry about Bob," I whispered.

I took a quick shower, slipped into a clean outfit and grabbed a washcloth to press on Noah's forehead. It was time to check if Bob had passed.

I did not want to approach the table where he lay. I knew the mess that he was in and was reluctant to look into his eyes as he crossed the rainbow bridge.

As I approached, he lifted his head.

He lifted his head.

He lifted his head!

I couldn't believe it. I hovered over him and inspected the wound. It was very deep, but it really was looking like something that he could survive if we had a vet to stitch him up. My heart jumped to my throat as I thought the craziest idea I had ever had.

Rushing to the closet, I grabbed a book on human anatomy. I opened it up and began to scan.

I had no idea if I could pull this off, but I needed to try. Noah needed me to try. Bob needed me to try.

If I were honest with myself, I needed to try. I had to prove myself that I was more than a liar, more than a manipulator, more than the mistakes that I had made. Maybe Noah would even forgive me, and we could move forward.

I grabbed the first aid kit, a shaving razor, some clean water, a sharp knife, and lots of rags. I put a pot of water on to boil, laid the anatomy book open nearby and began shaving around the wound.

I could save Bob. And even if I couldn't, I was damn well going to try.

CHAPTER 32

I don't know how much time passed—hours, at least. I was covered in blood and fur, thirsty and tired. It was time for me to take more pain medication, but I couldn't stop what I was working on. Stitch by stitch, minute by minute, I continued. Everything needed to be checked and rechecked. The anatomy book was based on humans, not dogs, and gave me a general idea of where everything should be, but in a very different shape. I had no surety about what I was doing and if it was right, but it was the best chance Bob had.

I heard Noah gasp and turned my attention to her.

"I think he might make it."

She looked at the gore everywhere and fumbled out some words. "What? How? Why? How is this possible? Where did you get a stethoscope?!"

"Let me finish this up first. Then we can talk. We should probably clean the blood up, too. In this summer heat, it won't take long to begin to rot." I turned back to what I was working on, trying to finish the last stitches, checking the pulse, wiping more blood off. Noah just stared.

"Noah, I need you here with me. You went into shock, but I need your help now. Are you going to be able to do it?"

As I finished up, Noah worked on the clean-up. I sat up to examine the stitches on the dog. It was messy but looked secure. Taking a deep breath, I scratched Bob's ears. I had crushed up some painkillers and put them in his mouth when I first started, but I was certain he was still in terrible pain. Speaking of pain, where were my drugs?

I helped Noah get everything cleaned up. We didn't have anywhere for the soiled rags to go, so I tossed them into the fire. We had enough blood smells permeating the cabin. We didn't need to invite the Rovers any more than we already had. Once I had Bob washed up to the best of my ability without putting him in more pain, I carefully carried him to a blanket laid on the floor by the fire. He licked my hand and then closed his eyes. Poor guy had a rough day.

I went to shower while Noah finished the last of the cleanup and settled on the couch beside Bob. The cold water was a relief, and it felt good to wash the sticky blood off of me. I dressed quickly and grabbed a couple of beers for Noah and myself.

After a while, Noah asked, "Okay, Doctor Duke. Any more surprises I should know about?"

I took a deep breath. Bob was far from out of the woods, and I didn't want her to have any false hope. "Noah, you need to know that he might not make it. I have never done anything like that before. Trinity was going to nursing school and had a box of books and her stethoscope in a closet. I was entirely guessing about a lot of the anatomy based on the diagrams of humans. I may have only saved him to have him die of my mistakes later. I did my best, but it might not be enough." That was only partially true. But it was me who wanted to learn more, so I bought the books and supplies.

She grabbed my hand and squeezed. "Duke, you tried. Even if he doesn't make it through the night, I am forever in your debt. I am amazed that he is still alive. I am amazed by you." She leaned in close, tilting her face toward mine. I turned away. I couldn't. I didn't deserve her love.

"Well, you would have done the same, I'm sure," I choked out. She looked hurt for a moment, then tried to recover.

"So, what exactly happened out there?"

"Can we talk about it in the morning? I need to process a few things. And I am beat. You want to sit up with Bob for a while, or you going to turn in, too?" I needed to get away from the situation. I was sinking deeper into this web of lies, and it was distracting me from what I needed to focus on survival. "Yeah, I will sit up with him. You can have the bed tonight; I will sleep out here. Good night."

"Night," I replied and quickly closed the bedroom door behind me.

"I have to tell her the truth," I said aloud to myself. What would that look like? *Noah, I have been lying about everything. I know a lot about the Rovers. I know where they came from and what they are doing here. This cabin is a honey trap for poor, unsuspecting women whom I try to manipulate into bed. I have been nearly stalking you for months, and now I am trying to use my fake dead wife to get you to sleep with me. But I am feeling guilty about it and keep digging these lies deeper and deeper in an attempt not to make myself look like a total dick.* Somehow, I think that would not get me anywhere good.

The worst part of it all was how much she trusted me. She looked to me for strength, for comfort. She was falling for me, and I didn't deserve it.

I tossed and turned for a long time, wrestling with my thoughts. I would have to tell her the truth before she found the album. I would just toss it in the fireplace. The lie didn't need to go any farther. No harm done; she never had to know the truth.

What could go wrong?

CHAPTER 33

The next night, I waited until she had gone to bed. It had been such a long day. We had studied Rover's carcass, giving me a chance to "learn" more about them without raising Noah's suspicions about what I knew about them. She is clever and made a lot of discoveries on her own. That woman never ceased to amaze me.

Once she had gone to bed, I waited, lying on the couch. I gave her a good half hour to fall asleep before getting up. I needed to get rid of that damned photo album. Once that was gone, the lies could end, and I would be home free. Relatively speaking, that is.

I pulled the album from the shelf. The cover had a design Tasha came up with. It was classy yet cheerful. I turned toward the fire, ready to toss it in.

I thought about my friends in the book. Would I ever see them again? Stevens, Drew, Carmicheal, even whiny little rookie Phillips. I sat on the couch and opened the album. My friends and their big, goofy grins. They thought the idea of fake wedding pictures was hilarious. They hammed it up big time. Tasha had brought some friends along and we had made such a great day of it. Each guy took a turn being the groom. One of Tasha's friends even swapped dresses with her so she could have a turn as the bride. We drank too much, laughed too loudly, and made some great memories. I had slept with Tasha that night. She made a few jokes about how I better watch myself, or she would make me actually marry her. I rolled my eyes and told her I wasn't the marrying type. She just kissed me and said, "We'll see."

I let my eyes rove over the book's pages. Would I ever see any of these guys again? Were they even alive?

My throat turned sour as tears threatened to spill out. My thoughts shifted to Noah. She would have looked stunning in that dress. The plunging neckline and lacy back were lovely on Tasha and her friend; however, on Noah, it would have been breathtaking. I closed my eyes for a moment, allowing myself to picture her in that dress. Her hair and makeup were done just so for me and me alone. Her long legs slicing their way out of the almost scandalous slit as she marches toward me. My heart pounded in my chest. Her smile takes over her perfect face as she approaches. My mind shot forward to the bedroom, envisioning all the things I would love to do to her as my wife. Not just a casual lay but a meaningful, deep connection. Intimacy. A passion that I knew she would bring. Another leap forward, and we are on a beach, her belly swollen with my child as I set up her chair in the shade and rush to bring her water. She laughs at me, her sound like the chiming of bells. A moment later, she is holding a tiny baby boy, bringing him closer to a little girl in a frilly dress. 'Say hi to your brother!' she says, and the little girl giggles, reaching out as tears glisten in her tiny eyes.

I jolted awake and out of the beautiful fantasy. Noah was standing over me, a look of horror on her face as she held the album, reading the title over again; "The Duke's, Tim and Trinity."

My mind reeled. I wanted to tell her the truth. I really did. I wanted to clear the air and start fresh. But the recent thoughts of our life together raged in my mind, a battle that I could not win. I needed to do everything I could to win her. Even if that meant the lie went deeper. I took a deep breath and let it out.

"Noah, I haven't been with anyone since Trin. I hadn't even kissed someone until you got me on the way here. It's been four years since they died, and yet I still can't believe that it's true. I always think that she is going to walk through the front door with our little boy on her hip, an arm full of wildflowers that they had collected, singing an old show tune badly. Trinity was my world, carrying my world. And I lost them. I lost them, Noah. That woman at Papa Ray's wailing and weeping over her missing babies—I couldn't even look because I knew her pain. And then to see that it was all a sick ruse to steal from others, I… I wanted to throw her to the monsters."

She took a shaky breath. "How long had you been married?" Noah asked.

"Six months, twelve days, twenty hours and forty-one minutes. She was due to deliver Matthew within a month. I had planned to take a month off to be with them when he was born. Man, I was so excited to be a father. I bought four different cribs before I liked the one we had in his room. I repainted the walls six times before I liked the shade of green. Trin teased me that she was supposed to be the one nesting." I looked down at the book in my hands, trying not to feel sick. What was I doing? This was twisted. But how could I escape now? So, I carried on.

"And then I got called into the chief's office. It was a Thursday—rainy cold. Trin was meeting her parents for brunch at her favorite bistro. It was ten in the morning, and the man who hit her was so high he jumped a curb and ran down four people without noticing. Just drove off. Chief said that they got a few details from witnesses but not enough to go off of. It took me months to track the guy down. When I did, he pulled a gun. Killed my partner, Martin, and put two rounds through me. I don't remember the incident, but another officer said she had to pry my bloody gun from my hand. I had beat him to death with it once I ran out of bullets." At least I could put a little truth into it. This had happened to me, but not when I said it had.

Noah took a shaky breath and asked, "Where did he shoot you?"

I stood up and lifted my shirt. I couldn't help but appreciate Noah's eyebrows shoot up of their own accord. "Here is one," I said, showing her the long scar along my ribs. I let my shirt fall and lowered the waistband of my pants down enough for her to see the round scar. "I nearly bled out on the way to the hospital, but I never stopped smiling. They say that revenge doesn't make it better, but I felt better that day than I had in a long time. I put that dog down."

Bob lifted his head and whimpered. "Ok, dog is too kind of a term. Monster. I put that monster down."

I sat back down. My heart ached from all these lies. I looked into her eyes, feeling immense guilt and shame. "Noah, I really like you. You are funny, quirky, tender, and thoughtful. Sexy, if I am being honest about it. But this place—this was ours. I just can't be with you here. I can't make love to you in the bed I shared with my wife."

She smiled as she took my hand. I did not deserve this woman.

"Duke, I wish I could take away your pain. I wish I had a magic wand that made it all just go away. Your unbelievable loss, the monsters taking over the world—all of it. But I don't, and I can't. What I can do is be here for you now. I really like you, too, Duke, but I will not pressure you in any way. This was your home away from home with your wife. That is a beautiful thing, and I won't undermine that. If you are ever ready to get involved, I will be here. If that day never comes, I promise to be your teammate and friend to the end of the road. I am not Trinity, and I could never replace her. But I could be the next chapter if you ever wanted that."

My heart burst open. I wanted her. I wanted to grab her and claim her right on this couch. I wanted to devour her, then tell her the truth about everything and try to fix it.

But I couldn't. Instead, I just leaned closer and took in her beauty. "I want to kiss you right now."

She smiled. "Not today, Duke. We both need some time. But I will allow you to share this very comfortable couch with me."

I couldn't help but grin as we made up the couch like a seven-year-old's sleepover, with pillows everywhere and limbs snuggled in tight. As I began to drift off, Noah said my name in the near dark. "Duke?"

"Yeah?"

"Is it okay if I still call you Duke? Or do you prefer Tim?"

I smiled at her thoughtfulness; I didn't deserve it, and she had no idea. "Whatever you want to call me, Noah. Good night."

"Dream sweet," she said, then fell silent.

It was not long before her breathing turned regular and deep. I rubbed my foot along her arm and trailed my fingertips along her bare legs. She was everything I ever wanted in a woman, everything I had ever imagined she would be and more.

Would I ever be good enough for her?

CHAPTER 34

Never before in my life had I been as scared as I was when Tasha arrived. I was angry at her for showing up. I had tried to make it clear that I was not her bug-out plan, but here she was. I sent Noah back into the house and faced Tasha.

"What are you doing here?" I asked her.

"What do you think? I decided that I am done living on the run, and I will not be told that you don't have room for a woman because you clearly have one here now. Who is she?"

"Tasha, you cannot stay here. We do not have the supplies for a third person."

"Tim, come on!" She reached out, touched my arm, and slid her fingers down until I jerked away. "We had so much fun together! I don't even mind sharing if the woman here is what you are worried about. Think about it!" Her eyes grew lidded and lusty. "Three-ways whenever you want."

I took a step back. "Not even an option. Please leave, Tasha. I am serious."

I heard the door open and turned to see Noah step out. There was a stubborn look on her face.

"Noah, get back in the house. I will handle this."

“Excuse me? I will not leave my HUSBAND out here to be grabbed and slobbered all over by some random ex. Anything you have to say to her, you can say in front of me.”

“Husband? Are you serious?” she asked, looking shocked. “Is she serious? You said that you had a friend staying here for a while, and there wouldn’t be room!”

“What do you mean, room? Who even is she? Is she planning on staying here? How does she even know where it is?!”

“Does she seriously not know who I am?”

My head began to swim. I couldn't think, couldn’t even breathe.

“Enough, both of you!” I shouted. Noah didn’t back down.

“Timothy Duke, you have one minute to explain what the heck is going on before I begin asking her questions.”

I took a deep breath. I just needed Tasha to leave without saying anything condemning.

“Look, Noah, I made some mistakes in the past. Some things that I wanted to take back and fix, but it doesn’t work that way.”

“Fix?! Mistake?! You want to say that we were a mistake?” Tasha shouted.

“Tasha, we were never a “we”! We had some laughs, but—"

She held up a hand in my face. “Don’t you even. Do not cheapen what we had.”

Anger overcame me as I threw her hand away. "You need to leave and never come back."

She turned on her heels and stomped back to her truck. I watched her leave, a flicker of rage building within me as she turned and said, "Enjoy the wedding pictures." She slammed the door and sped off, leaving a trail of dust in her wake.

I wanted to throw up. She had said it; she just had to say it. I stormed back into the cabin and slammed the door. Would Noah ever forgive me? Would she ever even look at me again? I wanted to scream, shoot something, and light something on fire all at once.

However, my anger was eclipsed by my fear. I couldn't lose her. I couldn't.

I looked around the cabin and began to tear everything that Tasha had touched—from the walls to the couch, everywhere. I threw it all into the fire. She ruined everything. She single-handedly destroyed the beautiful marriage that Noah and I had built. I roared my anger to the roof, swinging a fist at a picture of a duck that she had taken and framed. Glass shattered around me, scattering in a shower of blood and glass.

I knelt down in the glass, defeated. I couldn't believe that this was happening. Blood pooled under my hands and around my knees. I couldn't even feel it for the hurricane that was raging in my soul.

At least one, maybe two hours, passed before the front door to the cabin opened and footsteps approached me. I didn't look up. I didn't make a move. I just kept kneeling in the glass and blood.

Noah was the first to speak up. "I think we should go sit down and have a conversation about it."

I couldn't look at her. Shame clouded over me in an angry storm, tearing my heart out.

"Duke, if you have an ounce of decency in your body, you will stand up and face this like a man. I have a long list of questions that deserve answers."

"Promise me you will still love me," was all I could get out. My body ached, but not nearly as much as my heart.

"I cannot promise anything at this point, Duke. You either get up and talk to me, or I walk out that door and never look back."

I heaved myself off the floor. Pain shot through my knees as the congealed blood burst open, spilling a fresh wave of crimson down my legs. I couldn't look at her. I kept my eyes down as I walked to the couch and sat down.

"Noah, I—"

"Nope. Don't even start," she said, her tone clipped. "I am going to lay down some rules for this conversation. First of all, I will get your entire honesty about everything. Second, you do not cut me off while I am talking and I will do the same for you. We both get a chance to say our share. Third, if I decide that I am going to cut your balls off and feed them to a Rover, I will do it and make you watch. Any questions?"

I shook my head.

"Good. Now, from the top, tell me EVERYTHING you have been lying about."

I took a deep breath. This was going to be very hard. I cursed myself for even lying to her in the first place. What did I hope would happen, huh? What did I think I would gain? I shifted my gaze from the dried blood on the backs of my knuckles and looked into her eyes. They were red from crying. Man, how could I have put her through this? She was totally right that she deserved the truth. Without a preamble, I jumped right in from the beginning.

I talked for an hour, maybe more. From the way I used to watch her at work, to the captain's briefing on the Rovers, to the fake wedding album, and the made-up story of loss. The sun had set, and a chill had crept into the cabin—more than just the frosty glares she shot at me from the other side of the couch. When I had finished my monologue, I bit my lip, waiting to hear my fate.

"Noah, please know that even though I screwed up big time, I really do love and adore you. I could never measure up to what you deserve in a husband, but I want to keep trying."

She hadn't said a word, made a sound, shed a tear, or broken eye contact the entire time. I couldn't read her face. I had no idea what she was going to say or do.

Finally, she wet her lips and sighed. The words she spoke were calm and conversational. It made everything cut deeper. "Duke, you have betrayed my trust in a way bigger than I thought possible. You have taken advantage of me, hurt me, lied to me, and, worst of all, married me under the pretense of loving me. You are lower than the man who tried to rape me. You are less human than the Rovers. You do not deserve to sleep under this roof for another night."

My world collapsed. Tears sprang to my eyes, and fire clawed at my throat. "I deserve that, but

Noah, please, let me fix this. Let me make this up to you."

If I thought I was angry when Tasha first arrived, I was mistaken. Noah stood, and I swear, the shadows grew darker as her words assailed me. "You cannot fix what you have broken! You cannot mend a heart that you have been blown apart! You cannot love someone who you can't even tell a simple truth to! Your shame knows no bounds. Your betrayal is unforgivable, Duke. You disgust me, and I wish I had never met you and your cheap-shot guilt trips!"

Her eyes blazed with fire. Even Bob shied away from her wrath. I could do nothing. This woman had bled for me, sacrificed for me, loved me unconditionally, and I had betrayed her. Me—I could not place this blame on anyone else.

She sank into the seat beside me, her fury spent. "Duke, why? Why did you even start lying?

Why didn't you tell me the truth from the start?"

Her eyes sparkled with unshed tears. "I just wanted you to need me. Noah, you are such a formidable, capable woman. You make Wonder Woman look like a simp. I knew I had nothing of value to offer you, so I lied about the Rovers. Once that was done, I couldn't get out of it, so I just carried on with it, hoping I could stay ahead of the story. Then when we got here, I had all of these things that I couldn't just explain without looking like a total dick, so I lied about them, too. Then one thing led to another, and then... well, here we are."

Noah just shook her head gently. "How could you possibly think that making up a story about your murdered wife and baby for sympathy would never come back to haunt you? There is only so much forgiveness I have in me, Timothy Duke. I don't think that I can..."

She stood up and, without another word, walked to the bedroom and shut the door. There have been very few times in my life when I have cried uncontrollably. Behind closed doors when my parents died, when my childhood dog died. This put all other tears to shame.

CHAPTER 35

NOAH

From the moment I shut the door, I knew my life was about to change once more. Right then, I hated Duke. I would be lying if I said I hadn't thought about shooting him. Rage and sorrow ripped through my body. I sat on the edge of the bed and let my tears flow. My arm was killing me, and it made a good excuse to cry. I could hear Duke out in the living room, howling in anguish. Good. He deserved to suffer. He deserved to be eaten by a Rover. He deserved to feel a bit of the pain that he caused me.

After Tasha had left, I sat among the leaves on the cold ground, thinking, trying to put the pieces together. I could hear Duke trashing the place while I tried to fill in the gaps. Maybe she was a twin? Maybe she had actually divorced him?

Now that I had the facts of the matter, I sat there, aching. It felt like my heart was gone. When my ex cheated on me, I felt pain, but not like this. My marriage was a sham; my love had been built on a sand foundation. I couldn't think straight. I pulled out a pill bottle from the bedside table and popped a few tablets. I stared at the bottle in my hand, letting the dark thoughts creep in.

I had seen death. I had seen monsters. I had seen the dark side of humanity. I had seen the world torn apart and people turn on each other like starving wolves.

So why did I have to see this, too? The perfect man that I had fallen in love with was a shadow. He was an idea hiding behind a gilded mask. He was nothing more than a paper prince. And I had fallen for it. Maybe I should just end it—call it quits.

I crawled into bed and rolled over to face the wall. I knew I would not sleep much, but I needed rest. No sooner had I wrapped up in the warm quilt than I smelled Duke's scent all around me, making me sob all over again. Tears streamed out, and my chest heaved. I cried until there were no more tears, and exhaustion took over. I fell into a deep, dark, and thankfully dreamless sleep.

The next morning, I awoke before the sun. My heart felt hollow, and my head ached, not to mention my arm. I thought about going back to sleep, but now that I was awake, the reality of the previous day began to bombard me. I listened for any sounds of Duke being up and about, but there was nothing. He must still be asleep.

I didn't want to see him; I didn't even want him in the cabin. Would I kick him out? Would I just leave? Would I try to move on as though nothing had happened?

I opened the door and walked to the bathroom. It was dark and cold, and I needed to pee. After I relieved myself, I stood outside the bathroom, lost in thought. I was not ready to face Duke yet. I could just get some water heating up and take a walk, clear my head. I sneaked past the couch where Duke was sleeping and tiptoed to the small kitchen as quietly as possible, filling the kettle and getting it going. I slipped my boots on my feet and slid into one of Duke's flannels. As much as I hated him right now, I needed the extra layer.

I slipped out the door silently, breathing in the cold, pre-dawn air, appreciating the golden hue beginning to grace the eastern sky. Bob joined me; his furry face was a picture of happiness. For a moment, I was jealous of Bob. He didn't know about my heartache or Duke's lies. I wanted that.

I could hear the telltale clicking of Rovers in the distance, their sounds echoing through the misty forest. I knew to stay close to the cabin in case they showed up again, though the idea of Duke coming out for his morning run made my nerves frayed. I needed to clear my head.

"Bob, what am I going to do?" I lamented. "Duke not only lied to me, he deceived me on so many levels, I don't think I can ever trust him again. I wanted so badly for him to be real, for a man to love me as purely as I thought he did. But it was all a lie."

"Not all of it," Duke's words surprised me.

I started, turned around and scanned the cabin front for him.

"Up here," he waved at me from the roof. I felt my face flush at him overhearing me talk to Bob.

"I, uh, thought you were still asleep," I said, avoiding his eyes.

"I couldn't sleep. Came out here for a chat with the Big Guy," he said, glancing up at the star-strewn sky.

"Yeah?" I asked, crossing my arms. "He talks any sense into you?"

I could hear Duke smile. "He's trying to."

"Well, good. Someone needs to." An awkward silence followed as we both wrestled with our thoughts. "So, what do we do now?"

"That is in your court, Noah. I don't want to pressure you or manipulate you. I know you are raw after yesterday."

I was quiet for a moment while I gathered my thoughts. "I think that I need to get some coffee and breakfast in me. Then I think we need to clean up the mess you made inside. Then we need to clean you up. I saw the blood, and I am certain your stubborn ass didn't clean it up."

He chuckled lightly. "No, I didn't. I'll get the coffee going." He stood and began to descend the roof. As he walked past, he reached out to take my hand. I shied away from it, turning away from him. He took the hint and kept walking.

He worked on making coffee while I began to make breakfast. We don't have much variety these days, but rabbit and rice could make a good breakfast if you are hungry enough. Which I was. We ate in total silence. Bob seemed to realize that something wasn't right and ate his food quickly, then went off to the bedroom to sleep.

I could feel Duke's eyes on me as I cleaned up the dishes and began to sweep up the broken glass. I couldn't look at him yet. I still needed to think through what I was going to say to him. In any other situation, I would dump him, walk away and never look back. But this wasn't a normal situation. We relied on each other for survival. I knew that he had my back. I never doubted that, but could I forgive the lies and carry on with him as my husband? Just my partner? Just my survival roommate?

I felt Duke walk up behind me. I closed my eyes as his scent wafted over me. I wanted to punch him in the face and kiss him all at the same time. My heart hurt so deeply. His fingers gently, tentatively, grazed the sides of my arms, sending goose bumps up and down my spine. I didn't pull away, though I wanted to. "Noah, I know that I screwed up. I know that what I did was unforgivable. I wish that I could take it all back and start from the beginning with you. I would do it all over and do it right this time. But I cannot take it back. All I can do is spend every day for as long as I live, making it up to you if you will let me."

A jagged sob fought its way out of my throat. I tried to swallow it, which only sent a shudder through my body. I dropped the broom to the floor and sank down beside it. Once my knees hit the floor, the storm broke the dam. I sobbed with rage, fear, anguish, terror, uncertainty, heartache, and betrayal. Duke dropped next to me and pulled me into his arm, drawing me to his strong, broad chest. I resisted a little but abandoned the fight quickly. I needed comfort, and even if I wanted to stab this man's eyes out, I loved him.

I pounded a fist on his chest and sobbed harder. He held me gently, stroking my back with one hand and gripping my hair at the base of my neck with the other. "Let it out, baby. Let it out. Do what you need, whatever you need."

I looked up into his beautiful, smokey eyes and gave a small nod. Sitting up and pulling away from his chest, I reached over and decked him as hard as I could.

He yelped in shock and pain as I shook out my fist. Punching someone in the face is painful for both parties; don't let the movies lie to you about it. I met his gaze. Duke removed his hand from his bloody nose and wrapped his arms around me again. I punched him again for good measure. He groaned, closed his eyes, and took a moment to gather himself before looking me in the eyes again, giving a gentle nod. I fell into him, pounding on his chest again.

"Fight me back, Duke!" I yelled into his shirt. "Tell me I am crazy, call me a psycho, drop me on the floor and storm away!"

"I deserve whatever you want to dish out and more. I have no leg to stand on in this fight."

"Just stop! Yell at me! Something!" I pounded his chest again.

His only response was, "I love you. I will never stop loving you."

"You're a monster who doesn't deserve love! I hate you! I hate you!"

"I love you, Noah."

"Stop saying that!" I banged my head against his chest this time. "Stop loving me! I can't hate you if you don't fight back! You need to be a jerk so I can keep being angry! Just stop acting…. PERFECT!!"

I collapsed in a puddle of anguish and fury. He was a rock, a gentle, peaceful, loving rock. He just held me and let me fall apart. I was so furious that he didn't try to defend his actions. I was furious that he didn't try to make me the bad guy. He knew he was wrong, and he owned up to it. He wanted to make amends which pissed me off so much more.

I don't know how long we sat there. I woke up suddenly covered in dried blood, tears, and probably snot. Duke sat holding me gently, cradling me close to his chest. I looked up in his eyes.

"I love you, Noah," he whispered gently. A tear slid down his cheek. He looked so weary.

All the fight left me. I sighed and leaned into him. "I know, Duke."

"Can I get you into bed to rest? I will finish cleaning up the mess."

I nodded, expecting him to walk me to the other room. Instead, he stood up and picked me up gently, carried me to the bed and laid me down. He didn't try to kiss me, didn't try to pressure me. Man, I hated him right now.

"Duke!" I called as he turned his back to walk away. Our eyes met, and I sniffled. "Please sit with me."

Duke, looking torn and chewing on his lip, decided to do as I asked. He sat next to me and sighed, and I noticed his nose had dried blood on it, and one of his eyes looked like it was probably black. I thought of all the stitches, gunshot wounds, claw slashes, and teeth marks all over his body. I recalled all the misadventures we had faced and survived together. I thought of how he had saved my life on more than one occasion. How could he have faced all that and not been honest with me about the most basic things? Why the web of lies?

Finally, I worked out the words I needed to say.

"Duke, I love you. But I cannot trust you anymore. I don't know what else you could have been lying to me about all this time, and I don't want to find out. I know we should stay together for survival, but I don't think that I can live under this roof with you. I have to go. I think the sooner I leave, the better."

"Noah, please!" Duke dropped off the side of the bed and knelt beside me. "Noah, let me go in your place. If you cannot live with me, I respect that. I hate it, but I will not fight you on it. But please let me go instead. You need to be able to stay safe. I need to know that you will be okay."

I looked into his eyes. He had tears threatening to fall again, and it broke my heart so much more.

"This is your cabin, Duke. You should stay here, and I will figure something out."

"No, you won't. You will die out there in a day. I will go in your place."

"What makes you think you will survive longer than I will?"

He was silent for a moment. His eyes dropped, and he let out a sigh. "I know I won't survive a day out there, either. But I promised that I will love you until I die, and I mean to keep that promise, even if I only get one more day. Knowing that you will be safe and can survive is all I need. I will pack and leave as soon as I am ready."

With that, he stood and walked away.

I choked on a sob, my mind swimming. Was he really ready to walk out that door and face certain death because of me?

Who was the betrayer now? The thought strangled me. I sprang out of bed and ran to Duke. I tackled him in the living room, and we crashed on the floor hard. "Screw you, Timothy Duke."

Then I devoured his face. My lips struck him with all the anger and bitterness that I was holding, and he kissed it away. My hands yanked at his clothes as I searched for his body. His eyes widened as he pulled away from me, and a look of shock spread across his face. I snarled at him, pulling his face back up to mine while my other hand raked his muscular chest with fury. He replied in kind, his hands grabbing me by the hips and pulling me tightly against him. I groaned as his lips left mine to hungrily taste my neck. In a quick movement, he ripped my shirt clean off, the pain of my still-healing arm shooting through me, but I didn't care. I sat up on his hips and yanked at his shirt, which he struggled to remove, never breaking eye contact. His eyes were dark and stormy, full of desire. I bit my lip as his eyes trailed down my body to my bra, which he quickly removed.

He wrapped his arms around me, pulling my body close, his lips caressing and tongue tasting my flesh, groaning with pleasure and need. I rocked my hips against him, his arousal putting pressure on my sensitive parts, sending waves of pleasure through me. He reached down, grabbed my backside, and guided it up and down, getting a smooth rhythm going. I forced his arms away with a flick of my hands, and he met my eyes, his head tilting slightly in question.

"If you want me to ever be able to forgive you," I said in a ragged voice that dripped with need as I stood over him and slid my jeans down, "You are going to have to apologize to me in every way you can think of."

I stood over him, naked. He lay below me, eyes locked on mine. "Yes, my queen."

He sat up faster than I could blink and buried his face between my legs. The shock nearly knocked me over, but his strong arms kept me upright. He turned my body and set me down on the couch, continuing to lick and tease. I dug my fingers into his hair and held on tight as he took me for a ride that I had never been on before. It didn't take long for the waves of fireworks to shoot through my body, causing every muscle to jerk involuntarily.

He stood, cracked his neck, and said, "That's one," Then he dropped his pants. Duke grabbed me and spun me around so quickly that I was seeing stars, but not nearly as much as when he plunged into me. A gasp escaped my lips as he let out a throaty roar. His thrusts were hard and fast, desperate even. It didn't take long for both of us to reach the peak as we screamed each other's names.

We collapsed on the couch, heaving for breath. After a few minutes, once we came down from the high, he winked at me. "Two," he said. I lifted my middle finger at him. "If you insist."

He picked me up and carried me to the bed for the second time that day, but this time for a very different reason.

CHAPTER 36

t was close to dusk when we emerged from our bedroom. We had spent the entire day in bed together. To be honest, I was incredibly happy. We had a lot that we needed to work through, but I knew we could manage. We made dinner and then sat together on the couch to eat it. Bob looked rather annoyed at us, but I was sure he would forgive us once we fed him. Wrapped in Duke's oversized sweatshirt and no pants, leaning against his chest, I felt like we could take on the world. We had faced a relationship-shattering issue and came out together.

Duke stared into the fire, his fingers tracing swirls on the skin of my leg. "Duke?" I asked.

"Hmm?"

"Would you really have gone? Would you really have packed a bag and left, knowing you would most likely not survive?"

He was silent for a moment, taking a deep sigh, thinking about his answer. "I was ready to walk out that door no matter the consequences to me. My plan was to get to Papa Ray's and let him know what was going on so he could keep an eye on you, then just do my best until the Rovers got me."

"So even though you would probably die, you still wanted to make sure I was taken care of?"

"Always, Noah. After the last time, I left you and that scumbag attacked you, I swore I would never leave you unprotected again." He wrapped his arms around me and kissed the top of my head. I snuggled into his chest and closed my eyes. I don't know how much time passed as we watched the fire and felt contentment rolling over us before Bob started growling deep in his throat.

Duke's body tensed as we both held our breath. We had been blessed not to have an encounter with the Rovers for a while. I guess we were overdue.

I jumped up, dashed to the bedroom and grabbed both of our guns while Duke sneaked to the front door to look out the window. I joined him, handed over his gun, and checked my own for bullet count—full mag.

"How many?" I whispered.

"I can't see any, but it is totally dark out. No eyes reflecting, so that's good."

A loud crash in the bedroom made me shriek. I whipped around as Duke jumped in front of me, protectively holding me back with his arm. I held my pistol out, solid with a good base like Duke had taught me. "Stay behind me," he said in a rough whisper. I followed him, step by step, just like we had done a thousand times. The bedroom was dark, and I could feel a cold breeze coming in along my bare legs.

We were halfway there when the front door banged open with a dark figure blocking the exit. I barely had time to spin around when

Duke cried out in pain and fell to the floor. "Duke!" I screamed, dropping to his side.

"Like fish in a barrel, baby, just like you said!" a familiar voice called out from the bedroom doorway.

"Told you! Hey, sweetheart! You miss me?"

My blood ran cold as I turned to the figure in the doorway. Ricky stood inside with a shotgun pointed at Duke. I lifted my gun to face him when a cold metal barrel pressed to the back of my head. "There will be none of that, little thing! Drop it!"

I glared at Ricky, dropped the gun and laced my fingers behind my head.

"Ricky, take what you want, and you had better be gone before Duke comes around. He will tear you apart with his bare hands!" I spat at the man.

"I don't think so, Sister!" the woman behind me sneered, pressing the barrel harder against my skull.

"I am going to take what I want. And this time, there won't be anyone to stop me."

Bob had been lurking in the shadows. Once Ricky took another step closer to me, he attacked. Jumping at the vile creature disguised as a man, Bob filled his mouth with a chunk of Ricky's arm. A shotgun blast blew out of the gun, filling the air with pressure, an ear-splitting noise, and the acrid smell of gunpowder. I dove for my gun and grabbed it, flipping it on my back to cover the mystery woman who held me hostage.

My breath caught in my throat as I came face-to-face with the last person I expected to see.

Molly's look of shock was just as evident as mine. She didn't lower her gun but relaxed the grip a little. In my shock, I couldn't process the chaos around us. I was brought back by the sound of Bob's howl of pain. I looked away from Molly for a moment to see if my dog was okay. Ricky had beat his head with the butt of his shotgun and turned the thing to shoot.

"No!" I screamed out. Ricky froze and looked at me, giving me a wicked smile.

"What are you even going to do about it?" he taunted, then pulled the trigger.

The rage of a thousand exploding suns tore through me. My adrenaline surged strong enough to launch a spacecraft. I switched my gun to my good hand and emptied the clip.

Ricky's face showed shock for a moment, then nothingness as his carcass hit the ground, a grotesque marionette with his strings cut.

I jumped to my feet and whipped around to face Molly. Her face was ghostly pale, the whites of her eyes visible all around her irises, and her mouth slack as she stared at the bloody mess that she had brought into my home.

Fire burned in my veins as I lunged at her. She was on the floor for a moment, trying to fight me off as I choked the life out of her. Her gaze was terrified. I squeezed until my hands hurt.

"Noah, let her go," Duke's voice commanded me. I ignored him as I watched her life fade.

Suddenly, rough hands gripped my arms, prying them away from my victim. Molly coughed and choked, rolling on her side and gasping for breath. I turned to face Duke, my heart bursting. Pain, as I had never known, ripped through my body, and I screamed a war cry like none had ever heard before. Duke took the gun from Molly and turned to check Ricky. He didn't spend much time on the bastard. I sobbed as I stood, practically falling on my face as I stumbled over to my best friend. For the second time, I looked at his beautiful, silky fur covered in blood. He didn't move; he didn't make a sound.

Half of his torso was missing.

Duke grabbed me roughly and turned me away.

"Don't look. Noah, go sit down."

I fought my way out of his arms and fell to my knees beside my dog. Duke dropped down next to me as I screamed. I screamed out until my throat was raw and my breath was gone. Duke just let me. He wrapped an arm around my ribs, lifted me to my feet and guided me to the sofa. He lowered me gently, leaning me back and covering me with a blanket as the shock set in. I began to shiver and convulse uncontrollably.

He left me sitting there, added more wood to the fire, and then walked away. I heard his voice talking, but he sounded far away and echoey. “So, Molly, is it? You are going to have some explaining to do to my wife and me. I suggest you sit on that seat right there and don’t move a muscle. I won’t pull.

Noah off of you a second time.”

Molly made a whimper and must have found a seat to sit on. I just stared into the fire, not feeling anything. I was no longer cold, no longer sad, no longer alive as far as I could feel.

Duke came up to me a while later, knelt down before me, took my hands in his and kissed my palms. “Baby? You want to go to bed? I cleaned up the glass in the bedroom and got clean bedding put on.”

My eyes drifted to his. I shook my head gently and stared back into the flames. “Is he gone?”

Duke swallowed hard and dropped his head for a moment before giving a gentle nod. “Yeah, baby. He’s gone.”

“Can we bury him?”

“Of course, we will bury him. I will dig the hole and first light, and we can put him to rest together.”

I nodded as tears fell blandly from my eyes.

“Would you please go get some sleep?”

I looked into his eyes again. “Not until I talk to Molly.”

Duke looked conflicted, his eyebrows furrowing. "I don't know if that is a good idea for tonight.

You are still in shock and need some time to process what just happened."

"If I don't talk to her, I will need to kill her to fill this hole in my heart, and I don't think you want more blood in here," I said, my voice sounding hollow even to my own ears.

Duke sighed, lowered his eyes, and reached out to grab my hand. "Noah, there is no amount of violence that will ever fill a hole in your heart. You can't fill a void with more void. You have to fill it with something real." His eyes met mine as he squeezed my hand. "You have to fill it with love. We can talk to her, but remember who you are." He closed his eyes for a moment and whispered a silent prayer over me before standing up, then lifted me with him.

Once he saw I was steady on my feet, he led me over to the bathroom and coaxed me into washing my hands and face. He then turned around and led me back to the living room. I stole a glance at where Bob lay, his body covered in a white sheet with an angry, scarlet rose of blood blooming underneath. Ricky's body was gone; Duke must have thrown him out for the Rovers.

Once I was seated on the couch again, Duke looked into the kitchen where Molly was sitting. "Come here," he said in a commanding voice. Molly shuffled over to us, her eyes wide with fear as she looked back and forth between us. She had violent bruises forming on her neck.

I took a breath, closed my eyes, and tried to center my thoughts. Rage was trying to get the best of me, but Duke's words echoed in my head: *You can't fill a void with more void. Remember who you are.*

CHAPTER 37

I opened my eyes and lifted my chin. "Why don't you sit down, Molly?"

Her eyes shot to the other side of the sofa, back to mine, then to the door, and finally to Duke. She was cornered, and she knew it.

I sighed and pointed my chin at the couch. "Sit."

This time, she did, sitting only on the edge of the seat. Her leg began to bounce idly as soon as the weight was off it. For the first time, I really had a chance to see her. She had lost weight in the past few months, but I think we all had. Her hair was thin and stringy, her eyes hollow and bloodshot. Even though it was late fall, she had on a thin hoodie and ripped-up jeans with holey sneakers. Was she just in such rough shape from The Fall, or was she strung out?

Duke shifted his position to stand behind me, laying an encouraging hand on my shoulder. I looked up at him, and he gave me a gentle nod.

Looking back to Molly, I started where I thought I had to. "Molly, what happened to you after the fall?"

She looked at me with shock on her face. After a moment, she collected herself and found her voice. "I evacuated with my daddy, but he didn't make it. Them Rovers got him less than a week on the road. We were at my pawpaw's lake home, and they got us. I… I ran away as they ate him up."

I reached over and placed a hand on hers. "I'm so sorry, Molly. I know he was all you had."

She shrugged. "He was, but I wasn't sorry to see him go after everything he did to me over the years. He was mean, and he was a drunk, and he… He liked to watch me shower."

My stomach lurched. I gave her hand a gentle squeeze and asked her to continue.

"I was on the road on my own. I took Daddy's car, but I ran out of gas after a couple hours and had to try to make it on foot. I made it back to town and went back to the bar. I figured if the Rovers had already took everybody they were going to, then it might be safe to hang out, right? When I got to the bar, it was still standing, so I let myself in and locked up behind me. The power had been off for a while, so most of the food had gone bad, but there was some stuff to eat. I was sad and lonely, so I started drinking. When I got drunk, I didn't care about food, so I drank even more. I don't know how long passed before a few fellas came to the door looking to loot the place. I didn't have a way to defend it, so I let them in and tried to cooperate. They traded sex and booze for some food they had and a bag of pills. I don't really know what they were, but they helped me forget all the bad stuff and sleep.

"I basically survived by staying drunk and high enough that I didn't need to eat much and sleep all the time. Sometimes, guys would come and offer trades with me. The trades usually involved sex, but it got me the food I needed to keep going.

"Then one day about a month ago, Ricky…" Her eyes began to fill with tears. She let out a shuddering breath, barely holding herself together. "Ricky came to the bar. He took one look at me and said that I was the most beautiful woman he had ever seen. He was sweet; he didn't just screw me like the other guys did. He was nice and gentle about it, even asking me if I enjoyed it. Ricky was the first decent man that I had met in a long time, and I fell in love with him."

She could no longer hold her sadness in. Tears flowed freely from her eyes, and her body curled up into itself in anguished sobs.

I leaned over and took her hand again, giving it a gentle squeeze. This woman had had a rough life made terrible by so many abusive men that a few gentle words had overwhelmed her, even when those words had been spoken by a would-be rapist.

When she composed herself, she continued. "Ricky took me away from there. He had some provisions, and we were in love. We found some abandoned cars that hadn't been siphoned yet and took to the road. We turned into Bonnie and Clyde, stopping wherever we found people and robbing them blind while they slept. It may have been wrong, but why should they get to have everything as we have to starve? That's what he told me, anyway. And I was always so high. It was just a rush to see how much we could get away with.

"A few days ago, Ricky told me about this couple who had done him wrong, cheated him out of what was rightfully his and kicked his ass just for fun before throwing him out to the Rovers. He said it was time to pay them a visit and take back what was rightfully his. We parked away down the dirt road and walked through the woods to get here. Ricky told me about how dog whistles keep the Rovers away, so we always used them when we were on a job. He told me that I needed to break through the window to let you know I was here so he could come in the front.

"And then you killed him." Her voice grew angry and full of spittle. "You killed the man who loved me, the first good man I ever met in my life. He was going to marry me when this was all over and take me to Hawaii for a honeymoon!"

She was clearly delusional. The drugs, the abuse, all of it had wrecked this poor girl. My mind urged me to tell her off, but my heart said to let her keep her fantasy. She had had it rough enough without knowing what that psychopath was about.

I sighed and looked into her eyes. "Molly, I wish you had come under better circumstances. We would have helped you and shared what we could. I am sorry about what happened to Ricky, but you had to know that trying to take advantage of people was going to end badly. I have to talk to my husband about what we are going to do. You can sleep here tonight, but if you even think about trying to rob us, we will take your dog whistle and throw you out the door. Got it?"

She seemed to ponder this for a moment before giving a quick nod.

"Good. Now, we need to go to bed and try to get some sleep after this horrific day. You should sleep, too. You can have our bedroom as there is not anything of value in there for you to steal. If you are still here in the morning, we will happily help you before you leave. If you choose to leave the way you came, that is fine, too."

She nodded again and slunk out of the room, closing the door behind her.

Duke left his spot behind me and knelt in front of me, cradling my face in his hands. "Noah, that was an amazing amount of self-control, and I am so proud of you. But do you think it was a good idea not to tell her about Ricky and what he really was?"

"She has had enough trauma in her life. She is so strung out she won't survive long on her own.

Even with provisions, her time is limited. I want to let her live the rest of her time out in her fantasy."

"You have a good heart, my love, but I think you need to listen to your brain on this one. She is dangerous. She feels like we wronged her by killing Ricky, even though they were actively assaulting us at the time."

"I know that, but let me have this. I need to fill the void with something real."

Duke clenched his teeth and lowered his eyes. "I hate it when you do that."

“Do what?” I deadpanned.

“Let’s try to get some sleep,” he huffed. “Tomorrow is a long day.”

I nodded as my eyes welled with tears again—so much death. I was so tired of it. “Let’s just go to sleep,” I managed to whisper. Duke nodded, climbed up next to me, wrapped me in his arms and kissed my neck gently.

“I love you, Noah,” he whispered into the silence. It was peace in the eye of a storm. My heart was raw and bleeding for Bob, tormented over Molly’s story, and still bruised from Duke’s shocking admissions of the days prior, but we were going to be okay. We had been through so much and I knew it wasn't over, but as long as we had each other, we could continue to face each day, each fight. I fell into a pensive sleep with those thoughts swirling behind my exhausted eyes.

I was startled awake by Duke shifting his weight, leaning heavily onto me and letting out a deep, ragged breath. He coughed out a wet sound and gasped.

Shocked, I sat up and turned over, looking at him to see what was wrong. The woman standing behind him in front of the couch was silhouetted by the dying fire, making my mind reel, trying to put pieces together.

Then I saw the knife in her hand and blood pooling on the floor at her feet.

I jumped up and screamed, "Duke, get up, it's Molly! You were right!"

But Duke didn't move.

My eyes darted from Molly to the still form of my husband on the couch. There was blood on his back.

I looked back at Molly, horror tearing through me at the speed of rage. I lunged at her, not caring that she was holding a knife. I knocked her back to the floor and wrestled the bloody knife from her hand. Pressing the blade against her throat, I sobbed, "Why? Why would you do this?!"

She shot me a defiant glare and spat back, "You took mine; now I took yours."

"But we tried to help you! We gave you a place to sleep! We tried to show you mercy!"

She laughed wickedly. "You think it is mercy making me live without the man I love? Well, I guess you get to find out next." She lifted her head and yanked her neck along the blade, ripping open the flesh and spilling yet more blood in the place that had once been our safe haven.

CHAPTER 38

I stared at the warm, blood-covered corpse on the floor. I would have continued staring in shock until it turned cold if Duke's heaving voice hadn't snapped me out of it.

"Noah," he said, his voice sounding hollow and wet.

I jumped off of Molly and lunged toward Duke, trying to assess the damage to his back. The knife had gone in deep, piercing right through his ribs. She had actually stabbed a sleeping man in the back. Vomit threatened to come up as I tried to staunch the bleeding.

"Noah, stop. Help me sit up," Duke commanded.

"Duke, no, you have to lie still. You need to… I don't know what to do!" I was panicked.

"Please," Duke said again, coughing blood onto the couch in front of him. "I can't move enough to sit up, and I need to look at you."

Fear took over, and I started to sob. "I can take you to the compound! I bet they have a doctor there! They can get you fixed up in no time! Daisy! Or David! They can fix you!"

"Help me," he implored, his voice filled with desperation.

I reached across him and grabbed him by the ribs, lifting as gently as I was able with his assistance. I managed to get him sitting up and stable with a cloth on the wound to hold the blood in. I was about to run for the first aid kit when Duke's hand snatched my wrist.

"Sit, please, Noah. I need you to sit."

I sat beside him and wrapped his strong, calloused hand in mine. Looking into his eyes, I tried to smile. "We've got this, babe. I will get you there."

He gently shook his head. "No, sweetheart. This is it. I need to look at you again before I go."

"Shut up, Duke. You're not going to take yourself to the compound. I have to drive. You aren't going anywhere without me."

"Baby, look at me," he said, his voice growing weak and thready. He gently squeezed my hand.

"I gotta go home. I won't pull through this one."

"Don't you dare say that to me, Timothy Duke, or so help me, I will divorce you!"

He cracked a small smile and reached up to brush my face. "I will always love you. Someday, long in the future, when it is your turn to come home, I will be waiting for you. I will be ready for you."

Tears streamed down my face as I sobbed and shook my head. "No, we are going to get through this, Duke. Let me get your shoes, and we can be on the way."

He looked into my eyes, his focus wavering. "I'm so glad I was able to keep my promise to love you until my dying day."

Then his head tipped to the side, and his chest stopped moving.

Pain tore through me as I started to shake him. "Duke! No, Duke! Come back! I can't do this alone! I need you! I love you!"

Sobs ripped my throat to shreds, and I screamed out in rage and sorrow. My head fell to his chest, and I placed his still hand on my back, clutching his torso to me with all the strength I had. "Come back, Duke. Come back," I begged. "I love you, too."

I cried until I had no more tears left, and my throat burned like fire. Then I fell asleep, clutching my husband's body.

When I awoke, it was to a scene of horror and blood.

The sun was shining through the window on the front door, promising a lovely fall day to dig graves for my heart.

I pulled myself out of Duke's cold, stiff arms and began to cry all over again. He was truly gone. I had hoped that when I awoke, he would, too—with a smile, a kiss, and a cup of coffee.

Never again.

The emptiness I felt was like a black hole, pulling me into myself to leave behind a hollowed-out shell.

I would have wallowed in my sorrow if I could have afforded to. I couldn't today. Today, I had funerals to attend.

I stood and almost tripped over Molly's cold body, stuck to the floor by her own blood pooled around her head. Her cold eyes stared at me, mocking me. I turned away from her and looked toward the sheet that was draped over Bob's still form.

I had lost everything. Everything I loved, everyone in the world who mattered to me, was dead.

What was the point of trying to keep going? I had nothing to live for now. I wasn't spectacular at anything useful. I wasn't a medic, or an artist, or farmer, or anything that would help to rebuild the world. Did they even need me anymore?

I looked around at what had once been a happy home. One horrible night took everything beautiful away. The skin and flesh of a family had been stripped down to charred bones and rotting marrow.

I slowly walked over to the shelf near the front door where Duke kept our firearms and grabbed his gun. Then I turned, walked back to the couch and sat next to my husband one last time. I maneuvered his arm around me and leaned into him, seeking warmth but finding only death.

I cocked the gun and held it to my head. I felt that I should say a few words as this was our funeral. "Dearly beloved, we are gathered to honor the lives of Timothy and Noah Duke and their beloved dog, Bob. This family had its problems and had the scars to prove it." I looked over at Duke's gray skin and reached up to touch the scar on his face. "But they loved each other fiercely, knowing what was at stake if they ever gave up."

I closed my eyes and took a deep breath. "No wife ever loved her husband like Noah did. He was loving, gentle, dangerous, smart, kind, and generous. And Bob was the world's best boy. There was never a dog known to mankind that was as clever and protective as Bob, and he will be sorely missed."

I opened my eyes and took one final deep breath.

"Goodbye."

Then, I pulled the trigger.

CHAPTER 39

o tunnel of light, no grand heavenly welcome party, no streets of gold—nothing. Just a cabin full of blood and the click of an empty chamber.

Anger filled me then.

I jumped up and kicked Molly's corpse in the face, then strode outside. I grabbed the gun and shook it at the sky.

"Is this what you wanted, God? Huh? Having a good laugh up there?! You stole everything from me! You stole the love of my life! You stole my dog! You stole the world as we know it and filled it with stupid freaking monsters! And then, all part of your sick joke, YOU stole the BULLETS out of my GUN!!!!"

I let out a war cry and threw the gun into the air as far as I could. It fell harmlessly on the ground a few yards away. Racked with sobs, I dropped to my knees.

"I have always believed in You. I have always tried to follow you. I went to church. I prayed, and I read my Bible. Why did you do all of this to me?"

The wind picked up and some autumn leaves danced by like carefree faeries on the way to a party. I watched them for a moment before my eyes fell on some movement at the edge of the clearing.

I sighed. Rovers. Of course, Rovers. They could probably smell the blood and death lingering in the cabin from miles away. Slowly, I got up and watched the movement for a while. The Rovers stayed in the shadows, but I could faintly hear the telltale clicking sounds they made.

I thought about walking right over there and letting them eat me. That would not be as fast as a bullet, but it would be effective nonetheless. Instead, I walked over to the shed and opened the door. I stepped into the dark interior and looked around for the shovel. Not spotting it right away, I walked to the back wall and began searching under Duke's winter gear he had stored in there. I found the shovel buried beneath a coat and some coveralls. As I picked it up to carry out, something caught my eye. I moved the coat a little further and found a yellow piece of paper tacked to the wall. I leaned closer and took a sharp breath when I saw it had my name on it.

I pulled the tack out from the wall and put the paper in my pocket. I wasn't ready to read it yet; I had something I needed to do first.

Walking outside to the east side of the cabin, I thrust a shovel into the dirt and began to dig a grave.

Digging a grave is hard. First of all, you have to dig very deep, and second of all, being wracked with grief makes it hard to do much. Third, when you have an arm that was pretty much destroyed by monsters, you have to work twice as hard not to damage it more.

Thankfully, the Rovers stayed away while I worked, one scoop at a time, deeper, wider and longer. I dug until I had blisters and continued digging until they bled. Then, I dug even more.

The sun was high in the sky, already beginning its descent for the day when I finished. I climbed out with much difficulty and took to the next task.

I opened the cabin door and was hit with the smell of rot. Even in the cooler fall weather, it didn't take long. I washed my hands and wrapped them in strips of cloth to protect them a little. The next tasks were by far the hardest things I have ever had to do in my life.

I would rather have dug another hundred graves than to put the love of my life into one. I started with Duke, tipping his body forward on my shoulder and lowering him gently to the floor. Once there, I had to kick Molly's body out of the way and then pull Duke by his armpit toward the door.

"Wake up, Duke," I whispered the entire way. "Please wake up and tell me I don't have to do this. Please don't make me say goodbye."

He didn't wake up. I dragged him out the door and around the cabin, where I rolled him into the dark, ugly pit. His body hit with a sickening smack, his arm lying under him at an odd angle. I couldn't leave him like that, so I carefully climbed in and lowered myself to the bottom. I moved and adjusted him so he lay flat on his back, arms crossed over his cold, still heart. Taking a deep breath, I climbed back out and returned to the cabin for Bob. He was heavy, but I was able to carry my sweet boy over to the gravesite and roll him in next to Duke.

I was covered in dirt, blood, and sweat. I wanted to run away as fast as I could and never look back. I wanted to climb in with them and let nature take its course. Grief overtook me, and I dropped to my knees beside the pit, sobbing. I lay down and rested my head on the pile of dirt, looking down into the hole at them.

A scratching sound caught me off guard, and I whipped my head up to look behind me. There stood a Rover, not a dozen yards away.

I should have been scared. I should have cried out and run for the safety of the cabin. I should have made a loud noise to try to scare it away.

But I was tired and broken. I lay my head back down, looking back at Duke and Bob.

I could hear the Rover approaching; I could even smell it. I sighed as I prepared to meet my Maker, not even caring that it was going to hurt to be ripped apart and eaten.

The pain never came. Instead, the Rover approached me, looking down in the grave with me, clicking. I looked at it sadly and then looked back at Duke.

"That's my husband, Duke, and my dog, Bob. They were killed by monsters, but not the kind I was fearing would take them," I told the Rover. It shifted its gaze to me and tilted its head. It didn't start eating my face, so I continued. "We were in love. Duke and I made a great team. We had so many crazy things happen over the past few months that it feels like we have lived a lifetime together," I reflected aloud and looked back down at Duke and sighed. "We loved each other."

The Rover looked back and forth between Duke and me, seemingly curious about what was going on. Then, the world shifted, and something I never imagined could possibly happen took place right in front of my eyes. The Rover tipped its head back and let out a long, moaning howl. It was haunting and full of sorrow, yet beautiful and alive. When the howl ceased, the Rover looked at me and opened his mouth.

"Love e'ch-ther," it said in a voice so gravelly that I couldn't be sure that it actually spoke rather than made sounds that I put meaning to.

I stared at it, then nodded, pointing to Duke. "We love each other."

The Rover nodded and reached his long arm down to touch the side of the female torso. "Love e'ch-ther," it said again. I looked at them and realized what it meant. This Rover knew that we were mated and that I had lost him. And that I was grieving. Not only that, it seemed the Rover was mourning my loss with me.

I just stared in disbelief at the strangeness of it all. After a while, I began to push dirt in the hole. I couldn't watch as my love disappeared beneath the earth, and I needed it just to be done. I needed closure. The Rover watched for a moment, then reached down and began to push dirt in the hole with me. I smiled at it. "Thank you," I said, unsure how much the monster understood. It just kept pushing dirt until the hole was filled. I stood up and stared at the mound of dirt, wondering if the Rover was now going to eat me.

After a while, the Rover turned and walked back to the trees, disappearing in the fading light.

I watched it go, curious about what had just happened, but I knew my work was not yet finished. I still had another body to get rid of. This one would not get a grave.

I walked back into the cabin and approached the corpse that Molly had left on the floor of my home. Her blank stare seemed to follow me everywhere. Her final words echoed through my head and my heart. *You think it is mercy making me live without the man I love? Well, I guess you get to find out next.*

I knelt beside her and looked at her face, trying to remember the scared, abused, pimped-out girl who had been crying in the kitchen of the bar just months ago. She had wanted to be a vet but died a strung-out murderer. How many other people that were still alive had a similar story?

It was difficult to drag her body outside, though not as much as Duke's. I dragged her to the tree line and left her there for the Rovers. I didn't want to attract attention, but they would smell the death and blood either way. It seemed prudent to just leave her where they could easily find her, and then, hopefully, they would leave me alone.

Once back in the cabin, I looked around. There was gore everywhere and a rather large hole in the floor from the shotgun blast that had taken away my Bob. I also hadn't eaten anything in over 24 hours, and I needed to get the blood out of my hair.

There was just too much to focus on. I needed to keep myself busy, or I would collapse into despair, which oddly seemed like a great idea right about then. The best place to start seemed to be food. I washed my hands the best I could with the blisters and sores, then opened the cupboards to see what we had. Well, what I had left. I stared into the abyss of the cabinet, lost in my grief, with thoughts of Duke floating around my mind.

I would never be kissed by him again. He would never walk up behind me and wrap his warm, strong arms around me again. I would never have Bob's cold nose stuck in my face to tell me good morning again.

I was alone.

"Knock it off, Noah. Pull it together. You are not done yet. You get to grieve later," I said aloud to myself, refocusing on the food in the cabinet. Nothing looked good, though I knew I desperately needed to eat something. I closed my eyes and grabbed a can, opening the pop-top with out looking and grabbing a spoon to dig in.

It was cherry pie filling. Tears fell anew as I thought of Duke and the goofy face he made whenever I broke into a can of it. It was a sugar-filled heartache meal that soothed my soul.

After finishing, I began the cleanup process. Duke and I had a little left in the way of cleaning supplies, so I had to make do with what was available—mostly water and bleach. The process took me far into the night, and by the time I finished, I had a large pile of bloodied rags that would need to be washed the following day. Maybe I would burn them. I could decide that later.

For now, I needed to sleep. I walked into our bedroom and looked at the bed. It looked so cozy and warm, but I wasn't sure I would be able to climb into it. It would smell like Duke, and I knew it.

Steeling myself from the pain, I pulled back the covers and climbed in, pulling the quilt up to my chin. Taking a deep breath of Duke's scent, a sob shuddered from my chest.

I fell asleep crying again, and certainly not for the last time.

CHAPTER 40

I woke the next day to the smell of death and bleach. Simultaneously, my stomach craved food, and I felt the urge to vomit. The sun's light poked through the cracks in the boarded-up window, promising another beautiful and horrible day.

I made my way to the kitchen and stared at the hole in the floor near the front door. That would be my project today. I would fix that after eating. I opened the cupboard, grabbed the first thing I saw and walked outside with it, not caring what it was but knowing I needed strength.

I hadn't intended to go to the grave, but I found myself there anyway. I sat down gently next to the disturbed soil and cried; the open can of chili sat next to me, forgotten.

"Good morning," I said through the tears. "I wish you were here with me. I could really use someone to share this can of chili with me."

No one replied.

I sighed and looked up at the blue sky. Happy, silver-lined clouds floated by, mocking my grief with their freedom. "How could you do this to me?" I asked God again. He hadn't answered the last time, but maybe this time He would. "I mean, what did I do to deserve this? I was a Christian, I followed you, I trusted that you had a plan for my life and what did you do? You took everything from me. I had a job and a home. I had a mother who loved me. I had the best dog ever. I met the most perfect man who loved me. Okay, so not perfect, but he still loved me. Then you took it all away. Everything. What did I do to deserve this to happen to me?"

Again, no one replied. It made me so angry I began to scream at the sky, "You lost it! You lost my love! You lost my devotion! You never cared about me! You never knew me! Everything you have ever promised was a lie, and you are a liar! I hate you!"

I broke down and sobbed again, screaming into the loose dirt until my throat burned like fire. "How could you take them away?" I sobbed. I lay my face on the grave. "If you ever cared about me, now is the time to show yourself," I whispered.

A cool wind blew through my hair. A crow overhead cawed out a sorrowful call. Leaves rustled, and clouds scuttled along. The earth continued to turn.

Suddenly, I felt a sharp pain in my butt cheek. I jumped up and slapped at it, my hand coming away with a dead hornet. I glared at it and then at the sky. "You think this is funny?" I growled, angrier than I was before. I rubbed my sore butt cheek and put my hand in my pocket to get a better connection to the offending sting.

There was a piece of paper in my pocket.

I inhaled sharply, remembering the note I had found that Duke had left for me.

I yanked it out of my pocket and unfolded it, looking at his tidy handwriting over the page. I held it close to my chest and let out a shuddering sigh. I had forgotten it in the chaos and busyness of the previous day. Now, I desperately needed to read what he had written.

My sweet Noah,

If you are reading this, I am gone. While I am glad you found it, I wish you didn't have to. This is about the hardest thing I have ever had to write, but here it goes.

First of all, I am sorry. Sorry for all the pain I put you through, but also sorry that I wasn't strong enough to stay alive to protect you. I wanted to see you through this nightmare to the other side, but God had other ideas and while I don't claim to know what those ideas are, please trust that He has a reason for it. My part of this story may be done, but yours is not. You have to keep driving on, moving forward, and thriving without me. You are stronger than I ever was, Noah, my love.

Secondly, I want you to know that I have an emergency bank account set up in my name with you as the secondary benefactor. I set it up years ago and added you to the account the day we left for the cabin. While I don't know if money will be of any use ever again, I want you to know it is there and available for you to be taken care of. The account information is at the bottom of the page and also on the bookmark I always use.

Last of all, Noah, I need you to know that God is real and that He loves you. I have no idea why I am writing that, as you have always had more faith than I do, but I feel like you need to hear it right now. Maybe God is telling me to say it. I don't know. But there it is. He is real and He loves you even more than I ever did, which I kind of have a hard time believing.

Noah, I love you. I have many regrets from this lifetime, but meeting you and falling in love will never be one of them. You are the light of my life, and every day that I got to hold you and kiss you was the best day of my life.

Even though I am gone, this is not a goodbye letter. This is a "See you later." I will be waiting for you, Noah. I don't know what heaven is like, but I am glad that I have that to look forward to with you. I'll save you a seat next to me.

I love you, Noah. Every day, every breath, every beat of my heart, I love you. Be strong and keep moving forward. See you later, Killer.

With my entire heart,

Duke

P.S. Give Bob a kiss from me. Even if he is annoyed by it.

I read the letter over and over again. After I had been over it at least five times, I looked up at the sky and cried anew.

"I'm sorry, God. I'm sorry I doubted you. You knew what was going to happen, and I know for sure now that you have a plan for me. I'm still pissed that the plans don't involve Duke and Bob being here with me, but just knowing that there is a plan and a reason… I guess it just gives me hope."

I looked back at the letter in my hand, rereading the words my husband had so thoughtfully penned for me, when a small, white butterfly landed on the top of the page. I watched in fascination as it began to walk along the words, fluttering its wings. It hopped down the page, landing gracefully on the words "I love you." Overwhelmed by the moment, I stood up and turned my face to the warm sun, feeling the cool fall breeze caressing my face and gently pulling on my hair.

For the first time in a very long time, I knew everything was going to be okay.

EPILOGUE

TWO YEARS LATER

The wind outside tugged at my hair. I pulled my cap down further over my ears and tied the scarf a little tighter. Today was all about gathering firewood and clearing the snow off the roof so the solar panels could get some of the short-lived sunlight. If I wanted a warm bath tonight, it would be needed.

I trudged through the snow, keeping an eye on the tree line for any movement. The Rovers seemed to come around less often. They don't do well in the cold, and it seems that their numbers are dropping due to a lack of prey. The last time I had seen one was at least a month ago. It's hard to keep track of how much time has passed.

My path through the snow had filled a bit from the wind through the night, so I grabbed the shovel and began clearing the way to the woodpile behind the shed. I needed at least enough wood to get me through the next few days as I was planning to spend some time patching clothes, preparing some of the fish I had frozen in the shed, and getting the smoker going to take care of the game I had caught. A few days of inside work sounded like a dream. I shoveled my way to the grave and sat down to catch my breath.

"Hey, guys," I said. "I could really use some help today. Not that either of you deadbeats will be of any use." I chuckled at the lame joke I made almost every day as I sat here. "I miss you, Duke. I miss you every single day. It has been hard lately trying to keep up and move forward. I feel like it has been forever since we said goodbye, and I don't really feel like there is a purpose for me anymore. I know you want me to keep going, but I really just want to quit and be with you. It doesn't seem like there is an end to this. I haven't been to the compound in months. I haven't spoken to another human in that long, either. I know you said that I have to hold on, but why? What is important for me to stay here when I could be with you?"

The wind shifted and blew snow into my face. I brushed it off and stood up. "I love you, Duke. I'll see you later." As I turned to grab the shovel, I heard something that I had not heard in a very long time: the engine of a vehicle. It was too high-pitched to be a truck. I scanned the tree line, watching for movement and trying to pinpoint the direction of the sound.

After a few moments, I saw it: a snow machine pulled out of the woods, following the path of the small road that led to the cabin. I sprinted back inside and grabbed Duke's gun, checking the mag and chambering a round before walking back outside to face the approaching vehicle. A single rider approached and stopped a few yards away. I lifted the gun and braced myself. Although I wanted to talk to a living human, I certainly didn't want to seem vulnerable to a potential raider.

The rider lifted a leg, climbed off the machine, and trudged through the snow toward me with hands raised.

I was guessing that it was a man, based on build, but it was difficult to tell with the winter gear on. Whoever it was unclipped the helmet and pulled it off. My breath caught in my throat; I dropped the gun in the snow and fell to my knees in shock.

"Duke?" I uttered in a shaky breath, hardly above a whisper.

The man looked at me curiously. "Who are you?" he asked.

I was too stunned to speak for a moment. It was him, but his voice was deeper, huskier. His face was spot on, except for the full beard. I pulled myself to my feet and stumbled again, my legs feeling weak.

The man jumped forward and caught me before I could fall on my face. I looked up into his eyes and realized that this was not my Duke. This was a stranger with deep brown eyes, not the icy gaze of my husband.

I pulled back, snapping out of the shocked trance. I grabbed my gun and faced the man.

"I live here. Who are you?" I asked, trying to sound tough and recover from the shock.

"My name is Micah. Micah Duke. This is my brother's cabin."

Made in the USA
Monee, IL
09 March 2025